The Heirloom

GRAHAM MASTERTON

SPHERE BOOKS LIMITED
30-32 Gray's Inn Road, London WC1X 8JL

First published in Great Britain by Sphere Books Ltd 1981
Copyright © 1981 Graham Masterton

Printed and bound in Great Britain by
©ollins, Glasgow

'The devil is come down unto you, having great wrath, because he knoweth that he hath but a short time.'

—St John, 12:12

1 — Forebodings

How he managed to drive up to my door in that huge black van without my seeing him I shall never know. But I came around the side of the house with my sweeping-brush to tidy up some of the fallen eucalyptus leaves, and there he was, tall and silent, dressed in one of those long grey dusters that removal men and french polishers sometimes used to wear. His face was as long and pale as a calico kitbag, and his eyes were hidden behind the tiniest dark glasses I had ever seen. His hands were thrust into his pockets.

Behind him, neatly parked next to my Impala wagon, was the van. Old-fashioned, upright, and painted in a black so glossy that I could see a distorted reflection of the house and the eucalyptus trees in it.

'Mr Delatolla?' he asked, raising his cap.

'Who the hell are you?' I demanded. 'This is private property.'

'My name's Grant,' he said, mildly. 'I'm sorry to drop in on you without an appointment, but a friend of mine told me you might be interested in purchasing some unusual antiques.'

I glanced at the van. 'Oh, yes? Well, it depends how unusual they are. What have you got?'

He smiled a little. 'I'm not a time-waster, Mr Delatolla. I'm a house-clearer; and I can assure you that I only clear the best.'

'This is local stuff?' I asked him.

He nodded. 'I came down from Santa Barbara especially to do it. You've heard of the Jessops, of course?'

'You mean the Jessops who sell jewellery in San Diego or the Jessops who build aeroplanes at Long Beach?'

'The aeroplane Jessops. They have a house at Escondido.'

'I've seen it,' I told him. 'My wife always calls it the worst and only example of North San Diego Baroque. But surely none of the Jessops have died?'

1

Grant pursed his lips. 'No, no. Nothing like that. They're simply . . . restyling. They wanted to dispose of some of the extraneous furniture.'

'How extraneous?' I wanted to know. 'I don't buy garbage.'

'I know your reputation,' said Grant. 'If I didn't think you'd be interested in what I've got here, I wouldn't even have come along. Do you want to take a look?'

'Couldn't you bring it around to my store tomorrow?' I asked him. 'I'm supposed to be taking my son to the wild-animal park in about ten minutes.'

Grant looked away, across the tree-lined drive. 'I regret I have to be back in Santa Barbara by tonight.'

He said it in a strange, wistful way; and his voice was like the Sunday-afternoon breeze which rustled the leaves in the nearby lemon grove. He said nothing more to persuade me to look at what he had brought in that travelling hearse of his. He left it entirely up to me. And that, as I learned later, was one of the devices with which such antiques must be sold.

I checked my watch. 'Okay,' I told him abruptly. 'You open up the van, and I'll go tell my wife we're going to be running a half-hour late. I suppose a half-hour is going to be long enough?'

He nodded. It's strange, thinking about him today, because I can never quite remember what he really looked like. Sometimes I picture him like that French comedian Fernandel, only grimmer. Other times he appears in my memory as Jason Robards, or Richard Nixon. I watched him walk towards his van to open up the back doors, and it was like watching somebody walk through the shallow surf at the beach, an odd *wading* sort of walk.

I turned and went inside. Jonathan, my six-year-old son, was sitting on the Spanish-tiled floor in the hallway, studiously tying up his sneakers. Sara was in the kitchen, tidying up after preparing tonight's *carnitas* and *tortillas*. I came up behind her and kissed the side of her neck.

'Are you ready to go?' she asked me.

'Believe it or not, I have an antiques dealer outside,' I told her.

2

'Today? Sunday? *Here?*'

'He's from Santa Barbara. Apparently he has to go back tonight, otherwise I'd have had him call at the store in the morning.'

Sara wiped her hands on her flowery Danish apron, and then untied it. 'What's so important he has to come around on Sunday?'

'He cleared some furniture from the Jessop place at Escondido. Says they're redecorating or something like that, and they had one or two special pieces they wanted to get rid of.'

'They'd better be pretty special to interrupt your one day of rest,' warned Sara. She could be just as prickly as I was when she wanted to be. 'How long do you think you're going to be?'

'A half-hour. Not longer.'

Jonathan said, 'Are we going? I want to get in the car.'

'Not yet,' I told him, ruffling up his sun-blond hair. 'I just have to talk to that man outside for a couple of minutes. Then we'll go straight away. Faster than a speeding bullet.'

Jonathan squeaked the soles of his sneakers along the hallway in impatience. I warned, '*Jonathan,*' and he looked up at me and gave me one of those sulky, silly, persuasive little smiles, just like Sara's.

'I'll tell you what you *can* do,' I told him. 'Go chain up Sheraton in his kennel, and make sure he's got a bowl of water.'

''Kay,' said Jonathan, and skidded off.

Outside, on the asphalt driveway, the man called Grant had laid down a wide black velveteen rug, with black silk fringes. On it, he had already set out four dining-room chairs, two torchères, a circular Victorian bedside stand with a marble top, a pair of soapstone statues of fat naked ladies, and a lacquered Chinese-style Regency desk.

I walked around the furniture and statues and gave them a cursory once-over.

'Mr Grant?' I said.

'Yes?' He was struggling to lift down a brass-bound military chest.

3

'Mr Grant, I hate to have to say this, but if this stuff is any example of what you have to offer, then I suggest you pack it all up again and go. Not to put too fine a point on it, this is crap.'

He set down the chest and walked towards me. He was panting slightly from his exertions, and there was a decorative tiara of sweat across his forehead.

'These are simply make-weight items,' he said. 'You can have all these for nothing if you decide to buy the *pièce-de-résistance*.'

'I wouldn't have paid you anything for them anyway,' I told him. 'Come on, Mr Grant, this is junk-shop fodder. Those torchères don't even match. And what happened to that fat lady's left buttock? It looks like someone attacked it with a circular saw.'

Mr Grant nodded. He didn't seem to be denying how poor all these items were. But he didn't seem to doubt that I was going to take them, either. He stood there with his hands on his hips, regaining his breath, while I stared at him as meaningfully as I could and waited for him to say something. Anything. In back of the house, I heard Sheraton barking as Jonathan chained him up in the yard.

'Listen − ' I began, but Grant lifted a single finger to interrupt me.

'When you see the *pièce-de-résistance*,' he said, 'you'll change your mind.'

'All right,' I told him. 'Bring it out.'

'It's heavy. Why don't you step into the van with me and take a look?'

'What the hell is it? A busted ottoman? Really, Mr Grant, I can't − '

He looked at me, hands raised, his face wrinkled up into one of those expressions that says *now then, now then, don't get excited.* I looked at the van again, and for some reason I felt a sensation of prickly coldness. That kind of butterflies-in-the-palms-of-the-hands feeling you get before a tough examination in school. I hadn't felt like this since the previous fall, when I'd attended an auction in Los Angeles of the porcelain collection

4

that had once belonged to George Charovsky, the mass-murderer who used to live in La Jolla. Sara had coaxed me into bidding for a dancing shepherdess there, and I'd paid $875 for it. Three days later, I'd thrown it into the trashcan because I couldn't stand to have it around.

Let's just say that I'm sensitive to all things rotten. Rotten movies. Rotten paintings. And, more than anything – rotten people. People who mistreat their children, never take their dogs for a decent walk, and yell at their wives for no reason.

I'm not all that perfect myself. I drive badly. I snore when I'm asleep. I spank Jonathan when I shouldn't. But at least I believe in living, and letting live. You don't crap on my pumpkin-patch, and I won't crap on yours.

'Well?' asked Mr Grant, and waved his hand towards the open doors of the van.

I let out a tight, patient breath. 'All right, Mr Grant. But let's make sure that whatever it is you've got in there, it's worth looking at. I'm already ten minutes late.'

'Don't tell me you're *usually* so pressed for time,' he smiled.

'No,' I told him. 'I'm not. But it's Sunday, and so far you haven't impressed me at all.'

'I didn't intend to,' smiled Mr Grant. 'It's all part of the sales pitch.'

'Are you serious?' I asked him, as I took hold of the handrail, and hefted myself up into the back of the van.

'Never more so,' he replied. His voice was completely devoid of feeling. He held out his hand, and I helped him up. His fingers were as dry as corn husks.

'It's right in front,' Mr Grant said, and led me through a narrow and awkward avenue of nineteenth-century chairbacks and battered Victorian table-legs, until we had penetrated the furthest reaches of this mobile collection of unwanted junk, and reached the very front of the van.

In the corner, something was draped in a flour-sack. Whatever it was, it was tall and narrow, and it was made out of dark Cuban mahogany. I could just see one of its sides, burnished and carved, and the wood had a dark glow about it that you rarely saw in furniture made after 1860.

'Can you take off the sacking?' I asked Mr Grant.

'Take it off yourself, if you want to take a look,' he told me.

I hesitated. 'What is it?' I asked him. One lens of his tiny sunglasses was shining blind and bright as a quarter. It was stifling in the back of his van, and I was sure I could smell flowers. Gardenias. Or maybe stock.

'It's a chair,' he said. 'Take a look.'

I reached out hesitantly and grasped the coarse fibre of the flour-sack. I felt an extraordinary feeling, as if I were about to tear somebody's clothes off. Then I dragged the sack away and dropped it on to tne floor, and there it was. The chair from the Jessops' place at Escondido.

It was difficult to see very much in the darkness. Mr Grant had no torch, and no light rigged up; or else he wasn't going to switch it on, for reasons of his own. But I could tell at once that this chair was the real McCoy, a genuine and very unusual antique. There was something about it. A stateliness. A sense of proportion. And whoever had carved the back and the arms must have been some kind of furniture-making genius. There were snakes, and apples, and wolves' heads, and at the very crest of the chair, the face of a grinning creature that looked like a cross between a man and a sea-serpent. From what I could tell, the seat was upholstered in black leather.

'That's some chair,' I told Mr Grant. 'Can we see it in the daylight?'

'Sure. If you help me move all this other stuff, and lift it out.'

I turned back to the chair and peered at it closely. There was no question about it. It was carved mahogany, and very old. I'd never seen anything quite like it in my life.

'Where did Jessop get it?' I asked Mr Grant, as I helped him lift ten shield-back Chippendale chairs off the tail of the van.

'The chair? In Britain, I believe. He used to travel a great deal when he was younger. You ought to see some of the Italian antiques he's got out there at Escondido. He has two architectural landscapes by Guardi.'

It took us almost a half-hour to clear the back of Mr Grant's van. By the end of that time, my driveway looked like a garage‘ ‑ ‑

6

sale, and Sara had come out twice to complain. The third time she appeared, we were almost through, and I asked her to wait and see the chair.

'You've emptied all this stuff out for *one chair*?' she demanded.

'Sara,' I told her, 'it's something special. Just wait and see what you think of it.'

'I know what I think of our trip out to the animal kingdom,' she said, holding up her wrist and pointing at her watch. 'It's almost a washout. Well – *you* can explain it to Jonathan. Tell him we didn't go to the animal kingdom because of a chair. *I'm* not going to.'

'Will you just be patient?' I asked her. 'We're going to the animal kingdom, even if we have to go in the dark. But we have also to take a look at this chair. It's special.'

'God give me strength,' said Sara. 'I should have married a fish-market manager on the Embarcadero. At least he wouldn't be spending half of his precious Sunday afternoon buying pollock.'

Mr Grant paused, and stared at Sara carefully through his sunglasses. 'Mrs Delatolla,' he said, in that whispery voice. 'I'm real sorry for all the inconvenience. You must believe me. But, it had to be today.'

'A Sunday,' retorted Sara.

Strangely, Mr Grant nodded, his long mournful face going up and down like a rocking-horse that some child had just abandoned in an upstairs nursery.

'Yes,' he said. 'A Sunday.'

At last, we had cleared a way through the furniture in the back of Mr Grant's van. I tried to lift the chair myself, while Grant was kicking aside some loose ropes. Incredibly, I could scarcely lift it off the floor of the van, and I had to let it go. It thumped back into position, and the man-serpent face on the crest of the chairback seemed to be grinning at me in contempt. Even for solid mahogany, it was a monstrous weight. I'd hefted a solid mahogany wardrobe on my own before now, but this chair was ridiculous. Anyone who wanted to take it home would need a fork-lift truck.

'I can't believe how heavy this is,' I remarked to Mr Grant.

He turned. He was silhouetted against the sunlight outside of the back of the van. Beyond him I could see Sara standing impatiently amongst the forest of bentwood hatstands, Welsh dressers, bronze statuettes, library steps, and commodes. Jonathan was sitting on the stone kerb of the driveway a little further off, throwing pieces of bark and looking glum.

'I'll lend you a hand,' said Mr Grant, and came forward to the front of the van to help me. We took one side of the chair each, and gradually shifted it along the floor to the very edge of the tailgate.

'Not exactly Arnold Schwarzenegger the second, are you?' asked Sara, as I jumped down, sweating, from the back of the van.

'Do *you* want to try lifting it?' I asked her, annoyed. 'The damn thing weighs a ton.'

'I don't want to have anything to do with it,' she said, lifting her nose into the air into an exaggerated but serious expression of disdain. I knew it was serious because I'd tried before now to tease her out of it. When Sara lifted her nose into the air, you were dead, brother, and that was all there was to it.

'I hope you realise what all this is doing to my marriage,' I grunted, as I helped Mr Grant tilt the chair out of the back of the van, and lower it gently to the ground. 'I'm going to have to buy flowers, and perfume, and a bottle of Napa Valley Brut, and I'm not even sure the pharmacy's still open.'

'Don't worry about your marriage,' said Mr Grant. 'This chair will change your life.'

'Are you a marriage guidance counsellor, as well as a purveyor of second-hand sofas?' Sara asked him, cuttingly.

Mr Grant eased the back legs of the chair on to the ground, and then turned to Sara and took off his cap. 'Mrs Delatolla,' he said, 'I am nothing more than a clearer of houses.'

'You make yourself sound like an exterminator,' she said.

'Sara,' I snapped. 'For Christ's sake. Just leave it alone.'

'All right,' she said. 'I'm sorry. But if we're not ready to leave for the wild-animal park in five minutes, I'm going to

8

take Jonathan to Sea World, and you can stay at home on your own and play with your musty old furniture until you catch woodworm in the brain.'

'Hee, hee,' laughed Mr Grant, unexpectedly. I gave him the coldest stare I could manage but he was still smiling. An unsettling smile – more like a photograph of a smile than a real one.

'Listen,' I asked Sara. 'Can you just tell me what you think of this chair? Your calm, unbiased opinion?'

Sara walked around it. The back was even taller than she was, and she wasn't particularly petite. Five feet six inches in her naked feet. The arms were carved to look like entwined snakes, twisting their way right down to the feet, which were ball-and-claw. The seat was black leather, with a faint hint of blue, like a raven's wing; and when I pressed into it with my fingertips, it felt almost as if it were upholstered with something warm and alive.

'It's ugly,' said Sara. 'In fact, it's hideous. But I have to admit that it does have something.'

It was the decorated back which fascinated me. The splat – which is the centrepiece between the top of the chair and the seat – was thickly carved with what must have been hundreds of falling people, each of them only two inches long. They formed an intricate cascade of intertwined human bodies, all naked and all with their mouths stretched open in silent screams. I ran my fingers over them and the sensation was extraordinary. They felt bobbly and polished.

At the crest of the splat, the man-serpent face grinned with blind mahogany eyes and a wriggling mass of mahogany vipers for his hair. Two pythons formed the cresting rail along the top of the chair's back, their mouths open to regurgitate a curving stream of carved fruit and wolves' heads, which joined up with the snake-like arms.

'What do you think?' asked Mr Grant. I noticed that, once it was set down on the ground, he didn't touch the chair at all. Most antique dealers lean on their chairs in an easy, proprietorial fashion, as if the chairs actually belong to them; and they almost always tilt their chairs this way and that, just to

9

show you how snugly the frame has been put together, or how well the stretchers have been repaired.

Mr Grant treated the chair as if it were mine already, or at any rate as if it didn't belong to him. Maybe a chair like it only ever belonged to itself, I thought. It had such presence, such silent self-confidence, that it was hard to imagine it fitting easily and comfortably into anybody's home décor.

Jonathan came up and stared at the chair in fascination.

'What are all those people doing?' he asked me, at last.

Mr Grant, his hands clasped tightly in front of him, said, 'I believe they are tumbling from Hell into Sub-Hell. They are not very pleased about it, as you can see.'

'Why don't they have any clothes on?' asked Jonathan.

'They're going for a swim,' I put in. I gave Mr Grant a disapproving tight-lipped look for pre-empting my right to answer the first question. I believe in telling Jonathan the truth, but all that baloney about Hell and Sub-Hell, wherever that was, well, that was all baloney. Rotten baloney, at that.

'May I sit on the chair?' Jonathan said.

'Sure,' I told him.

'No,' said Mr Grant, quickly.

'There's no harm in letting the boy sit on the chair,' I told Mr Grant. 'Don't you ever sit on a chair before you buy it?'

Mr Grant came forward and stood between Jonathan and the chair. He was still smiling, in that peculiar unreal way, but I could see that he wasn't going to let Jonathan go past him, no matter what.

'Why can't he sit on the chair?' Sara wanted to know. 'Are you afraid it's going to fall to pieces or something?'

'It's not a – child's chair,' smiled Mr Grant. 'And apart from that, I don't usually allow people to sit on my chairs before they buy.'

'Well, in that case, we'll just have to go without the pleasure,' I replied. 'Do you want me to help you lift the chair back in the van?'

'Excuse me?' asked Mr Grant.

'You heard me,' I told him. 'Do you want me to help you lift the chair back in the van?'

'You're not going to buy it?' His affability vanished like steam off a sidewalk, and he was suddenly, inexplicably, alarmed.

I shook my head. 'No, I don't think so.'

'But – my dear Mr Delatolla – I was quite sure that you would. If I'd known – '

'I'm sorry,' I said, shaking my head. 'It's a very interesting piece. Obviously unique. Late eighteenth-century domestic, I'd guess. Made in Massachusetts or possibly Pennsylvania. The basic proportions are probably based on designs in Chippendale's *Gentleman and Cabinet Maker's Director*, as far as I can tell. Excellently interpreted, too. And with all this inventive carving around the back and arms . . . well, that's almost genius.'

'And you don't *want* it?' asked Grant, aghast.

'No, I don't,' I said firmly. 'Come on, Mr Grant, be serious. I'm dealing with customers who live in condos and seaview apartments with strictly limited room-space. They want their furniture on a particular scale, in a particular style. Light, spindly, and elegant, that's what they go for. But this thing . . . it's amazing, I admit . . . but it's like someone blowing the Trump of Doom right in the middle of a piccolo concert.'

'Mr Delatolla,' said Mr Grant, 'if you buy this chair, I'll throw in everything you see around you. Everything. Even that cheveret. Even that tea-kettle stand, and that's Chippendale.'

I glanced at Sara and Sara glanced back at me. There was a cool breeze blowing across the driveway and both of us communicated a feeling that there was something terribly wrong about all of this.

'Is any of this stuff stolen?' I asked Mr Grant, directly.

'Stolen? What are you trying to say?'

'I'm not trying to say anything. You seem awful anxious to get rid of it, all of a sudden.'

Mr Grant took off his sunglasses. His eyes were bulgy and pale, and were as unmemorable as his face. Sometimes I recall that they were dark, or that one of them was milky and blind. Sometimes I can't remember them at all.

'Listen, Mr Delatolla,' he pleaded, 'all of this stuff is honestly and genuinely mine. I swear it. But I have to get back to Santa Barbara tonight, and I don't want to take it all with me. That's the only reason. I mean, you're right. What I said before was just sales talk. It's not very good stuff. So what's the point of my carrying it all the way back up the coast? I might just as well offload it here for whatever I can get.'

I narrowed my eyes. No house-clearing agent had ever spoken anything like this to me before. Mr Grant was actually *begging* me to take all of this furniture off his hands.

'How much do you want?' I asked him, cautiously.

'Ten thousand, and that doesn't even cover my expenses.'

I paused. The chair alone had to be worth $12,500, or even more. None of the rest of the stuff was very good, but I had plenty of contacts in downtown San Diego who could sell it off for me. I stood to make $15,000–$20,000 clear profit, all for the sake of a house-clearer who couldn't wait to get home to Santa Barbara.

'Do you have a card? Any form of identity?' I asked Mr Grant.

'Sure,' he said. 'Here.' And he handed over a card that read 'Henry E. Grant, Antique Dealers, Houses Cleared, Antiques Bought & Sold. Member of the Association of California Antique Dealers.' There was an address near the beach in Santa Barbara.

'I'll have to think it over,' I said, turning the card over and over between my fingers. 'I mean, this chair, there's no way to put an accurate price on it. No way to compare it with anything. It could be worth half a million, or five dollars.'

'Eight thousand,' said Grant. 'And that's as low as I can go.'

Sara said, 'Ricky . . . do you really *want* all this junk?' She knew like hell that I did, especially at eight thousand, but she was playing her usual game of beating other dealers down just by pretending to talk me out of whatever it was they were selling. I've had dealers end up by ignoring me completely, and haggling hysterically with her.

'I wouldn't say no to one or two of the pieces . . .' I mused. ·

'But, well, I don't know . . . if you don't think it's a good idea . . .'

'Seven-five, but no lower,' put in Grant. His voice was very whispery now.

'Seven thousand five hundred? For all of this?' I asked him.

'Just take it,' he said. 'Send me a cheque in the mail.'

'Hold on one minute,' I asked him. I leaned over and murmured in Sara's ear, 'Make sure he doesn't leave.' Then I walked quickly into the house, and into my library. I leafed through the North San Diego County telephone directory until I found '*Jessop*, Samuel F., San Miguel, Escondido'. I punched out the number and waited while the ringing tone went *bzzzz – bzzzz – bzzzz –*

'Jessop residence,' said a wary voice. A woman, maybe sixty years old or older.

'Oh, hallo,' I said. 'You may not know me – in fact you probably don't – but my name's Delatolla. Rick Delatolla. I'm an antiques specialist, in Rancho Santa Fe. No, an *antiques* specialist.'

'I'm sorry,' said the woman. 'We don't want to buy anything, and we have nothing to sell.'

'No, please – this isn't a sales call. I just want to tell you that a man called Grant is around here at my house this afternoon with some items of antique furniture – some tables and secretaires, things of that kind, some dining-room chairs – yes, that's right – and, well, he says he got them from the Jessop house at Escondido.'

There was a lengthy pause. Breathing. Then the woman said, 'Yes, that's true. A man called Grant did come around last week. He cleared one or two pieces of furniture from old Mr Jessop's study, and from some of the guest rooms. We're having that part of the house restyled.'

'I see. So Mr Grant's genuine.'

'Oh, yes, he's genuine. No question about it. I believe he was known to one of old Mr Jessop's business partners, and that's how we came to use him. He comes from Los Angeles, I think.'

'Santa Barbara,' I corrected.

'Well, whatever,' said the woman.

'Is it possible you can tell me anything about the chair?' I asked. 'I'm having a difficult time pricing it, and I was wondering if you – '

'Chair? What chair?' asked the woman.

'There are several, actually. But the one I'm particularly interested in has carving all the way up the back, and a kind of a beast's face on the crest. You must know the one I mean. It's not exactly the kind of chair you can overlook, is it?'

'I don't know what you mean,' said the woman. 'We have never had a chair of that description anywhere. Not in this house, nor at San Clemente.'

'Are you sure?' I frowned. 'Mr Grant certainly gave me the impression that he'd gotten it from you.'

'I expect you were mistaken.'

I held the receiver away from my ear. 'Yes,' I said. 'Yes, I expect I was.'

'Is there anything else?' said the woman's voice, tinnily.

'No, no, thank you. You've been very kind. I'm sorry I disturbed you.'

I set down the phone and stood thinking for a moment. I was sure that Grant had told me the chair came from Escondido. Hadn't he told me that old man Jessop had brought it back from Europe? But even if he hadn't, the woman had betrayed something in her voice. A hurriedness. A sense of anxiety. The same sort of let's-get-it-over-quick impression that I'd gotten from Grant.

It seemed like old man Jessop's furniture wasn't very popular. Particularly the chair. In a way, I could understood it. The chair was one of those pieces of furniture you come across from time to time in the antiques business that are works of brilliant craftsmanship and superior design, but which nobody in their right mind could stand to have in their home. I remember buying a love-seat once from a collector in Los Angeles, and it was all carved out of South African yellow-wood into the shape of two embracing kaffirs. An incredible achievement, but a terrible piece of furniture to live with. It took me two years to sell it, at a $300 loss.

I walked back along the tiled hallway and out into the front garden. Sara was still standing there, surrounded by the bric-à-brac that Mr Grant had unloaded on to the driveway. Jonathan was there too, only a couple of feet away from her. Grant, however, had gone, and so had his black van.

'Sara?' I called, hurrying down the steps. I took her arm. 'Sara? Where's Grant?'

She turned her head around slowly and stared at me. For a moment her eyes looked unfocused. Then she said, 'Grant?'

'Grant – the guy with the furniture. I told you to keep him here.'

She slowly, slowly shook her head. 'I don't remember any Grant.'

'Sara?' I asked her, more gently. 'Are you sure you're okay? Sara, there was a guy here with a black van . . . a guy in sunglasses. I told you to make sure that he didn't leave. Sara – are you kidding me, or what?'

'A black van?' she frowed. 'Yes, I remember.' Then she looked bright, and pointed down the driveway to the road. 'Yes, he just left. Only a minute ago. You missed him by seconds.'

I hunkered down beside Jonathan. He was staring at me with the same dreamy expression as Sara. I waved my hand from side to side in front of his eyes, and he blinked and smiled at me, but at the same time he still seemed to be distant, and disconnected.

'Jonathan,' I asked him, 'did you see what happened? What did the man do to you?'

'He went,' said Jonathan, simply. 'He said he had to go, and he went. He told me to look at the chair.'

'Sara?' I said. 'Is that what Grant told you to do? To look at the chair?'

Sara thought, and then nodded. 'That's right. Jonathan's right. He said it was such a fine piece of carving, I ought to look at it more closely. Particularly the face, he said. It was the cruellest, most loving face ever. That's what he said. More like life, than carving.'

I turned around and looked at the face on the crest of the

chair myself. There wasn't any question about the subtlety with which it had been wrought. Solid Cuban mahogany, shaped and smoothed until it had taken on the shape of a man-serpent's face. You could almost feel the bones underneath the skin, even though it was nothing but wood.

I checked my watch. It was two o'clock, which meant there was still time to drive out to the wild-animal park. Personally, I didn't feel like going any more – not that I'd been crazy about going in the first place. But I felt that it would probably be a good idea if I took Sara and Jonathan away from the house for an hour or two, to freshen up their minds. Maybe they'd remember what had happened when Mr Grant had left.

'Give me ten minutes to hump the best pieces in the garage,' I told Sara. 'The rest of the stuff – well. If anybody comes and steals it, they'll be doing me a favour.'

'You're going to keep the chair?' asked Sara, a little stiffly.

'I'm going to get rid of it as soon as I can,' I told her. 'As soon as I can find anybody to give me eight thousand dollars for it, it's out.'

'I don't like it,' she said, emphatically, in the same way she'd say 'I don't like zucchini' or 'I don't like old Charlie Chaplin movies.' Then she walked quickly back to the house, taking Jonathan by the hand as she went. They disappeared inside, and the front screen door banged a loud *period* to the arrival in our lives of old man Jessop's chair.

My life hasn't always been wealthy, but I guess you could say that it's always had a certain eccentric style. I was conceived in the front (and only) seat of a ridiculous three-wheeled automobile called a Davis, a Californian 'fancy car' of the mid-1940s which seated four people abreast. Few of these cars were ever built, but one was enough for me.

My father, whose square Eisenhower-generation face still stares short-sightedly from the photograph frame in the living-room, was a house plasterer. I guess I should be loyal and romantic, and say that he could plaster two rooms in a day, and that the walls would be as smooth and flawless as silk. In fact, my mother told me the year after he died that he hadn't ever been particularly good at his job. His workmates had called him 'Sloppy Joe', or 'Old Trowel and Error'. His real ambition had been to set himself up as a bookie. A *bookie*, can you imagine it? If only he had. I would have spent my childhood on the track at Santa Anita.

Instead, I was brought up in Anaheim, in one of those crowded uninteresting streets you pass on the way to Disneyland. My parents wanted me to be a dentist, for God's sake; and every time they introduced me to anyone they would fold their hands and smile smugly at me and say, 'This is Ricky. He's going to be a dentist.' I used to have nightmares about wet salivating mouths, and wire braces that nipped me like skeletal lobsters.

The dentistry thing kind of petered out after my father died of lung cancer in 1958. My mother became fussy, over-indulgent, and if I'd announced that I wanted to join the circus as a fire-eater's assistant, I think she would have said, 'Oh, yes, dear. Whatever you want,' and given me a dollar for gasoline. I drifted through high school, playing moderate football, bad baseball, and even worse piano. I dated pretty girls with pony-tails and spots. But then, everybody I knew had spots.

The only teacher I really liked a lot was a young guy called Panov who spoke in a thick Hungarian accent and taught woodwork. His family had immigrated to California from Europe just after World War Two, bringing with them most of their old furniture and paintings. Since the war, Panov's father had lost most of his money on stock speculations, and the family lived in a tiny, tacky little house in West Hollywood. But Panov took me back home there one day for *borscht*, and inside of that tiny, tacky little house, there was a riot of antiques. Tables, wardrobes, commodes, mirrors, chairs – the contents of a seven-bedroomed mansion crammed into a three-room shack. We spent the whole afternoon clambering around it, and over it, and under it, while Panov explained to me the beauties of eighteenth-century dovetailing, the wonders of walnut marquetry, and the joys of fluted legs.

I went into that house liking Panov as a friend and a teacher. I came out, five hours later, realising that he'd become a whole

17

lot more. He'd become my inspiration, my mentor. He'd shown me a completely new world that I'd never really been aware of, and it was the most exciting and beautiful world you could imagine. After I graduated, I took a course in fine art and antiques at UCLA, and I learned about Chippendale, Hepplewhite, Sheraton, and Gillow. I could tell kingwood from pearwood, splats from stretchers, and frets from friezes.

I also met Sara. She was tall, almost beautiful, and remote. She had long shiny blonde hair that blew around her in the California sunshine like the gold that the princess spun in *Rumpelstiltskin*, and hazel-coloured eyes. I'm being romantic now, but Sara was just about the one person who could make me feel that way. All soft focus and 'cellos, and Bach, and the shimmer of a tear on trembling lower lashes.

Sara was majoring in Renaissance history, and that was why she occasionally joined my art classes. I used to wink at her across the lecture-hall – big, broad, suggestive winks, real construction-site stuff – and she used to stick her nose up in the air and ignore me. My best friend Carl Watkins said I was wasting my time. Sara Horton, he said, had been a classic case of frigid little rich girl ever since high school.

Carl was right, sort of. But Sara's diffidence was a result of shyness rather than snobbery. I suspected it the moment I first saw her, walking across campus with her books held against her breasts, her mouth pouting in a fashionably Brigitte Bardot moody expression, her long legs striding along in a pale blue mini-skirt. She told me later that she always used to have this fantasy that she was starring in a French movie, with subtitles.

After two or three months, I grew impatient with the way she consistently ignored me and stuck her nose up at me. What did she think I was? Some kind of leper? So I took the steering-wheel in both hands and madly but deliberately rear-ended her shiny firetruck-red Ford Mustang convertible host outside of the campus gates. Crunch. She screamed at me for almost fifteen minutes. What a careless moron I was. How could you do it? Men like you should have their licences revoked and their things cut off. But after I'd told her I was sorry, not just ordinary sorry but abjectly and unconditionally sorry; and the only reason I'd rear-ended her was because I hadn't been able to take my eyes off her beautiful hair; and in any case I'd pay for all of her body-shop expenses out of my student grant, well, she calmed down, and nearly smiled. And once she'd nearly smiled – once haughty Sara Horton had actually nearly smiled – it was all over except for two delirious sunny years of going steady, of Paul Masson wine and Bob Dylan concerts and smoking grass, and then a picture-postcard wedding at her parents' house in Pasadena, with white cake and black Cadillacs and sobbing aunts and orchids, and a nice cheque from Pops to help me get started in the antique business. Pops, as it turned out, owned half of Seal Beach – the half where the oil is.

I felt like I'd played at living, and won.

We found Rancho Santa Fe one weekend in spring, when we were driving through North San Diego County. It's a small, prim, hyper-respectable community nestling in the sandy-coloured hills about seven miles inland from the Pacific Shore at Solana Beach. It only has half a dozen streets – tidy, sunlit little thoroughfares with names like *Paseo Delicias* and *La Flecha*. It has two stores, a gas station, a post office, and an elegant restaurant where you can sit amidst expensive Mexican decor and eat salads and fish and gâteaux and talk about the tiresome problems you've been having with your decorator. At the end of the main street, half-hidden amongst the eucalyptus trees, is The Inn, where elderly visitors roll bowls across the lawns, or cover their faces in the *Los Angeles Sunday Times* and sun their grey-haired bellies.

In normal circumstances, Rancho Santa Fe would have been too quiet for us. Victor Mature had retired there, and you can't get any quieter than that. But Sara was expecting our first baby by then, and the family doctor had cautioned her to take things real easy. What was more, there was an antique shop for sale halfway along main street, in a shady and attractive little mall, and if ever there was an ideal site to start up in the antiques retail business, this was it.

Two months later, we moved into our two-storey oak-shingled house in a lemon grove just half a mile outside of town, with a pool and a verandah and bougainvillaea growing wildly all over the patio roof. Three months later, I opened the doors of Richard J. Delatolla, Antiquités et Objets d'Art. Four months later, Sara was driving home from seeing a friend in San Diego when a tyre burst on her estate wagon. The wagon skidded off the freeway, rolled down a twenty-foot embankment, and landed on its roof. She lost the baby, a girl, on her way to hospital.

Now, in the waning light of a Sunday afternoon, we were sitting with Jonathan under the mock jungle thatch of the refreshment parlour at the wild-animal park. Jonathan, in spite of Sara's protests, was munching his way through a hot dog that was more catsup than sausage, and I was sipping a large paper carton of cold beer. Sara was very quiet, and hadn't touched her lemon tea.

'What's wrong?' I asked her, after a while.

She looked up, and made a face that meant, I don't know, nothing. The fringe of the jungle thatch cast a ragged, flickering shadow across her forehead.

'You're not still thinking about that chair, are you?' I said.

Jonathan said, 'Why didn't that man let me sit in it, Daddy?'

I reached over and wiped the splotches of catsup off his chin with a paper napkin. 'He was just being careful, that's all.'

'Careful about what?' asked Sara, with a suddenness that was almost aggressive.

'I don't know. Careful. An antique is an antique.'

'What's that supposed to mean?'

I raised my hands in surrender. 'Nothing, as a matter of fact. I just didn't know what to say. Listen – you're upset about something, aren't you?'

'Of course I'm not.'

'Don't tell me you're not upset,' I insisted. 'I know when you're upset. We've spent the whole afternoon staring at lions, and zebras, and performing elephants, and parrots, and you haven't said a word. You haven't even said how goddamned boring you think they all are.'

'They're not boring,' Sara retorted. 'I never said they were boring.'

'You never said *anything*.'

She leaned forward, her expression intent. 'I don't understand what could have happened to me,' she said. 'It was like – fainting. Blacking out. But I haven't blacked out like that since I was in the third grade.'

I sat back, and toyed with my carton of beer. 'Maybe it was just some kind of auto-suggestion. Grant told you to look at the face, and somehow your subconscious mind thought it seemed hypnotic, so for a minute or two you were actually hypnotised. *Self*-hypnotised, not really hypnotised. You can't believe that a wooden face on a chair can actually – '

'Do you know what you're saying?' demanded Sara. 'You're saying that I was so dumbstruck by a piece of furniture that I stood there like the town idiot with my jaw hanging open while Grant walked off, climbed into his van, backed up, and drove away. That's what you're saying.'

'Okay,' I told her, 'that's what I'm saying.'

'But it's impossible, Ricky. Things like that just don't happen.'

'They must happen. I mean – well, it *happened*, didn't it?'

'Not the way you're trying to suggest.'

'Well, what way? He gave you a quick squirt of "Ignore Me" gas? He vanished in a puff of smoke?'

Sara didn't answer. I took a sip of beer and watched her. She kept twisting the ends of her hair around and around in her fingers.

'Listen,' I said gently, 'what are you trying to tell me?'

She hesitated, searching for the exact words to express what she felt. 'I'm trying to tell you that it was the chair. It has a kind of charisma.'

'A *charisma*?'

'Don't make fun of me, Ricky. I really and truly believe that there is something about that chair which made me lose consciousness while Grant drove out of the grounds.'

'I see,' I nodded. Somehow, Sara was making me feel depressed. I mean, however odd it was that Grant had managed to leave the house without her noticing him go, there had to be some rational explanation for it. Maybe Sara was starting to suffer from pre-menstrual tension again. Maybe Grant had worked some kind of stage conjuring trick on her – now you see me, now you don't. But the trouble was that Jonathan hadn't seen him leave, either, and there was no way that Jonathan was suffering from PMT.

'Jonathan,' I asked him. 'Did that man really go without you seeing him? Or did you get a little teentsy look at him?'

Jonathan was gnawing at his breadroll like one of the rabbits in the children's enclosure.

'Jonathan,' I repeated. 'What happened when Mr Grant left? I want you to think what happened. *Think*.'

He slowly put down his roll. Then he turned to stare at me with an expression that actually frightened me. Haughty, cold, and utterly severe, as if he were a ruthless old man whose cruelty and determination had somehow been brought into question. Almost immediately, though, his face softened, and tears started to trickle down his cheeks.

Sara reached over and hugged him. 'There, baby,' she said, stroking his hair. 'Don't worry about it. You don't have to think what happened if you don't want to.' Then she looked across at me and said, 'Now see what you've done.'

'I haven't done *anything*,' I protested. 'All I did was ask him to think what happened in that moment when Grant left the house. What's so terrible about that?'

'He doesn't want to think about it, that's all.'

I let out a long, exasperated breath. 'Jesus Christ. A guy does a magic vanishing act in my driveway. My wife and my son are the only witnesses. And do you think either of them will tell me what the hell happened?'

Jonathan raised his head from Sara's arms. His eyes were blotted with tears. 'I saw *you*, Daddy,' he whispered.

'What do you mean, you saw me? You couldn't have seen me. I was in the house, making a telephone call.'

'I saw *you*, Daddy.'

'When?' I wanted to know. 'When did you see me?'

Sara held Jonathan even more protectively. 'Don't say any more, darling,' she told him. Her eyes were fixed on me so fiercely that I felt as if I was growing horns or something.

'You were sitting on the chair,' said Jonathan. 'You were sitting on the chair but you looked funny.'

'Funny? How?'

'I could only see the top of you. Your legs were disappearing down the crack at the back of the chair. I tried to tell you not to go down the back of the chair, but you didn't want to listen. You were smiling at me. I was frightened.'

I stood up. Then I sat down again. I couldn't think what to say. Jonathan stopped crying, and sat solemnly on his chair, staring at me with a pale face. Sara stroked his arm.

'Listen, Jonathan,' I said at last. 'You know for a fact that I was inside the house, making a telephone call. So what you thought you saw was only imagination. It was only inside of your head.'

Sara said, 'Jonathan's right, Ricky.'

'Right? What do you mean he's right? Don't tell me *you* saw me sliding down the back of the chair, too?'

She shook her head. 'No. If I did see anything, I can't remember what it was. But I do know that I had a terribly strong feeling when I blacked out.'

She held her cheek as if she was remembering that someone had slapped her, and stared at me with watering eyes. These weren't the tears of romance, either, or of 'cellos, or of too many carafes of Paul Masson wine. These were the tears of uncertainty, and fear.

'Ricky,' she told me. 'I felt sure you were going to die.'

2 — Witherings

When we arrived back home, the furniture was still standing where we had left it on the driveway, although the wind had somehow blown the black velveteen rug across to the other side of the house, where it was tangled up in the bushes like a broken umbrella, or a snared bat.

Sara climbed out of the car without a word, and reached into the back seat to wake Jonathan up. He had nodded off as we passed Lake Hodges on the way back through Escondido.

It was dusk, and the insects had started chirruping. A warm breathy wind stirred the leaves of the eucalyptus trees overhead. I unlocked the front door, switched off the burglar alarm under the stairs, and then walked through to the den at the back of the house, where two wide sliding doors looked out over the pool patio. I switched on the lights around the pool, and then slid the doors open.

'You want a drink?' I asked Sara, as she helped a tousled Jonathan up the stairs to bed.

'Aren't you going to put away the rest of that furniture?' she asked me.

'I'll have Miguel come up and do it tomorrow. I'm bushed.'

'I thought you were a nocturnal.'

'I am,' I told her. 'But that doesn't mean I have to be an *energetic* nocturnal, does it? Besides, Miguel likes heaving furniture around. I wouldn't like to deprive him of any fun.'

'I'll be down in a moment,' said Sara.

I went to our eighteenth-century inlaid corner cabinet where I kept the bottles of drink, and built us each a large Rum Collins. Then I stepped out on to the red brick patio, and stood for a while listening to the sounds of the evening, and watching the last crimson dust of the day stir itself slowly into the darkness of the woods.

Sara came out after a few minutes in her blue silk kimono.

'Jonathan sleeping?' I asked her.

She took her drink. 'He says he wants to go see it all again next week. Especially the lions.'

'He was lucky to see those lions. Usually, they're fornicating behind the rocks.'

Sara let out a short, strained laugh.

'About this afternoon – ' she began.

'Forget it,' I told her. 'It was all weird, and unpleasant, and right now we can't think of any explanation for it. But that doesn't mean we have to let it faze us, does it?'

She leaned on my shoulder. 'I guess not. It was just that the feeling I had was so powerful. That's why I didn't want to tell you at first.'

'Sara, my darling,' I said, with as much conviction as I could manage, 'I am not going to die. Not in the immediate future, anyway. When I'm a hundred and eleven, maybe. But not yet.'

She walked across to the other side of the patio. I stayed where I was, drinking my cocktail. I heard her rearranging the cooking utensils on top of the brick barbecue.

'Maybe we should invite the Wertheims over next week,' she said. 'Dry martinis and burned steaks.'

'I never burn the steaks,' I retorted.

'Oh, no? What about that time we had the Salingers over?'

I shrugged. 'That was an experiment.'

'An experiment?'

'Sure. I was trying to determine if it could ever be possible for human beings to thrive on carbon.'

Sara said, 'It's cold tonight, don't you think so?'

'It's summer. How can it be cold?'

'I just feel cold,' she insisted. 'Don't you think there's a wind?'

'You want to go inside?' I asked her. 'I could light a fire if you really want me to.'

'Unh-hunh. Maybe I'll just take a swim. The water looks nice and warm.'

Both of us liked the pool water at a steady 75 degrees, and as the evening air cooled off, the surface steamed like a Florida swamp. Sara dipped her toes in, and then peeled off her blue silk kimono and hung it over the back of one of the patio chairs. Underneath, she was naked – still as slim and tanned as ever, with those small tip-tilted breasts and narrow hips. She lowered herself slowly into the water, and ripples widened through the steam. I sat myself down on the side of the pool cross-legged, and watched her as she struck out for the other side.

'You should come in,' she called, her hair streaming all around her. 'It's really relaxing.'

'I'll think about it,' I said, lifting my glass to her. 'Personally, I prefer to sit and watch you, sexy.'

She swam a few side-strokes, and then trod water at the deep end. Her body was distorted and refracted by the ripples, and for a moment I had a curious feeling that I was watching something out of a dream.

'You know something,' I called. 'I think we both need a vacation.'

'We would have *taken* a vacation by now if we could only agree on where to go,' she called back.

'So what's wrong with marlin fishing in the Gulf Stream?' I asked her.

'For a six-year-old boy? Most of those marlin weigh more than he does.'

'He could catch sardines.'

Sara flippered around in a lazy circle. I was just about to ask her if she wanted another drink, when she shrieked out, '*Ricky!*'

My heart clamped tight like a wrench. I leaped up, kicked off my shoes, and jumped into the shallow end of the pool with one almighty splash, wading out towards her as fast as I could.

'It's okay!' I yelled. 'I'm coming!'

'No!' she shouted. 'It's not me! – *it's not me!* Look on the patio!'

I didn't understand at first, and I had already reached her by the time I realised that she wanted me to turn around. But when I did, I stared in complete disbelief at what I saw.

Sara's blue silk kimono, which she had draped over the back of one of the chairs, was on fire. Flames were licking up one of the sleeves, and part of the back was already charred.

We watched in shocked silence as the kimono was gradually consumed. Thin fragments of burning silk rose into the evening sky, and then sank back to the patio again like the feathers of a shot raven.

Gripping Sara's hand, I waded to the side of the pool, and heaved myself out. Water clattered from my clothes on to the concrete edge. I reached down and helped Sara out, too; and still holding hands we approached the patio chair.

'Did you see it?' she asked me. 'It just . . . caught fire.'

I raised my eyes and scanned the evening sky. 'Must have been a stray charcoal spark from somebody's barbecue. That's all I can think of.'

'Can you *smell* anybody's barbecue? The Johnsons are away in Philadelphia.'

I sniffed. 'I'm not sure. But maybe the spark was just carried on the wind. It happens.'

'But the way it simply caught fire . . .'

I led her back towards the house. She was right – the night had grown unseasonably chilly, and she was naked. By the time I got her inside and slid the doors shut, she was trembling all over. Her nipples were stiff and tight, and she was covered in goosebumps.

'Straight upstairs, have a hot shower, and then I'll fix you another drink,' I told her. 'You can borrow my thick towelling wrap.'

She kissed me, her lips cold and shaking. 'At least I know you'd never let me drown,' she told me, and then she went padding off to take her shower.

I went to the windows and stared out at the patio chair for a while. It *must* have been a stray spark that had set light to Sara's kimono. There wasn't any other explanation. On a summer evening, a red-hot speck of charcoal could be wafted on the wind for miles, and still set fire to anything it settled on. Sheriff Young had told me that, and he'd had to deal with more brushfires than I'd sold wheelback chairs.

I fixed two more drinks, and carried them through the living-room. It was long, the living-room, with a pitched ceiling, and a big old-fashioned fireplace with brass firedogs and brass-handled irons. The walls were plain and whitewashed, so that they didn't detract from the two magnificent early-American paintings we had hanging at either end of the room. One was a John Singleton Copley, a second version of his famous 1778 picture of a naked mariner being rescued by his friends from the gaping jaws of a shark. The other was a dark portrait by Gilbert Stuart of a serious colonial gentleman in a periwig and a black hat. I switched on the spotlights that illuminated both pictures, and then went to the fire and stacked on a few split logs.

'Ricky!' called Sara, from upstairs. I had a match out of the box, just ready to strike, but I left the hearth and walked to the foot of the stairs.

'Everything okay?' I asked her.

'Sure. I feel better for a warm shower. Did you leave your towelling wrap downstairs?'

'I don't think so, unless I took it off in the library this morning.'

'Could you go look for me?'

I crossed the tiled hallway and opened the library door. Somebody had drawn the drapes in there, and it was unusually dark. I reached for the light switch, but when I found it, and flicked it down, nothing happened. I hesitated at the door, and frowned. The lights had been working all right last night, and there were six of them – bracket-lamps all the way around the walls – so it couldn't be anything as simple as a blown bulb. Maybe the fuse had gone on the downstairs lighting circuit – but if that had happened, the living-room lights wouldn't be working either. I pushed open the door a little way and peered inside.

It was absurd, but I was suddenly convinced that someone was inside the library, watching me. I strained my eyes, and I could just make out the corner of my desk, and the light from the hallway reflected on the side of my Olivetti typewriter. I listened, but all I could hear was the busy rustling of the bougainvillaea in the evening wind outside.

'Ricky?' called Sara.

'The lights have gone,' I called back. 'I won't be a minute.'

I took a step forward, and it was then that I was sure that I saw a hostile pair of eyes. Slanted, like an animal's eyes – a wolf, or a fox – but strangely fluorescent. I stayed where I was, holding my breath so that I could pick up the slightest sound, but my heart was banging hard enough to convince the people across the road that I was putting up shelves.

The eyes, slowly, blinked.

'Sara,' I said, in a warning voice. I don't think she heard me 'Sara, there's something in the library.'

Now I could just detect a faint grumbling growling noise. It sounded like the rattle of breath in a fierce animal's throat. Maybe a coyote had accidentally wandered into the house through the patio doors, or even a mountain lion. Maybe something had escaped from the wild-life park, and it had managed to make its way here. A tiger, or a puma, or something.

'Who's there?' I snapped, trying to sound brisk and authoritative.

There was no reply. The low growling went on.

Gradually, I backed out. There was a telephone on the wall in the kitchen, only fifteen feet away, and I reckoned I could retreat discreetly and quickly enough to reach it before whatever it was in the library decided to come after me. I had a vivid memory of some black-and-white photographs that I'd seen years ago in *Look*, of a zoo-keeper being hideously mauled by a lion. Blood, bones, and anguish. And what had that doggedly jovial guide at the wild-animal park said this afternoon? 'Don't worry, folks, lions aren't dangerous unless they decide to eat you.'

I was halfway down the corridor, backing away on tippytoes, when I saw the lights in the library begin to brighten again. They didn't flick on abruptly, like they do when you've mended a fuse, and you switch the power back on. They shuddered and faltered, gaining strength in intermittent surges, as if they were recording the heartbeat of someone who had nearly died, and was now struggling to recover. There was a curious *blueish* effect to them, too, that reminded me of wild electricity from a lightning-rod.

I hesitated. The sensible adult thing to do was to run straight to the telephone and call the sheriff's office. Help, help! There's a wild animal in my library! But now that the lights had flickered back on, my fright began to ebb, and my curiosity began to take over instead. If there really *was* a puma in my library, it was probably just as alarmed as I was, and the chances that it would pounce on me were pretty remote. In any case, what were the odds on it really being a puma? About one in a million. It was far more likely to be a stray dog, or a wandering cat. And what would Sara say if three police cars came howling into the drive for the sake of a bewildered local mongrel?

Cautiously, I crept back to the open doorway. The lights around the library were bright now, and shining normally. And there certainly wasn't a lion there. Not even a puma. There wasn't even a yowling cat which had lost its way, or been tempted into the house by the smell of Sara's *carnitas*.

'This is crazy,' I said to myself, quite loudly. I took two or three steps into the room, and looked around. Nothing seemed to have been disturbed. My latest 'Antiques Newsletter' for the San Diego *Evening Tribune* was still in the typewriter, with that awful opening sentence, 'Tired of Tiffany? Brassed off with brass? Here's an idea for brightening up your home that wxjl . . .' and that was as far as I'd got.

I went to the window, opened the drapes, and tested all the handles. They were locked, two of them with security keys. But I was right in the middle of drawing the drapes closed again, my arms outstretched, when I saw in the darkness of the window a reflection of myself and the room behind me.

I felt a cold shudder down my backbone. I couldn't help it. I didn't even want to turn around, but I knew that I had to. Besides, the reflection of my own frightened face in the window-pane was more than I could take.

In the corner behind the door, placed right up against the wall so that I hadn't noticed it when I first walked into the.

room, was the chair. Tall, forbidding, and secretive. A nightmare created out of burnished mahogany and old leather.

I walked towards it, curious but shocked, the way you walk up to a road accident. I stopped when I was only a couple of feet away. For some reason, I didn't feel like touching it. It had an aura about it, a tight self-possession, which warned me to keep my distance. I stared at the writhing snakes, and the bulging fruit, and the screaming figures who endlessly tumbled from the cresting rail down to the seat, and I thought of Mr Grant and his tiny dark glasses, and what he had said about 'Sub-Hell'.

I stared, too, at the man-serpent's face on the crest of the chair – a face with slanted animal eyes and a mouth that seemed to find its own deep depravity a cause for amusement. The eyes looked exactly like the eyes that I had seen glowing at me in the darkness, before the lights came on, and yet they couldn't have been. I wouldn't have been able to see anything more than the left-hand arm of the chair from the library doorway, even supposing the lights had been working. To have faced me from the darkest recesses of the library, the way those eyes had faced me, the chair would have had to move *by itself* more than thirteen or fourteen feet, and that was obviously out of the question. It couldn't have been Sara playing a practical joke on me, either. I could scarcely budge the chair myself, and *I* was the one to whom Sara always passed the pickle jars for opening. Sara couldn't even have *dragged* the chair across the library, let alone lifted it.

I peered at the face more closely. It was a study in cold ferocity. The eyes seemed to take in everything and give nothing back. It was the face of a devil.

I thought: stop it, for Christ's sake. This is nothing but an antique chair. Wood, leather, springs, and horsehair. That's all.

Yet – how had it managed to get into my library from the garage, where I had left it this afternoon? I had locked it in with a six-lever padlock, and when I had arrived back at the house from the wild-animal park, I had seen for myself that the padlock was securely in place. Maybe Sara *might* have found a way to heave the chair around the library in the dark – although my logical mind rejected the whole idea of it as totally insane. But there was no way she could have carried it into the house from the garage. Absolutely no way at all.

I looked at the chair for a long time, and then I said, 'I know what you're up to. You're trying to confuse me. That's what you're trying to do.'

The chair didn't answer, of course, but then it never would. I paced backwards and forwards thoughtfully in front of it, like an evangelist preacher on a Saturday evening, sober with the prospect of sin.

'I'm going crazy,' I told myself, and the chair as well. 'I put you into the garage this afternoon and I locked the door. You can't be here. There just isn't any way.'

The man-serpent grinned at me in mahogany amusement.

'Sara!' I shouted. 'Sara!'

She appeared in the library doorway wearing the top of my old blue-striped pyjamas.

'Didn't you find that wrap yet?' she asked me.

'Look at this,' I told her, waving towards the chair. The sight of it made me feel unaccountably frustrated and angry. She looked at it, and then shook her head.

'I don't see what you're so mad about.'

'I'm mad because it's here, in the library.'

'I think it suits the library.'

'Sure it suits the library. The only point is, who put it here?'

She crinkled up her nose. 'I don't understand you.'

'What can you possibly fail to understand? Who put it here, that's all I'm asking!'

'You mean – *you* didn't?'

'No, Sara, I didn't.'

'But there hasn't been anybody else in the house. I mean – Marianna comes tomorrow to clean up – but she couldn't have moved this chair anyway.'

'Neither could you,' I pointed out.

'Then who . . . ?' she asked, and her words faded in the air like a smoke-ring, an evanescent question to an answer·

that seemed timeless and old and peculiarly frightening.

'I don't know who,' I said, in a husky voice. 'All I know is that Mr Grant's wonderful chair is going to go straight back in the garage; and that in the morning I'm going to telephone him in Santa Barbara and tell him to come collect everything he's left here. I don't know how I could have been dumb enough to let him get away with selling me all this junk. It's junk, and that's all.'

Emboldened by Sara's presence, I bent over the chair, gripped hold of the serpentine arms, and heaved. To my surprise, I was able to lift it quite easily. It was heavy, yes – but no heavier than any other mahogany armchair. She opened the door wider for me while I staggered out of the library with it, along the corridor, and into the kitchen. She unlocked the back entrance, and I took it out into the night, across the driveway, and back to the garage. I set it down on the asphalt while I examined the padlock. Nobody had tampered with the lock, or the hasp. Whoever had brought the chair out of the garage must have had a key. I unlocked the padlock, lifted the garage door, and shuffled the chair inside. It was dark in the garage, and it smelled of varnish and gasoline and antique furniture. I slammed the door shut, relocked the padlock, and walked back to the house.

Sara was in the living-room, warming her hands by the fire. I sat down heavily on the tapestry-covered sofa, and said, 'That's the last time I buy anything creepy. I mean that. That chair's too damned creepy for me.'

'You bought that creepy old Tarot pack in Indiana.'

'Well, sure. But that wasn't as creepy as this. Can you believe it? The chair found its way into the library, even though nobody touched the lock on the garage door, and nobody we know is strong enough to lift it.'

'Maybe Miguel came around while we were out. Have you thought of that? He always fancies himself as an interior designer.'

'If Miguel came around, why didn't he leave a note? And why didn't he take the stuff that was lying around the driveway? Besides, he doesn't have a key to the garage.'

'Ricky, don't ask me,' Sara protested. 'I don't know anything more about it than you do.'

I reached for my drink, and took a cold fresh mouthful. 'Maybe we're just tired, and tense,' I told Sara. 'What a goddamned Sunday.'

'You still didn't find me your wrap,' she said.

'You've got the fire,' I retorted. 'That should keep you warm. And, besides, whenever I see a nice log fire blazing, it puts me in mind of love-making on the hearth-rug.'

'Oh,' she said. 'It does, does it?'

I kissed her. A small, affectionate kiss at first; as cute and romantic as an old-time Valentine card. But then I kissed her longer, and deeper, and my tongue probed her mouth. She closed her eyes, and I felt her breath on my cheek. She touched my neck with her fingertips, and then her hand strayed downwards and unbuttoned my shirt.

Slowly, an open-mouthed actress in a freeze-frame movie, she settled down on the shaggy rug in front of the fire. Her eyes sparkled with the orange flames that danced around the logs. Her lips were parted to kiss me. I opened her pyjama coat and held her breasts in my hands, squeezing and fondling them until her nipples rose between my fingers. Then I touched her between her thighs where the firelight made her moisture glisten like maple syrup in the fall sunshine.

She held my penis in her fist, its head reddened in the fire's glow, and guided it urgently between her thighs. Then her flesh swallowed it, and I thrust into her as deeply and passionately as I could. Hair tangled with hair, blonde and brown. And I remembered.

I remembered!

'Sara,' I said. I could hear how haunted my voice sounded. She opened her eyes. Stared at me.

'Sara, listen. Did you light this fire?'

A long, uncomprehending pause. How far must the world have rotated on its axis in the time it took for Sara to grasp what I had asked her.

'*Me?*' she said. 'I came downstairs and it was already alight. You told me you were going to – '

I knelt up straight. 'Sara, I didn't light it. I had the match in my hand but I didn't light it.'

'Darling, *of course* you lit it.'

I shook my head. I *knew*, damn it. Sara had called down for the bathrobe, and I'd been right on the brink of striking the match, but I hadn't. I stood up, naked, and I walked across the living-room towards the library.

'Ricky – where are you going?'

'Don't ask. I'm probably wrong.'

'Wrong about what?'

I didn't answer her. I went straight to the library door, threw it wide, and switched on the lights.

Just as I'd feared, there it was. Right in the centre of the room this time. Dark, tall-backed, upholstered in black. The chair that only ten minutes ago I had locked up in my garage.

'Sara,' I said, and she must have heard the shock in my voice, because she came running over straight away.

She stared at the chair, and then at me.

'You said you were going to put it in the garage,' she said. 'Ricky – you said you were going to put it in the garage.'

'I did,' I said quietly. 'But it doesn't seem to want to stay there.'

She held her hand over her mouth.

'Oh, my God,' she breathed. 'Oh, my God, I can't believe it.'

'I'm going to try it one more time,' I told her. 'I'm going to take the chair out into the garage, and I want you to stand here and keep watch. It's my experience with mysterious happenings that they don't stand up to close scrutiny with the lights on.'

'What experience have *you* ever had with mysterious happenings?' Sara asked me.

I stared at her. 'Well, none,' I admitted.

'Ricky,' she whispered, 'I'm frightened.'

'There's nothing to be frightened about. It's only a chair.'

'But *it moved by itself*. You locked it in the garage and it came back. Through two locked doors.'

I walked around the chair, without touching it The eyes on

35

that mask-like man-serpent's face didn't follow me around the room, but I had the oddest feeling that they didn't have to. The man-serpent looked as if he could sense everything that was happening without having to move. Then I thought to myself: *What am I saying? It's wood. It can't move.*

'Maybe it's an hallucination,' I suggested. 'Maybe there's something in the timber. Some kind of aromatic quality, like a drug. Peyote, yage, something like that. Maybe I only *imagined* I took it out into the garage.'

'Ricky, you know that's not true,' said Sara.

I rubbed my face. My chin felt prickly and uncomfortable. 'It's a theory, that's all,' I said, without much conviction. 'But you can't tell me the chair actually walked along the corridor on its own wooden legs. I mean, for Christ's sake.'

Sara said, 'Did you shave this morning?'

'Sure I shaved this morning. You saw me do it.'

She didn't say anything else, but continued to stare at the chair as if she expected it to jump at her.

'What did you say that for?' I asked her.

She glanced up. 'What did I say what for?'

'Why did you ask me if I'd shaved?'

'I don't know. You just look stubbly.'

'Well, thanks.'

'You don't have to be sarcastic,' she said. 'Perhaps your razor needs a service. My father always used to use an old-fashioned straight-razor.'

'Your father used to walk around with more plasters on his chin than any man I ever knew.'

There was a lengthy, awkward silence, while we both stood beside old man Jessop's chair like guests at a cocktail party who couldn't think of anything to say to each other. The clock at the far end of the library began to chime the hour.

Eventually, I said, 'Let's try it, shall we? You wait here, and I'll take it back to the garage.'

Sara brushed her hair back from her face. 'Supposing it – '

'Supposing it what? Supposing it comes strolling in here on its own?'

'Ricky, it got here before.'

'I know. That's just what we're trying this experiment for. To find out how.'

'I'm not sure that I want to know,' she said, in a voice so soft that I could scarcely hear her.

Nonchalantly, I rested my hand on the chair's cresting-rail, and pointed to the man-serpent's face with the commercial ease of an auctioneer. 'Don't tell me this thing scares you. It's a piece of furniture. It looks scary, I admit. But it's nothing more than a rather singular item of eighteenth-century American Chippendale.'

'Does it scare *you*?' asked Sara.

'Are you crazy?'

'I was just asking. The last time you talked this way was when we thought someone had broken into the house.'

'Well, you're right,' I said. 'It scares me.'

We were both silent again. Then Sara said, 'Let's wait till the morning.'

'You think either of us are going to be able to sleep until we know what's going on here?'

'I don't know. No, probably not.'

I bent down, and took hold of the chair's mahogany arms. 'In that case, let's give this experiment just one try, shall we? Keep all the lights on, take hold of the poker, and wait here. That's all you have to do.'

'Don't you think you'd better put some clothes on?'

'Who's going to see? The Johnsons are on vacation, and apart from that it's nine o'clock on a Sunday evening.'

'It's still light outside.'

'That's the moon. If you're really worried that a stray Winnebago full of Girl Scouts is going to pull in to the driveway and that twenty innocent eyes are all going to stare at my penis, then I'll wait until it goes behind a cloud.'

'Ricky . . .' smiled Sara.

Still holding the arms of the chair, I turned around to her and gave her a hard, serious look to show her that I wasn't really joking. The only reason I was teasing her was because I didn't know of any other way to suppress my feeling that something very powerful and very frightening had come to lodge itself in our house tonight. No wonder people laugh so much at death, and funeral parlours. How else can you deal with the dark charade they really represent?

I had a sensation at that moment of incredible foreboding, as black as the nodding plumes on an old-style horse-drawn hearse, as wild as a coastal typhoon.

Then I tried to lift up the chair.

I yelled: '*A Aaaah!*' and whipped my hands away. Because the *instant* I had attempted to heave the chair off the floor, those snake-like arms had *wriggled*, as dry and as muscular as real snakes. I stood away from the chair, my hands raised, and you could tell how frightened I was by the way my balls had tightened up like a pair of shrivelled walnuts.

'It's alive,' I managed to choke out.

'Ricky?' asked Sara, reaching out for my hand.

'I tried to pick it up and the damned thing's *alive*!'

'Ricky, it *can't* be. It's wood. You said so yourself. It's only a piece of furniture.'

I shivered, and rubbed my arms to try to stir up my circulation. All of a sudden I felt intensely cold, as if someone had left the window wide open, and a freezing draught were flowing in.

'Never mind what I said,' I told Sara. 'I tried to pick it up just then and those arms felt exactly like live snakes. They *moved*, Sara. It was like holding on to a couple of goddamned boa constrictors.'

Sara walked across to the phone. 'Who are you calling?' I asked her.

'Who do you think? The police.'

'The police? What do you think the police are going to say?'

She had lifted the receiver, and was about to punch out the number. Then, slowly, she laid the receiver down again. 'I'm not sure. I'm not even sure what *we're* going to say to *them*.'

I said, 'The first thing I'm going to do is get dressed. Look – my towelling wrap's over there. Put that on. I'm not having any damned chair staring at you while you're naked. Not a chair with a face like that.'

The man-serpent grinned at me sightlessly.

'All right,' said Sara, tying up the white wrap, and circling around the chair. 'Now what are we going to do?'

'We're going to wait until ten o'clock, which should give Mr Grant plenty of time to get home to Santa Barbara, if he's not home already, and then we're going to give him a call. We're going to tell him to get his ass down here as quickly as possible, no arguments, and to pick up all of this junk he's left here. Including, and *especially*, this chair.'

'Do you think he will?'

'If he doesn't, I'll get in touch with the California Antique Dealers' Association and have him struck off their register for shoddy practice. And I'll sue him for misrepresentation. *And* I'll bust him in the mouth.'

We retreated into the living-room, locking the library door behind us, although it was quite obvious that the chair didn't consider locks to be much of an obstacle. It was one of those ritual gestures that any human being would make, I guess. Why do we say prayers, or light candles for our loved ones? They're all part of our endearing frailty in the face of sinister and cataclysmic forces that we can neither control nor understand. And don't think I'm usually this philosophical. It was just that during that first terrifying night, I began to realise what it's really like to be helpless. What else could I do but lock the door?

We walked into the living-room. It was cold in there, too, and I went over to the fire to poke a little more life into it. To my surprise, it had almost completely burned out. There was nothing left of the logs I had stacked on it only a half-hour before but mounds of soft grey ash, glowing with cinders.

'Sara,' I said. 'Will you take a look at this fire?'

She came closer. She raised her hands to feel its dying warmth. 'It was blazing,' she said. 'When we were making love just now – it was really burning up.'

I raked through the hearth. A soft cold wind blew from nowhere at all, and some of the powdery ash sifted across the rug.

· 'Something's wrong here, honey,' I said. 'Something's very badly wrong. I think we'd better go up and check that Jonathan's okay. I don't want anything happening to him.'

We left the fire and went upstairs. At the top of the stairs, there was a long landing carpeted in light gold, and our five bedrooms came off it on either side. Jonathan's room was way down at the far end, past a row of framed engravings of American birds of prey, Mississippi kites and sharp-shinned hawks and California condors. There was a fan-shaped window at the end, too, and the extraordinary thing about it was that it was already bright with the misty blue light of dawn.

'Am I going nuts or is it morning?' I asked Sara. I'd taken my watch off downstairs, when we'd been making love. All she could do was shake her head in confusion.

'It can't be morning,' she said.

We hurried down the corridor to Jonathan's room. Sara flung open the door, and there he was. Safe, and still asleep. Tucked up in his early-American patchwork quilt in his bright little room with its brass-bound bureau, and red-and-white wallpaper, and some of the gaudy paintings that he'd brought home from playschool. Sara leaned over and kissed his cheek. I saw a tear glistening in her eye, a tear that fell on her son's pillow. I stood by the door and said, 'At least it hasn't affected *him* – whatever it is.'

'There's really something here, isn't there?' Sara asked me, as she quietly closed Jonathan's door behind her. 'I mean – that chair's brought some kind of evil spirit in with it.'

'I don't know,' I said, and I didn't. 'I'm still willing to admit that we could be suffering from overloaded imaginations. Don't ask me how, or why. But can you actually believe that it's something to do with the supernatural?'

'What else could it be?'

'Come on, Sara. The supernatural? Demons and devils and invisible forces that throw all your pots and pans around the place? It just doesn't happen.'

'What about *The Amityville Horror*?'

'Didn't you read that article in the papers? They proved that half of the things that were supposed to have taken place at

Amityville were – well, they were exaggerated, to put it kindly.'

Sara turned towards the window. It looked out on to our sloping side garden, and the picket fence that surrounded the lemon grove. The rising sun was shining through the dark green leaves of the lemon trees, and the sharp-coloured citrus fruits looked almost as if they were fashioned out of wax.

'Ricky,' she said, gently, 'about a half-hour ago it was nine o'clock in the evening. We'd only just come home from the wild-animal park. Now, it's morning. Are you trying to say that what we're experiencing isn't supernatural?'

'We could have slept by the fire without realising it.'

'Ricky, we didn't sleep by the fire.'

'But maybe we did.'

'We *didn't*, for God's sake! Don't you think I know if I've been to sleep or not? It's morning, and I'm tired, and I haven't closed my eyes even once!'

'What the hell do you want me to say?' I shouted at her. 'I don't know where the night's gone any more than you do! I'm trying to rationalise it. Trying to explain it.'

'What for? Can't you question it? Can't you challenge it? Can't you suppose just for one moment that it might be something outside of any kind of explanation at all?'

I couldn't answer that, and I didn't try. The truth was that I was only seeking answers to what had happened during this briefest of nights because I had Sara to take care of, and Jonathan, and if I once admitted that our house had been possessed by some species of supernatural force, I was admitting that I couldn't protect them against it. Maybe I was acting like a stereotypical husband; but I didn't know how else to behave when there was a chair downstairs that could apparently move itself through locked doors at will, and a night that I had thought was just about to begin had vapourised away in front of my eyes.

I thought of the wall-clock in the library. When we had been examining the chair it had struck the hour. I could remember the strokes in my head. *One – two – three – four – five*. I should

41

have realised then that the chair was turning our whole world upside-down.

While Sara took a shower, I went to our bedroom and dressed. Our bedroom was decorated all in white – with a white shag rug, white figured bedspread, and white furniture. The only relief was a huge unfinished oil painting by Gustave Moreau, the French symbolist. It showed an androgynous figure in a crown and white robes, standing in a dark and exotic temple. The figure was obviously supposed to be reacting to something in surprise and possibly terror, but nobody would ever find out to *what*, because Moreau had died in 1898 and left over a third of the picture as blank canvas, with only a few rough sketches on it.

I put on a dark blue shirt and a pair of cream linen jeans. I looked at myself in the mirror over Sara's dressing-table, and I saw that she was right. I'd shaved this morning – or what by now must be *yesterday* morning – but there was at least twenty-four hours' growth. In some weird way, the arrival of that chair had taken a whole slice of time out of our lives. It had tampered with our entire perception of day and night.

I shaved quickly, and splashed on some English Leather. Sara came in from the bathroom, her hair wound into a towel-turban, her eyelashes spiky with wet. As she rubbed herself dry in front of the mirror, I stood behind her and touched her on the shoulder and said, 'Listen. I didn't mean to shout at you You have to understand that I'm trying to look after you.'

'I know,' she nodded. 'But you won't be able to look after us unless you face up to reality.'

'You call a half-hour night reality?'

'It's reality as far as we're concerned. I don't know how it happened, but we lost eight hours someplace, and there isn't any question in my mind at all that Mr Grant's chair was responsible for it.'

I kissed her ear, the wet stray curl of her hair. 'You're a wife in a million,' I said, 'and a lover in a billion.'

'You've had a billion lovers to compare me with?'

'Don't be so pragmatic.'

'I can't help it. I'm made that way. Most women are. And that's why I can face up to what's going on here while you can't. All this stuff about protecting us.'

I kissed her again, but Sara shook her head, and said, 'Not now, darling. Let's get rid of the chair first.'

I stepped back. 'They should have run over Kate Millett with a truck when they had the chance.'

I went to the telephone, picked it up, and punched out the number of Grant Antiques in Santa Barbara.

'You're calling Grant?' asked Sara, as she combed out her hair.

'You bet.'

The phone rang and rang and rang. After a while, I sat down impatiently on the edge of the bed. I had almost given up the call when someone picked up the phone at the other end, a grave-sounding man with an East Coast accent.

'Hallo? Henry Grant, Antiques.'

'Oh, hi. Is Henry Grant there, please?'

There was a silence that I can only describe as 'difficult'. Then the grave-sounding man said, 'I regret not.'

'Do you expect him back today? My name's Delatolla. I'm an antiques dealer from Rancho Santa Fe, near San Diego.'

'I'm sorry, Mr Delatolla. But I'm afraid Mr Grant has met with an accident.'

'An accident? What kind of an accident? Is it serious?'

'As serious as it could be. He was returning from a buying trip yesterday evening when his van collided with a concrete pier on the Santa Ana Freeway.'

'You're trying to tell me he's dead?'

'I'm afraid so. The van – the van caught fire. He didn't have any chance to escape whatsoever. He was burned to death.'

I smoothed the tense muscles at the back of my neck. 'I see. I'm really sorry.'

'Was there anything I could help you with?' asked the grave-sounding man. 'I'm Mr Grant's attorney, Douglas Eckstein. I'll be doing whatever I can today to clear up his outstanding business affairs.'

I cleared my throat. 'As a matter of fact, Mr Grant left me with something of a problem. He came around here yesterday afternoon with a whole pile of antiques, none of which were particularly valuable or interesting to me, but he unloaded them all on to my driveway to show them to me, and then he took off in his van before I could tell him I didn't particularly want them.'

'He left some antiques with you, without asking for payment?'

'A whole heap. And the trouble is, I don't want any of them. Do you think you could arrange to have them collected? There must be twenty or thirty thousand dollars' worth here. I don't really want to be responsible for them.'

'Will you hold on for just a moment?' Mr Eckstein asked me. He must have clamped his hand over the phone, because all I could hear for the next few moments was two or three muffled, distorted voices. After a while, though, he came back on the line.

'Mr Delatolla,' he asked me, 'do these antiques include a certain carved chair, with a sort of face on it?'

'You've got it.'

'Well, Mr Grant left a letter of instructions with his office before he went off to San Diego County, and he stated specifically in this letter that if he were to leave this particular chair with anyone, no matter whom, no matter whether it was paid for or not, we could take it that the chair and any other objects that came with it had been accepted by the beneficiary as a gift, and that we were to take no action to recover it.'

I ran my hand through my hair. I could hardly believe what I was hearing. 'What are you talking about, Mr Eckstein?' I asked him. 'I never accepted the chair either as a gift or a sale. All I want to do is get rid of it.'

I was bending the truth a little — but since Henry Grant was no longer around to prove that I had offered him $7500 for his antiques, and since the chair had turned out to have such unpleasant and unsettling effects on my household, I think I was justified.

But Eckstein was adamant. 'Mr Grant's instructions are

quite clear,' he told me. 'He has written in the plainest language possible that we should not take the chair back from whomsoever has accepted it, *under any circumstances*, and those include financial inducements, no matter how substantial, and even threats of physical duress.'

'You mean you wouldn't even take it back at gunpoint?'

'Mr Grant's instructions are quite unequivocal.'

'Listen,' I snapped, 'this is crazy. I don't want the damned thing.'

'I'm sorry, Mr Delatolla. I am not empowered to take any action to help you.'

'Those instructions that Mr Grant left you . . . they don't constitute a legal will. And apart from that, there's nothing in writing which says this chair belongs to me.'

'There's nothing in writing which says it belongs to anybody.'

'What are you trying to pull here?' I shouted. 'I've got all this junk here, cluttering up my driveway, and you're trying to tell me you won't clear it away?'

'That's precisely it,' said Mr Eckstein, in his Brooks Brothers voice. 'But I'm willing to send you a cheque to cover the expenses of removal and disposal.'

'I'll sue,' I retorted.

'Whom will you sue?' asked Mr Eckstein smoothly. 'Mr Grant? Or his business, which is going to be wound up? And what for? For an unwelcome gift? An embarrassment of free antiques? You'd be laughed out of court, even if you could find a lawyer to take your case.'

'I'll dump the stuff on your doorstep,' I threatened.

'Well,' said Mr Eckstein, 'you can try.'

'What's that supposed to mean? That's not a threat, is it?'

'I don't know. What do you think?'

'I think you're just another oily sardine with a licence to practise law.'

I banged the phone down, and sat on the bed with my arms folded, simmering. Sara was watching me in the mirror, and she combed her hair slower and slower and finally laid her comb down.

'That didn't sound very promising,' she said.

'Grant's dead,' I told her. 'That was his attorney on the phone. It seems like he crashed on the Santa Ana Freeway on the way home. The van caught fire, and he couldn't get out.'

'Ricky, that's awful,' she said.

'It's more than awful. Grant's lawyer said he won't take the chair back. Apparently Grant left him a letter saying that he shouldn't accept it back no matter what. Not even if we went around there and pointed a sawn-off shotgun at him.'

Sara frowned. 'He was that serious about it?'

I stood up, and went to the bedroom window. 'You bet,' I told her. 'If you ask me, Grant had been having as much trouble with that chair as we had last night. He was just driving around, looking for some sucker to dump it on.'

I let out a breath. 'It was just my luck that the first sucker in line was me.'

'Can't you just drive the chair back to Santa Barbara and leave it on his attorney's doorstep?' asked Sara.

'That's one way. The other way is simply to take it out into the yard, chop it up, and burn it. Of course, I could always put it in the shop window, and try to sell it.'

'But that might mean that whatever – well, whatever spirit this chair has inside of it – that might mean that you'll pass it on to somebody else. And you wouldn't want to do that, would you?'

'I don't know. I think I'd rather do anything than keep it here. I mean that, Sara. That chair is definitely hexed.'

I heard a rustling, scurrying noise which made me look towards the window again. At first, I couldn't quite believe what I was seeing. Then I stepped closer and peered out over the slope of the side garden, and what I saw there made me feel as if I'd stuck my fingers into an electric plug. A thrill of sheer fright, and unreality.

'What is it?' asked Sara, standing up. 'Ricky – what's out there?'

'Fall,' I said, in a hushed voice. 'Sara, it's *fall*.'

All around the house, whirling down from the eucalyptus trees, flew showers of dead leaves, brown and curled-up and·

46

twisted. Even the leaves of the bougainvillaea had turned brown, and the carefully-nurtured grass along the side of the driveway seemed to have shrivelled and dried. The leaves were blown into drifts by the morning breeze, and the drifts rippled as if they had a life of their own.

The whole garden was withering, and it wasn't at all difficult for either of us to guess why.

3—Returnings

We walked out into the morning, into the yard, and we held hands with the bewildered innocence of children. The leaves still blew from the branches of the eucalyptus trees around the house, and our feet rustled through them like the feet of ghosts walking through a dried-up memory.

It was always quiet out here in Rancho Santa Fe, but today the air seemed especially cold and especially still.

We went as far as the picket-fence, and there we saw how pervasive the influence of old man Jessop's chair had turned out to be. Even the leaves of the nearby lemon trees were curling up, and the lemons themselves had turned green with mould.

A little further away, however, the trees were still thriving, and the eucalyptus we could see waving in the distance were quite healthy.

I reached over the fence and tugged one of the rotten lemons off the tree. I squeezed it in my hand and it ran between my fingers like dust. Sara stood a little way away, watching me, her hands clasped around herself as if she were cold.

'Ricky,' she said, 'we just have to get that chair out of the house.'

I brushed the dust from my hands and nodded. 'I'll put it in the station-wagon and drive it along to the dam at Lake Hodges. A hundred-foot drop into the reservoir race should sort it out.'

'I'll come with you,' she said. 'Just let me get Jonathan ready.'

While Sara went upstairs to wake Jonathan up and dress him in his chequered cowboy shirt and his denim dungarees, I went along to the library, tapping the key in the palm of my hand with all the nervousness of a jailer in a madhouse. I stood outside the library door for over a minute before I plucked up the nerve to push the key into the lock and turn it. Then I nudged the door with the heel of my hand so that it swung open.

The chair was still there, in the centre of the room, illuminated by a single beam of sunlight which fell across the carpet from the half-drawn drapes. Its mahogany gleamed as dark and rich as before. The man-serpent's face, with its crown of twisted vipers, still smiled at me with lips of wood, still mocked me with eyes that could never see. I walked into the room, and stood looking at the chair with a tight-chested feeling that was nothing short of controlled terror.

I had been frightened before. Once, in a car crash, when I thought I was certainly going to die. Once in New York, when I was rousted on Tenth Avenue by three young punks with knives and a car antenna.

But the fear I had felt before had always been immediate – a surge of hyped-up adrenalin and self-protective instincts. Whereas the fear I felt when I stood in the presence of old man Jessop's chair was something else. It was a slow-burning dread that seemed to freeze me rather than jolt me into action. It was a dark, ancient certainty that whatever I did to help myself, this chair was going to overwhelm me.

I remembered reading about the way two hundred aeroplane passengers behaved in Saudi Arabia when their aircraft caught fire and they had absolutely no way to escape. They sat where they were, paralysed. And the same thing happened when thirty gamblers were trapped by a fire in a club in England. They stayed at their tables, screaming but unable to move, while the flames roasted them orange.

Looking at that chair, I suddenly wished that I had never read anything gruesome or frightening in my life. Because that chair seemed to stir up in my mind the very worst fears I could think of. It made me feel so damned *weak*.

I circled around it. After the last time, when the arms had writhed in my hands like snakes, I wasn't at all sure that I wanted to pick it up. I touched the cresting-rail quickly with my fingertips, and nothing happened, but I still didn't feel particularly inclined to lift it.

I thought for a moment. Then I left the library, went outside to the garage, and took down a coil of nylon rope, which I usually used for tying chairs and bureaux on to my roofrack. I went back into the house, loosening the rope as I walked, and returned to the library.

The chair was still there. It hadn't moved. Or, at least, it didn't appear to have moved. There was something about the way the sunlight was illuminating the man-serpent's face which gave me a disturbing suspicion that it had altered its angle slightly.

I licked my lips. I shouldn't let the goddamned thing start getting to me. It was a chair, right? A spooky chair, admittedly, but a chair and nothing more.

Working quickly, I threaded the nylon rope under the arms of the chair and pulled it tight. Then, twisting the rope around my hand, I started to drag the chair across the library carpet, and out through the door.

By the time I was halfway down the corridor to the kitchen, I was gasping for breath, and smothered in sweat. That chair was so incredibly heavy that I could scarcely move it. Each time I took a fresh grip on the rope and pulled, I felt as if the ball-and-claw feet were actually *digging in*, like a tug-o'-war, and resisting me. Where the chair had passed, the carpet had been roughed up into two deep tracks.

As I reached the back door, Sara came downstairs with Jonathan. Her face was white and strained, but she managed a quick smile.

Jonathan said, 'Hi, Daddy. What are you doing?'

'What does it look like I'm doing? I'm pulling this damned chair out of the house.'

'Ricky,' Sara admonished me.

I stopped pulling for a while, and wiped my forehead with the back of my arm.

'I'm just trying to get this real heavy chair into the yard,' I corrected myself. 'I'm going to load it on to the wagon, and then we're going to take it for a ride.'

Jonathan ran his finger down the cascade of carved wood at the side of the chair, and looked thoughtful.

'Jonathan,' I warned him, 'I don't want you to touch it, all right? I'd rather you didn't touch it.'

'It's all right,' Jonathan told me, in an unusually flat voice.

'It's not all right,' I retorted. 'I don't want you to touch it, and that means don't touch it. You got me?'

He looked up at me, and smiled. 'Yes, Daddy.'

Sara had brought out a bag of Pepperidge Farm cookies and a carton of milk so that Jonathan could eat his breakfast in the car. After a short struggle with the rope and a couple of sharp kicks, I managed to drag the chair over the back step, and along by the side of the house to the front driveway, its feet scraping and bumping on the quarry-tile path.

Jonathan, following me, looked up at the trees and said, 'What's happened? All the leaves have fallen. Mommy, it's just like New England!'

Sara put her arm around him, and smiled. She didn't tell him what had happened. There wasn't any way that she could.

The rest of the furniture that Mr Grant had left on our driveway was still standing there, drifted up with dead leaves. It looked disturbingly like a collection of tombstones in a cemetery, the kind you might put up to mark an antique dealer's last resting place. A long-case clock, tall and silent. A bow-fronted bureau. A leather-topped writing-desk.

I pulled the chair as close to the tailgate of my wagon as I could. As I searched for my keys in my tight jeans pocket, Sara lifted her head and said, 'Is that the telephone?'

I listened. At first I couldn't hear anything, but then I picked up the muffled *brrrnnggg-brrrnnggg-brrrnnggg* of the phone in my library.

'I'll answer it,' said Sara. 'You just get that thing on to the wagon. And make sure you tie it down.'

I opened up the tailgate, pushed aside some old brass castors which I had picked up in a junk store on Morena Boulevard in the hope of repairing an early American bed, and tugged the chair right up to the wagon's rear bumper as if it were a disobedient dog. In the morning sunlight, it had lost nothing of its dark charisma. It was like a black hole which drew everything towards it and let nothing escape. Jonathan raised his hand as if he wanted to run his fingers down the contours of the tumbling, hell-bent people who formed the central splat of the chair's back, but I said, 'Ah!' in that sharp warning way that parents do.

'It won't hurt me,' protested Jonathan.

'Never mind,' I told him. 'Just keep your hands off.'

I went round to the back of the chair, planning to heave its back legs off the ground and tilt it into the back of the wagon. But at that moment the front living-room window opened and Sara called out, 'Ricky? It's Bill Everett, from the store. He wants to know what time you're coming in.'

'What time is it now?' I called back.

'The clock in here says a quarter of nine.'

'Well, tell him eleven o'clock. That should give us all the time we need.'

There was a pause, and then Sara leaned out of the window again. 'He says he wants a word.'

'Tell him I'm busy.'

'I already did. He says he still wants a word.'

'Okay,' I sighed.

I lashed the nylon rope which held the chair to the Malibu's rear bumper. Then I said to Jonathan, 'Listen – I have to talk to somebody on the phone. Why don't you go feed Sheraton until I'm through?'

'Can't I stay here and look after the chair for you?' Jonathan asked me.

'No, you can't. Now, Sheraton's hungry. Go give him some Gravy Train, and a dish of water.'

'But Daddy – '

'Will you go do what you're damned well told to do?' I snapped at him. 'And make sure you leave this chair alone. Don't touch it. Don't go near it. And that's an order.'

'Okay,' he said, turning away with flushed cheeks.

I went inside the house and impatiently picked up the phone. It was Bill Everett, my assistant, a moustachioed lunkhead from the University of California at Santa Cruz whose idea of an antique was a '62 Chevy. But he was willing, and eager to learn, and he had a certain surfing-bum appeal about him which attracted those fastidious upper-class ladies who liked to browse through the store. I often caught them eyeing Bill through the handles of a Royal Worcester vase, and unconsciously licking their ice-pink lips. It must have been something to do with his tangled blond hair, which looked as if it had been dried by the sun; or maybe that sloping Neanderthal forehead which looked as if it contained just enough primitive instincts to keep a rampant lady happy, but very little else.

Compared with Bill, I looked too much like a half-Italian smartass, all university degree and shirts by Cerruti. A kind of suave Petrocelli. *Italians* never think I look like a half-Italian smartass, mind you. They always think I look like a Southern California smartass. But Italians only accept you as a brother if you have spaghetti hanging from your ears, and your pockets crammed full of Chianti bottles, and you drive a Fiat Mirafiori with *O Sole Mio* going at full blast on the stereo. My father would hate me for saying that, but he was the same. 'Without opera,' he used to proclaim, 'the whole world would suffocate.' Opera, for Christ's sake. Pizza. I was still grumbling to myself when I said, 'Yes, Bill. What's going on?'

'I had some British guy in this morning. He says he has one or two things to sell. But he's also interested in that japanned cabinet.'

'Really?' The japanned cabinet was priced at $135,000, and a few cents. It was late eighteenth-century English, with a beautifully carved stand and surmount. I'd bought it from one of the retired movie actors who shuffled around Rancho Santa Fe, living out their retirement on memories, golf, and cameo appearances in *Charlie's Angels*.

'He said he could call back. But he'd like to know when. And since you didn't show up at your regular time this morning, I thought I'd check.'

'Okay. Tell him eleven. I should be able to get into the village by then.'

There was a pause. Then Bill said, 'Is everything all right?'

I glanced towards the window. 'Sure. Everything's fine. Why do you ask?'

'I don't know. Sara sounded kind of spooked. You know what I mean?'

'I don't think I do, no.'

'All right,' said Bill, 'I'm sorry I brought it up. As long as everything's okay.'

'Yes. Everything's okay.'

I put down the phone, and went back outside into the morning sunshine. The chair was right where I'd left it, lashed to the back of the wagon, and there was Sara in her pink dress, waiting for me amongst the crisp leaves of our own unnatural autumn. But also, like figures in a Norman Rockwell painting, there was Jonathan, running across the driveway, and there was Sheraton, our golden Labrador and guard dog, bouncing and bounding around the car.

'Sheraton!' I shouted. 'Heel!'

Sheraton, as usual, ignored me. I swear to God that if ever I'd tried to climb over the fencing around our house, instead of driving in through the front gate, that dog would have torn my legs off.

'Sheraton!' I repeated.

The dog finally stopped leaping up and down, and stood not far away from the wagon's tailgate, panting and wagging his tail. But as I came closer, he retreated towards the chair; and when I was only a few feet away, he actually jumped up on to the seat and sat there, staring at me with his great lolloping head on one side, and his tongue hanging out. I took a few paces towards him, trying to look like an Angry Master.

'Sheraton, you'd better get off that chair,' I cautioned him.

He let out a low, rattling growl. I stopped, and stayed where I was, because for some reason that growl reminded me far too much of the animal breathing I had heard in my library last night.

'Sheraton,' I told the dog, more apprehensively. 'Sheraton, I want you to move your ass off that chair. I mean it.'

Sheraton growled again.

'Ricky?' asked Sara. 'What's wrong with him? He usually does what he's told.'

Jonathan cried, 'Sherry! Come on, boy!' in that high, piping voice of his, but Sheraton ignored him. Trust me to christen a dog after a goddamned sideboard.

'Sheraton,' I said, in my real *this-is-it* tone – the tone that Jonathan always recognises as a final and absolute signal that it's time to go to bed. 'Sheraton, get off that chair.'

Sheraton stared at me for one second more, and then suddenly he yelped out loud in pain, and twisted his body first one way and then the other. Then he was off that chair like a bat out of hell, and running across the lawn towards the back of the house as fast as I'd ever seen him.

'Ricky, something's wrong with him,' said Sara. She didn't have to say any more, because I was running after that dog as if he'd snatched my annual tax rebate.

I followed him around to the paved patio in back of the house, beside the pool pump enclosure. He was sitting outside his kennel, shivering and panting, and when he looked at me his eyes rolled around so that I could see the whites.

'Sheraton, steady boy,' I called, in what I hoped was a reassuring voice. 'Come on, now. Steady, boy. Steady.'

I knelt down beside him, and he allowed me to stroke his head, and rub his trembling flanks. At first, I didn't think he'd been injured. But as I ran my hand through the thick golden hair around his flanks, I felt the matted wetness of blood.

Sara had come around the house now, and bent over to pat Sheraton's back.

'He's hurting,' I said. 'Somehow, that goddamned chair's hurt him.'

Sara took a cloth from the pipe beside the pump enclosure, and dipped it in the pool. While I held Sheraton still, she mopped away the blood from his coat, and tried to see where he was wounded.

'It's hardly anything at all,' she said, at last. 'Look – it's not much more than a puncture. Maybe he scratched himself on the carvings when he jumped up.'

I peered closely at the wound. It was a single, circular pinprick. Nothing serious. Already, the blood was starting to coagulate and form a scab.

'What do you think?' asked Sara.

'I don't know. It doesn't look like the kind of scratch he would have got from catching himself on the carvings. And what made him jump up in the first place?'

I fastened Sheraton's collar to the long chain that was stapled to the side of his kennel, and gave him another soothing rub around the neck.

'If you dab some antiseptic on it,' I told Sara, 'I'll go load the chair into the wagon. Sheraton should be okay while we go out to the lake. It won't take us more than twenty minutes, there and back.'

'You're sure we ought to leave him?'

'He doesn't look badly hurt, does he? And he's stopped shivering now. Maybe the chair just gave him a fright. Dogs are supposed to be susceptible to all kinds of vibes that we can't pick up, aren't they?'

Sara looked around at the flaking trees, and the dried-up grass. 'That chair gives off more than vibes,' she said.

I went back to the station-wagon. Jonathan, obediently, was standing a few feet away from the chair, waiting with one of his serious, grown-up expressions on his face. I ruffled his hair as I came up to him.

'Sherry's okay now,' I reassured him. 'He's scratched himself a little, that's all. It could have been a bug bite, or something. But he's quite okay.'

Jonathan said, 'The chair spoke to me.'

I was bending over, just about to tilt the chair into the back of the wagon. I said, 'What?'

Jonathan came closer. His face was grave, and I knew that he was telling me the truth. 'The chair spoke to me,' he said. 'When you were gone, it said, *"Break the windows. Break the wagon's windows."*'

I stood up. The man-serpent looked as malevolently self-satisfied as before; but whatever it looked like, I knew that it was fashioned out of nothing but mahogany. And mahogany, as far as I was aware, wasn't capable of speech. Oh God, I hoped it wasn't.

'You imagined it,' I said.

56

Jonathan shook his head.

'It said, *"Break the windows."'*

'So what did you say?'

Jonathan didn't answer at first. He was clearly very frightened. I hunkered down beside him and held him in my arms. There were tears in his eyes because he couldn't understand how a chair could talk to him, and how it was fall in California when it was really summer, and why Daddy and Mommy were so anxious to get rid of this dark, peculiar piece of furniture.

'Listen,' I said, gently. 'There's something real funny about this chair. I don't know what it is. But somehow it makes people think they see things and hear things they don't want to hear or see. It's like a kind of magic chair, you understand me? But it's not very nice magic. So, what we're going to do, we're going to take this magic chair out to the lake, and we're going to throw it away, for ever.'

'Okay,' Jonathan nodded, through his tears.

I stood up. 'Jump into the wagon, and then we'll go. You can sit in the front seat with us.'

I went back to the chair. I paused a moment, and then I seized hold of its legs and heaved it into the back of the wagon. Its cresting-rail just fitted under the roof-lining, although its back was so long that I couldn't fit its legs completely inside, and I had to lash the wagon's tailgate closed with the nylon rope.

Sara came around from attending to Sheraton, flapping her hands to dry them. We all climbed into the front seat of the Impala, and I started up the engine and backed out of the driveway.

We had to drive through the centre of Rancho Santa Fe to join the road which led out to Lake Hodges. It was sunny and quiet, as usual, and the only people I saw on the streets were two old friends and customers, moseying along to the Post Office to collect their Monday-morning mail. There are no house-to-house mail deliveries in Rancho Santa Fe, and the Post Office is a daily gathering-place for anyone who wants to gossip about money and real-estate prices and whatever happened to the good old days. Next door to the Post Office is a supermarket called Jonathan's, and we always used to joke with Jonathan that we had bought him there, for fifty-nine cents.

We left a trail of summer dust behind us as we left town and drove along the sweeping road that took us through the hills. The sky was raked with high cirrus clouds, but they would probably burn off before mid-morning.

Lake Hodges is a grey-surfaced reservoir which lies amongst the wooded hills on the way to Escondido like a pool of mercury in the fold of a dark-green blanket. As we approached it from the west, we saw the narrow concrete dam which holds the water back, with its cascading over-flow plunging nearly a hundred feet to the rocky riverbed below.

I pulled off the road on to the rough parking area, and turned the wagon around. Fortunately, it was too early for sightseers or tourists, and the only other vehicle in sight was an oily old Mack tanker which was toiling its way up the grade in a cloud of filthy exhaust.

'Do you want me to help you?' asked Sara.

I shook my head. 'I think I can manage. Just stay there. This shouldn't take more than a couple of seconds.'

I untied the rope which held the tailgate closed, and then wrenched at the chair until it toppled from the back of the wagon and fell sideways on to the ground. It looked defeated, lying like that. More like an ugly piece of old furniture than some species of evil spirit incarnate. It was only fifteen feet or so to the edge of the precipice which overlooked the dam, and I decided to risk carrying the chair with my bare hands.

Tentatively, I touched one of the arms. It felt like wood. I turned the chair on to its back, and took hold of the other arm. That felt like wood, too. So far, no nasty surprises.

Sara called, 'Is everything okay?' and I gave her a wave to show that everything was.

I lifted the chair on to its ball-and-claw feet, and then I picked it up by the arms and began to carry it slowly over to the precipice. The chair was heavy, but not abnormally heavy, and I had the feeling that whatever influence it contained, wherever it had come from, I had it licked.

The man-serpent face watched me without emotion as I sweated and struggled to carry the chair over the uneven ground. Up above, the sun had already frittered away most of the clouds, and it was growing uncomfortably hot. All I could hear was the rushing of the reservoir water as it slid down the long steep face of the concrete dam, and foamed on to the rocks below.

At last, my chest heaving in and out like the bellows of a harmonium, I reached the very brink of the precipice. I stood there for a half-minute, to get my breath back, and then I lifted that damned chair as high as I could, and launched it out into space.

Instantly, like a suicide who ties himself to a boulder, I was plucked off the edge of the precipice after it. *I couldn't let go!* My hands were fastened tight to the arms of the chair as if my flesh had grown into the wood.

There was a blur of rocks, sky, sliding gravel, and bushes. I was tossed end over end, battering my face and body against the chair and the cliff, until something inside of me commanded *let go, for Christ's sake, let go!* And then the chair tumbled away on its own, and by some split-second miracle I slid into the roots of a tough old bush, and was brought up short in a scratchy, bruising, mind-jolting shock.

I lay there, almost halfway down the face of the precipice, gasping and coughing and thanking God. Far below me, I glimpsed the chair falling into the foamy river, and then disappearing.

Sara appeared, wide-eyed, at the brink of the precipice above me.

'*Ricky!*' she screamed. '*Ricky!*'

'I'm okay,' I called back. 'Not very okay, but reasonably okay. Just a few bruises.'

'Oh my God, I thought you'd been killed.'

'So did I,' I told her, wrestling my way out of the roots, and standing up. My nose was bleeding, and I had to wipe it on my arm.

'Can you climb back up?'

I looked around. 'I think so. If I edge my way along this ledge a ways, as far as that big rock there, I should be able to make it easy.'

It took me ten minutes of sliding and slipping and clawing at roots to reach the top, while Sara and Jonathan watched me in apprehensive silence, but at last I made it. When I got there, I hugged them both, and we stood for a long time without saying anything, a small family who loved each other very dearly.

'What happened?' asked Sara. 'I was watching you in the rear-view mirror and you just – *fell*.'

'I think the chair made a last effort to get its own back,' I said. I brushed twigs and mud from my shirt and jeans. 'I threw it over the edge, but right at the last moment I couldn't let go of it. It was like my hands were stuck fast. The chair went over, and I had to go over with it.'

'Is it gone now?' Sara asked me. 'Is it really gone for good?'

'You can't go any gooder,' I smiled, dabbing at my nose with a tissue. 'I saw it fall into the river, and disappear under the water, and that's what I call *gone*.'

We got back into the wagon. 'How about a celebratory drink?' I suggested. 'Let's all go along to The Inn and share a bottle of champagne.'

'Don't forget you have an appointment at eleven,' Sara reminded me.

I checked the clock on the dash. 'We have twelve minutes. If we can't finish a bottle of champagne between us in twelve minutes, then we don't deserve to celebrate.'

It only took us a few minutes to drive back into Rancho Santa Fe. I parked the wagon in the sloping parking lot outside of The Inn, and then we walked along the brick path beside the neat-clipped lawns and manicured hedges to The Inn's front door. The morning was sunny and beautifully calm, and I put my arm around Sara and gave her a squeeze of affection. We may have lost the night to old man Jessop's peculiar chair, but we were alive and well on one of those balmy Southern

California days that makes you feel richer and younger and almost religious.

They brought us a frosted ice-bucket of Domaine Chandon in the high, airy drawing-room, where we sat on chintzy sofas amidst antique furniture and The Inn's collection of old decoy ducks. I ordered a fresh orange juice for Jonathan, but I fizzed it up for him with champagne, and he laughed because it tickled his nose. Then Sara and I raised our glasses to each other, and drank a silent toast. We didn't need any words.

At ten after eleven, I left Sara and Jonathan at The Inn and walked across the street to the store. There was a sand-coloured Rolls-Royce Corniche parked by the kerb, with its hood down. I walked in through the store doorway, and the Russian troika-bell jingled pretentiously behind me as I crossed the brown-carpeted floor between the softly-illuminated display cabinets.

My appointment was waiting for me, a tall tanned man of about forty, with swept-back hair that was tinged with grey, and that kind of hawkish profile that you only seem to see at English country houses. He wore an off-white suit that must have cost him $750, and a yellow silk shirt.

Bill, standing behind the counter in his usual rumpled denim suit, said, 'Hi, Ricky. This is Mr David Sears.'

I shook hands. 'I'm sorry I'm late. I was having a small celebration with my family.'

'It's not your birthday, is it?' asked Bill, worriedly.

'No, it's not my birthday. It's just – well, one of those days when you feel you have to celebrate.'

'Not too many of *those* in the antiques business these days,' said David Sears, in an accent like clipped-up tea-leaves. 'I usually expect to turn over well above six million dollars on each of my annual visits to California. But this year, well . . . a dismal lack of buying power has fallen over the land.'

'I'm surprised I haven't met you before,' I told him.

'I'm not,' he replied. 'I don't usually come as far south as San Diego. I can generally do all the buying and selling I need to do in Los Angeles. Expatriate English film stars are suckers for anything antique, and anything that reminds them of home.

My most effective sales incentive is to promise to send them a pound of English sausages every week for a year, air charter, wrapped up in paper with Dewhursts the Butchers printed on it.'

'Are English sausages really that good?'

'Not really,' smiled David Sears. 'The only real attraction is that they're not American sausages. Find them too bready, myself.'

'Can I offer you a drink?' I asked him. 'A cup of tea?'

'A Tab, actually, if you have one.'

'Sure. Bill? Do you want to go across to the market and get us a six-pack of Tab?'

'I'm dieting,' admitted David Sears shamefacedly, patting his stomach. 'I'm afraid I have an inexhaustible appetite for Pacific lobsters. I *could* drink tea, I suppose, but Americans make tea too well for me. I like it thick and stewed, with rather a lot of milk. Criminal, isn't it? But most English people do.'

'Bill told me you were interested in that japanned cabinet.'

'Yes, I am quite,' said David Sears. 'What sort of price are you asking for it?'

I walked across to the cabinet and opened it up. 'It's English,' I told him, 'as you can probably guess. Late seventeenth century – undoubtedly japanned after the publication of Stalker and Parker's treatise on japanning. Good baroque carving around the top and the stand.'

'I had a pretty close look while I was waiting for you,' said David Sears. 'It's one of the best examples of japanning I've seen for a long time. So much of it was done by gifted amateurs, wasn't it? I saw a frightful example in San Francisco, and they were asking eighty-five thousand for it.'

'You could take this one away for ninety-three,' I told him.

'Hmm,' he said.

I grinned. 'I'm afraid there can't be any "hmm" about it. It's either going to have to be "yes" or "no". That's my rock-bottom price.'

'I'll have to think about it,' he said. 'You don't mind if I think about it?'

'Of course not. Was there anything else you were interested in?'

'Nothing much, old boy. Although you don't happen to have a cheapish long-case clock anywhere, would you? I have a lawyer friend in Los Angeles who's been decorating an apartment for what you might call *a lady companion* of his. He doesn't want to spend a fortune . . . he's too canny a lawyer for that. But he did ask me to keep my eyes peeled for a cheapish long-case clock.'

I suddenly thought of the clock that Mr Grant had left standing in my driveway. I hadn't looked at it very closely, but it certainly wasn't anything special. Enough to satisfy the whims of a lawyer's mistress in LA without breaking the bank. And if I gave it to David Sears at a reasonable price, he might think more favourably about paying ninety-three grand for my japanned cabinet.

'Listen,' I said, 'why don't you come back to The Inn with me and help my wife and I to finish off another bottle of champagne? Then come along back home for lunch. Someone brought round a pretty low-priced long-case clock over the weekend, and you might like it. There are one or two other bits and pieces there, too. You never know. You could find yourself picking up some bargains.'

David Sears brightened. 'Do you know something,' he said, 'that all sounds like a jolly good idea.'

Bill came back with the Tabs, but I told him to keep them in the ice-box at the back of the store. There were always going to be plenty of long hot afternoons when nobody called by for hours, and on afternoons like that we'd be glad of them.

'Everything's okay, is it?' Bill asked me, as I opened the front door for David Sears.

'What do you mean?'

'You look kind of bruised, that's all. Like you jumped off a cliff or something.'

I touched the abrasions on the side of my cheek. 'It's nothing. But you're right. I did jump off a cliff.'

Bill gave me an odd, quizzical look; but when I slapped his

shoulder and grinned at him he went back to the counter with a rueful, silly smile. 'Ask a silly question . . .' he said.

I closed the store door behind me. Outside in the sunlight, David Sears was just starting up his Rolls-Royce.

We ate guacamole and cheese salad out on the patio, under the leafless trees. David Sears had been curious when he arrived about the ravaged appearance of the vegetation around the house, but I told him that our Mexican gardener had mixed up weedkiller with fertiliser, and accidentally sprayed most of the grounds with a lethal dose.

'You sacked him, of course?' asked David Sears, sipping cold white wine.

I cut my throat with my finger, and nodded.

Over on the far side of the yard, Sheraton was sleeping beside his kennel. He hadn't eaten his lunchtime bowlful of food, but apart from that he seemed to have recovered from his experience with old man Jessop's chair. Every now and then he wuffled and turned over, or semi-consciously patted a paw at the flies which danced around his nose.

'This is a lovely place you have here,' remarked David Sears. 'I hear that property comes pretty pricey in Rancho Santa Fe.'

'Oh, I wouldn't say that,' I told him. 'You can pick up a two-roomed shack for less than a quarter of a million.'

'Doesn't the peace and the quiet ever get on your nerves?' David Sears asked Sara.

Sara looked at me. 'I don't know,' she said. 'Ask me tomorrow, when I've had some sleep.'

'I like to travel myself,' said David. 'One month I'm in London – then I'm here in California. Next month I'm off to Italy. Of course, I don't have a family to take care of. Or, rather, I don't now.'

'Divorced?' asked Sara.

'No,' said David, with a tight smile. 'Margaret died in a fire. Very tragic business, really. More than five years ago.'

'No children?' Sara asked him, sympathetically.

'Er, no. No children.'

The rest of the meal finished rather lamely. Then, while our

64

maid Hortensia cleared away the dishes, Sara and Jonathan both went upstairs to rest. David Sears and I smoked small Havana cigars by the pool, and finished the last of the wine, and then I suggested he look over the furniture that Henry Grant had left with us the previous afternoon. Miguel had driven up from the store during lunch in his dilapidated Hiace pick-up and shifted it all off the driveway and into the garage.

I led David around the house and across to the garage. I unlocked the padlock, and threw back the doors. David strolled amiably inside, still puffing at the end of his cigar. He bent over a small walnut bureau, and tugged open its drawers. He tapped the veneered top of a bedside table. Then he peered at the long-case clock, opening up the front and closely examining the face.

'It's not an English clock,' he said, after a while. 'It looks as if it might be Canadian. There was a clockmaker in Quebec called DuPlein who made quite pretty clocks in the 1830s. They weren't masterpieces, but they were sound; and this could be one of them.'

'I'll throw it in with the cabinet,' I said, watching him.

'You mean *gratis*?'

'That's right.'

'Well . . . that certainly gives me more food for thought.'

I cleared my throat. 'You don't have to make your mind up right away. But I do have to warn you that one of my wealthier local ladies has been making eyes at that cabinet for a few weeks now, and she's one of those old ladies who likes to pounce suddenly – just when she feels in the mood. Out comes the cheque-book, and away goes the furniture.'

David looked at me, and nodded. 'I understand. But never fear. I won't keep you waiting very long.'

'Is there anything else here which interests you?' I asked him.

He gave the contents of the garage a cursory glance. 'Nothing that strikes me as first-class. What was all this – a house-clearance job?'

'That's right. One of our North San Diego luminaries is remodelling his home.'

'There wasn't anything else?'

I shook my head. 'What you see is what there was.'

'Nothing . . . *unusual*?'

The way he said that, standing there with his cigar in his mouth, his hands on his hips, struck me for some reason as peculiarly alarming. I thought to myself, he can't know about old man Jessop's chair. Not unless he's already met Henry Grant – or visited the Jessops. Yet why should I be feeling unsettled about it? According to Henry Grant's attorney, the chair was mine to dispose of however I wanted to; and if something's yours, even if it's a Rembrandt, there's no law in the world which says you can't flush it down the toilet if you want to.

David Sears crushed his cigar butt out under his foot. Handmade shoes, in light tan. Then he raised his eyes, and said, 'Well, I suppose in that case I'd better be off.'

'You wouldn't like some coffee? Some Tab?'

'No, thank you, really. I've imposed on you too much already. I'll call you first thing tomorrow and let you know about the cabinet and the clock. I'm staying at Presidio Place with some friends of mine.'

'All right,' I said. 'If you really have to rush off.'

He tapped his forehead with his finger. 'There's one thing,' he said. 'You *did* promise to show me your Copley. Would you mind awfully if we went in and took a look?'

'Not at all,' I said, and led him into the house through the front door.

We were halfway along the corridor when the telephone in the kitchen began to ring. Hortensia was outside, clearing away the lunch plates, so I told David Sears to go right ahead into the living-room, and hooked the phone off the wall.

'Oh, Ricky?' asked a woman's voice. 'Is Sara there? It's Helen Fallbrook.' Oh, God, I thought. Helen 'The Babbling' Fallbrook. That's all I need.

'Hi, Helen, how are you? I'm afraid Sara's resting right now. She had a bad night. Can I take a message?'

'It's only about Wednesday's bridge night. I'll call her tomorrow, shall I?'

'Great idea,' I said, and briskly hung up.

Helen Fallbrook would undoubtedly tell Sara tomorrow that I had been 'extraordi-*narily* abrupt', but right now I couldn't face one of her gushing monologues about how wonderfully she had redecorated her breakfast parlour, 'in *turquoise*, of all the daring colours, my dear'.

I found David Sears in the living-room, standing admiringly in front of my Copley.

'This is very fine,' he remarked. 'If I didn't think that you wouldn't part with it for any price I could possibly name, I'd name you a price for it.'

'You're right, I'm afraid,' I told him. 'This is one work of art that's staying right where it is.'

David nodded a couple of times. 'How about the chair?' he asked me.

'Chair? What chair?'

He looked at me with a face that seemed to have been washed in white wine vinegar – tight-lipped, questioning, sour.

'You don't have *two* chairs as fine as that, do you?' he said.

'I don't know what you're talking about,' I retorted. 'The only antique chairs in the house are the dining-room chairs, and they're not very good quality shieldbacks.'

'Are you putting me on?' said David. 'I mean, I really don't mind if you don't want to sell it . . .'

'What chair?' I demanded.

David raised his arm and pointed towards the library. 'The chair I saw standing in the library when I walked past. The big mahogany armchair, with all the carvings on it.'

'*What did you say?*' I whispered.

'The big mahogany armchair with all the – '

I turned my back on him in mid-sentence and walked towards the library door as if I was under the influence of sodium pentathol. Blurry, but single-minded. I pushed the library door wide and stood there staring at it and I couldn't help shaking with sheer dread.

'It's a magnificent piece of work,' said David, right behind me.

'You really want it?' I asked him hoarsely. I couldn't take my eyes off it. The man-serpent appeared to be laughing now, his jaws wide open in demonic amusement. His eyes were alight with terrible glee.

'Want it? I'd give you twenty-five thousand for it. It's a masterpiece.'

I finally managed to turn and look at him. 'I'll take ten. Do you have a truck?'

'Well, my dear chap, I can't take it with me *now* . . .'

'Take it now or don't take it at all.'

'Well, that's a bit abrupt, isn't it?'

'It's my day for being abrupt.'

'I thought you were celebrating.'

I closed my eyes tiredly. 'I was,' I told him. 'Now, can you take the chair away or can't you?'

'I can arrange it if you absolutely insist.'

'I do. I'm sorry.'

'All right, then. If you can help me lug it outside, I'll stow it in the back of the Rolls.'

'You lug it outside. I'm not touching it.'

David raised his eyebrows. 'I must say you're rather prickly,' he told me. 'Most of your colleagues in Southern California are normally so laid-back . . . so *benign*.'

I took in a sharp breath. 'Just – get rid of the chair, will you?'

'Very well.'

I stood and watched him as he half-tilted, half-dragged the chair out of the library and along the corridor. By the time he had reached the kitchen, he was trembling with effort, and he had to stop to take off his smart white coat. He folded it fastidiously and laid it over the back of one of the kitchen chairs. Hortensia, who was stacking the dishwasher, took one look at David and the chair and crossed herself.

At last, David had succeeded in carrying the chair out on to the driveway, and pulling it behind him until he reached his Rolls-Royce.

'I'm afraid I won't be able to lift it into the car by myself, old boy,' he called out.

'You'll just have to,' I said. 'I'm not touching it, and that's my last word.'

David took out a handkerchief and mopped carefully at his forehead. Then he executed an athletic knees-bend, what the Army physical training instructors call a burpee, and grasped the frame of the chair in both hands.

It was at that moment that, from the back of the house, we heard an agonised shriek of terror and pain – a cry that was so desperate and vocal and prolonged that it could almost have come from the throat of a human being.

But I knew it wasn't a human being. It was Sheraton.

4—Consumings

The dog came barrelling around the side of the house before I'd run even two or three paces. I'd never seen a dog run that way before and I hope I never have to again. His eyes were maddened and his mouth was billowing with frothy blood and he was jerking and convulsing and rolling over.

'*Sheraton!*' I yelled, and tried to catch him as he ran past me. But he was twisting and turning too violently, and as he came to the downward grade in the driveway he tumbled sideways and collapsed.

I started towards him but David raised his hand and shouted, '*Stay away!*'

'He's sick!' I protested. 'The dog's out of his mind with agony!'

'That's why you have to stay away!' David insisted. 'It could be rabies!'

I ventured a little closer. Sheraton was lying on his side now, gasping and foaming. I guessed David was right. It could be rabies, from a squirrel bite, maybe; or a nip from a bat. But Sheraton raised his head and stared at me with an expression of such tortured desperation that it was all I could do to stay where I was.

I heard the screen door bang behind me. It was Sara, disturbed by the noise.

'Ricky!' she called. 'Ricky – what's wrong?'

'Keep back,' I warned her. 'Call Dr Isaacs, urgent. Tell him that Sherry looks like he's gotten rabies.'

'*Rabies?*'

'He's convulsing, and foaming at the mouth. Now, will you please hurry?'

The screen door banged again as Sara went back inside. I glanced at David for reassurance but all he could do was shrug.

Sheraton was silent for a few minutes, but then he began to whimper, soft and low, as if he didn't have the strength to complain any more loudly. A wet stain spread across the driveway and I realised that he'd urinated.

'You ever seen a dog like this before?' I asked David.

'I don't know. I saw a dog that was knocked down by a car once. But it didn't froth the way yours is frothing.'

Sara came to the door and said, 'Dr Isaacs is coming as fast as he can. He shouldn't be more than fifteen minutes.'

'He's coming by mule or something?' I snapped.

Sara came out and stood beside me, taking my arm. 'Poor Sheraton. He looks just awful. You don't think we'll have to have him – ?'

I shook my head. 'It's impossible to tell. It could be anything. Maybe he ate some rat poison. I don't know.'

Slowly, Sheraton's belly began to convulse, in deep, shuddering ripples. He rolled on to his back with his legs held weakly in the air, but in a horrifying way the convulsions in his abdomen seemed to gain in strength. Soon, his head was being flopped this way and that by the muscular force in his body, and his legs were slapping uselessly against the asphalt.

It looked as if there were actually something *inside of him*, some other creature with far greater strength, and that it was wriggling and stretching itself and trying to get out.

Sara was clutching my arm so tightly that it hurt, but I was almost glad of the pain. It was my only anchor on reality. Neither of us spoke as the bulging and contracting in poor Sheraton's belly grew to a furious shaking, like some enraged madman trying to shake coins out of a fur coat, and the dog's tongue suddenly slid out of the side of his mouth and hung across his upper jaw.

'The chair,' whispered Sara suddenly. 'You didn't tell me the chair was back.'

'I wasn't going to,' I told her.

'But it's back!'

Sheraton screamed. It was the most hideous sound I ever heard in my life – a dog screaming for mercy. And then his bowels were stretched inexorably open, wider and wider, and a

71

black insect head emerged, slick with intestinal mucus, like a giant woodlouse.

'Oh, Jesus God,' I said, and my stomach went over. I was so frightened that I couldn't even run away.

With a ghastly tugging motion, the insect gave birth to itself out of Sheraton's bowels, and for one moment of total dread it stood on the driveway motionless, while its black jointed back dried off. Then, with a scuttling rush that made all of us jump back in terror, it ran towards the mahogany chair, slithered up on to the seat, and disappeared down the crack between the back and the black-leather cushion. I had one last glimpse of its earwig-like tail as it disappeared.

I helped Sara across to the steps, and we both sat down. David came over and leaned against the rail of the verandah, his face grey.

'Cigarette?' he asked me.

I shook my head.

He took out a lighter and clicked it three or four times before it worked. Then he unsteadily lit a cigarette and stood there smoking in nervous silence. None of us wanted to look at the chair, but none of us could take our eyes off it.

Sara, without making any sound at all, began to cry.

'You know what we have to do now,' I said to David, as I stroked Sara's hair.

David looked at me expressionlessly.

'We have to chop that damned chair up, set fire to it, and burn it to ashes,' I told him. 'Then we have to spread the ashes as far apart as we can. We have to destroy that chair, and I mean totally.'

'This isn't the first – incident – then?' asked David. 'I heard your wife say that the chair was back.'

'Look around you,' I said, pointing to the leafless trees and the bare hedgerows. 'We were given that chair yesterday afternoon and since then we've been through hell. But never again, I promise you.'

'You tried to get rid of it?'

'That's where I was earlier this morning, throwing it into the river at Lake Hodges.'

'And it came back by itself, undamaged?'

I said softly, 'Yes. It came back by itself.'

David stared at the chair for a long time. Then he said, 'What makes you think you'll be able to get rid of it by chopping it up and burning it? Won't the same thing happen?'

'I don't know. But I'm willing to give it a try. That chair is absolutely evil and absolutely powerful. It's hell on four wooden legs. I don't know why it's visited itself on me and my family. I don't know what its purpose is, or whether it even has one. I don't think I care to know. I just want it destroyed. Utterly, so that it can't *ever* come back.'

Over on the driveway, Sheraton lay dead, his body bloody and ripped. David left the verandah, circled cautiously around the chair, and went to the trunk of his Rolls-Royce. He unlocked it, took out a plaid travelling-rug, and tossed it over Sheraton's remains.

Hortensia came to the door. 'Everything okay?' she asked, staring at us as if we were a party of picnicking lunatics.

'Everything's fine, Hortensia, thank you,' I told her. 'Never been better.'

David came back across the driveway, his cigarette dangling between his lips. 'Listen,' he said, 'let me try to take the chair away from here. Let me just pack it into my car, and drive off, and put as many miles between you and this chair as I possibly can.'

'You're not saying you still want it?'

'Why shouldn't I still want it?' asked David. His voice was noticeably sharp.

'With that oversized bug hiding in the upholstery?'

David glanced back towards the chair. 'I'm not so sure that bug was real.'

'It wasn't real, huh? And I suppose what happened to my dog wasn't real? What are you trying to pull here?'

'I'm not trying to "pull" anything,' said David, in a very English tone. 'I'm just saying that what you perceive with your eyes isn't always what's really there. I know – *something* about the occult – and one of the first things you have to remember when you're dealing with occult forces is that they manifest themselves in all kinds of extraordinary ways.'

I bit at my thumbnail. 'You didn't really come here for the cabinet, then?' I asked him.

'What do you mean?'

'Oh, come on, David. I'm not stupid. And you're not very good at disguising your real interests. If you'd wanted that japanned cabinet, you'd have written me a cheque on the spot. It's perfect, and you know it, and it's a steal at ninety-three grand. I could drive it up to LA tomorrow and offload it for a hundred and ten, maybe more.'

David said nothing. His cigarette burned away between his fingers. Sara, her eyes still glistening with tears, raised her head in curiosity.

'You came to Rancho Santa Fe for one thing only, David,' I told him. 'You came for that chair.'

'Well,' said David, dropping his cigarette at last, and crushing it out, 'I suppose I'll have to come clean.'

'I wish you would.'

'Do you think we might have a drink?'

'I guess so. What about the chair?'

David made a face. 'I don't think it's going to run off.'

We went inside to the breakfast-room, where I poured us each a large glass of chilled pinot chardonnay. David sat on a stool at the breakfast counter, and tiredly ran his hand through his hair. The afternoon light shone through the white venetian blinds on to the white tiles, and the room seemed like a diffused photograph.

'I've known about the chair for some time,' said David, his head lowered so that I couldn't see his face. 'I didn't mean to deceive you in any way, or "pull" anything, as you put it. But you've already experienced for yourselves how – difficult the chair can be.'

'You heard about it in England?' I asked him.

David nodded. 'More than that. I *saw* it in England, about fifteen years ago, before Sam Jessop acquired it.'

'Then Jessop *did* own it. I called up yesterday to check, but some woman there denied all knowledge of it.'

'Oh, Jessop owned it, all right. He bought it from a banker friend of mine called Williams. I made an offer for it myself once.'

'Williams said no? Or was he asking too much for it?'

'He wasn't in what you might call *a position to sell*.'

'What position was he in? Standing on his head?'

'You don't understand. He *couldn't* have sold the chair even if he'd wanted to. The chair can never actually be sold in the vulgar meaning of the word. I can buy it from you for ten thousand dollars – as indeed I am attempting to do – but it may be necessary for certain other obligations to be fulfilled before the chair decides that it actually belongs to me.'

Sara said, 'I don't even know why you want it. It seems to do nothing but cause damage and frighten people.'

'That's because it has a fundamentally malevolent aura. It was made that way.'

'I don't understand you,' I said.

'Well,' David explained, 'the story is that the chair was originally made in England in 1780 on the order of the Earl of Beckenham. Young Beckenham was a notorious gambler, who sometimes lost three or four thousand pounds in a night, and in those days that was money. He wanted a chair to sit in while he played which would give him "the luck of the devil". That, incidentally, is how the expression was first coined.'

'Go on,' I told him, refilling his glass.

'Beckenham went to all the famous cabinet-makers of the day, but all of them turned him down. His credit was shaky, and apart from that, none of them liked the idea of what he was proposing. By accident, however, he spent a night in Derbyshire, and there he came across a cabinet-maker and wood-carver called Thomas Unsworth, who was responsible for some of the most inspired furniture ever to come out of the eighteenth century.'

'I've heard of him,' I nodded. 'Wasn't he crippled, or something?'

'He liked to put it about that he was crippled . . . but in fact he had a growth on one side of his head which made him frightening for most people to look at, and smell rather offensive. His isolation from normal society and the company of women had made him a little peculiar, to say the least. He was said to believe in the black arts, and to eat cats, whenever he could catch them. He undertook to make Beckenham's chair for him for six thousand pounds, and Beckenham agreed.'

'And then?' asked Sara. 'Did Beckenham's luck improve?'

'So it was said,' nodded David. 'By the turn of the century, he was a wealthy man, and he was so lucky at the tables that most of the London gamblers refused to play with him. He died, though, in mysterious circumstances, at the age of fifty-four, and it was found that all the trees and flowers on his estate had died away. Where the chair went after that, I simply don't know . . . there are no records of it having been sold before Beckenham's death, and it doesn't appear on the inventory of furniture at Beckenham Hall that was made the following week.'

'But this malevolent aura you were talking about . . .' said Sara.

'Oh, yes,' David replied. 'The chair had a malevolent aura about it all right, and – as you've unhappily found out for yourselves – it still does. It has a malevolent aura in just the same way that the rood-arch of a church has an aura of sanctity. Because in just the same way, this chair is a gateway.'

'A gateway?' frowned Sara.

'That's right. It exists not only in the real world as you know it and I know it . . . but in an unreal world as well. And because of that, it somehow forms a nexus through which certain things . . . certain *influences* . . . can freely pass.'

'Did this banker friend of yours ever tell you where he got it from? This Williams?'

David shook his head. 'I asked him once, but he was very reluctant to talk about it. That wasn't unusual for him – he didn't like to talk about his personal life at all. But he once mentioned that it could only be bought and sold by what he called a runic transaction, whatever that meant. He never explained it to me, and he never sold me the chair.'

'Was he successful? I mean, was he rich?'

'Who, Williams? My God, yes. He was one of the richest men I ever knew. He had two Gainsboroughs and a Van Gogh. And you ought to have seen his country house, in Surrey. He owned the landscape as far as you could see.'

'So *he* had the luck of the devil, too.'

David shrugged. 'You could say that, yes.'

I stood up, and walked across to the window. 'So did old man Jessop. Right up until five or six years ago, Jessop's were nothing more than a struggling company who built aeroplane components for Boeing and Douglas and McDonnell. Then, all of a sudden, everything changed. They landed a contract for cruise missile systems, and all kinds of subsidiary stuff. Old man Jessop became a millionaire overnight.'

'I've passed his house in Escondido,' said David. 'It's quite something, isn't it?'

I swallowed wine. 'Hideous taste, but quite something.'

There was a pause, and then David said, 'I really don't know anything more.'

'You still haven't answered our original question.'

'Which was . . . ?'

'Which was why do you want the chair at all? The Earl of Beckenham may have made his fortune with it, and your friend Williams may have used it to get rich. So might Jessop, apparently. But look what it's done to us.'

David looked away. His aquiline profile was silhouetted by the sunlight flooding through the blinds. 'Perhaps you didn't want what it had to offer,' he said, cryptically.

'Meaning?'

'I don't honestly know. The truth is that I'm not acquiring the chair for myself. I'm not supposed to be telling you this, but I'm acquiring it on behalf of a client. He's an influential man, and I do a great deal of business with him, so obviously I'm not going to betray his confidence. As a matter of fact, I didn't even ask him myself what he wanted the chair for. As long as I can deliver it to him intact, that's all I'm concerned about.'

There was a sudden buzz at the back doorbell. I went to

answer it, and it was Dr Isaacs, wearing a limp fishing-hat pinned with flies and a camouflage jacket. His plump little feet were encased in monkish sandals, and the legs of his pants were still wet from the river. He was panting hard.

'I came as fast as I could,' he said. 'They told me it was an emergency.'

I took his arm and led him around to the front of the house. 'I'm afraid Sheraton's already dead, Dr Isaacs. It was like some kind of rabies. You know, convulsions, foaming at the mouth.'

I lifted the plaid travelling-blanket. Dr Isaacs was fumbling to find his spectacles, but when he had carefully perched them on to his nose, and focused on Sheraton's remains, his jaw dropped as if he were about to sing the first chorus of a barbershop quartet.

'*Mr Delatolla,*' he breathed.

I turned. I'd been looking away, because right then there were few sights I was less inclined to see than the torn-up body of the dog I had raised, loved, and cared for. But what I did see was something else altogether – something that gripped my throat with nausea, and made me toss away the travelling-blanket as if it were on fire.

Sprawled out on the asphalt were grey translucent lumps of glistening tissue that looked like intestines and membranes and heaps of body fat. No dog, just guts. And what was even more sickening was that it was all thick with blowflies, which rose up when I threw away the blanket and then settled again.

'What happened?' asked Dr Isaacs, in a shocked voice. 'Mr Delatolla, *what happened?*'

'I don't know,' I told him. I started to retch, but I managed to hold it back. 'You'll just have to forgive me, that's all.'

'Should I call the police or something?'

'The police?'

'Well, if someone's done this to your dog . . .'

'Nobody did it to my dog, Dr Isaacs. It was an accident.'

'But how – ?'

I took his hand. I was sweating and shaking as if I had pneumonia, and Dr Isaacs was staring at me with an expression of alarm and sympathy, like trying to take care of Hamlet.

'You'll just have to forgive me,' I repeated. 'Please. It's been a bad day.'

Dr Isaacs turned around again and balefully regarded the grey remains on the driveway.

'I'm afraid I'm going to have to make a report about this,' he said. 'That poor dog's been *annihilated*.'

'Okay,' I told him. 'You make a report. Tell the ASPCA that one of your clients who normally treated his golden Labrador as if it were a loyal, dignified, and trusted friend, suddenly and inexplicably went out of his head and reduced the animal to a grey pulp. Tell them that. And don't expect me to bring anything around to your clinic again. Not even a turtle.'

Dr Isaacs began to retreat down the driveway, where his pale blue Le Baron was parked.

'I can't pretend it never happened,' he called, from a safe distance. I think he believed I might chase after him and hit him, and for a dizzy moment I think I might have done. I stood and watched him drive away, his tyres skittering on the road, and it was only when he was gone that I looked again at the chair, standing tall and dark beside David's Rolls-Royce, a grotesque memorial to my dead Sheraton. I could almost feel the influence of that chair as if it were a sonic vibration in the air, the same way that you can feel the humming power of a high-voltage electricity cable. It affected everything around it – the temperature, the trees, the grass, and the flowers. It even affected my temper. And there were no squirrels around today like there usually were, foraging for oranges.

I performed, by myself, one simple and grisly task. I went to the garage for a shovel, and scraped up what was left of my dog. Then I buried the remains under a yucca in the back yard. The soil clung to the soft intestines, and I filled the hole in with the quick, jerky movements of fright and disgust.

Back in the breakfast room, Sara said, 'What happened?'

'With Dr Isaacs? He thought *I'd* done it.'

'You didn't tell him about the chair?' asked David, putting down his glass of wine.

'You think I'd tell him that? He's quite convinced I'm crazy already. He says he's going to have to report me to the ASPCA.'

Sara said, 'Don't worry. I'll call Ruth in the morning and straighten it out.'

I poured myself another glass of wine. I was getting slightly drunk, particularly after all that champagne we'd finished off at The Inn, but then I reckoned I deserved to.

'Tell me, David,' I said. 'What do you think your client's going to *do* with that terrible chair?'

David turned the stem of his wineglass around and around between his fingers. 'I really don't know. My instructions are simply to get hold of it.'

'The question is . . .' I asked him, 'what was Henry Grant doing with it? I mean . . . if it couldn't be sold in the ordinary way . . . only by "runic transaction" . . . what was he doing with it? And why did he bring it around to me? And, most of all, why did it take such a liking to me and my house that it wouldn't leave?'

'I wish I knew what to say,' said David, with an uncomfortable little smile.

I leaned forward. 'I think you know what to say but you just aren't saying it. After all, your knowledge of what this chair's all about does seem to be conveniently patchy. A whole lot of rich historical detail which could be fiction or could be fact. But not very much in the way of helpful, up-to-date, meaningful input.'

'I'm sorry it appears that way,' said David. 'I assure you that I've been as straightforward as my professional code allows me to be. Perhaps it's really rather better if I leave.'

'Taking the chair with you?'

'Of course.'

'Well, there's no way. Because I'm going to go out there now, and I'm going to chop that chair up into firewood.'

David went pale. 'Really,' he said, 'I wouldn't advise it.'

'You wouldn't, huh? So what *would* you advise? Maybe you'd advise me to sell you the chair so that in less than an hour it can come back to my library like some kind of goddamned hellish homing pigeon? Is that it? Or maybe you'd advise me to give it to you for nothing, just so that I can get the damned thing out of my life? For all I know there's nothing wrong with the chair at all, and you've been doping my drinks so that I've missed out on eight hours of sleep, and spraying my garden with defoliant, and poisoning my dog, and trying to drive me and my family crazy.'

'Ricky – ' interrupted Sara. 'Ricky, you know that none of that's true.'

'I don't know what's true and what isn't!' I shouted. 'All I know is that I've had two unwelcome visitors in the last twenty-four hours, and both of them have known more about that chair than I have! Well, maybe David here and Henry Grant don't mind using me as a go-between, but I object. And just to show you how much I object, I'm going to break that chair into pieces!'

David pushed back his chair and stood up. 'Ricky, please,' he begged me. 'I know how you feel. I know you're angry. But if you try to damage that chair you'll regret it.'

'I'm not going to damage it, buddy. I'm going to smash it to smithereens.'

David reached into his back pants pocket and took out a Security Pacific cheque book. He scribbled out a cheque for ten thousand dollars and held it out to me.

'Here,' he said. 'This completes the sale legally. You take the money, I'll take the chair, and we'll leave it like that. Okay?'

I wouldn't even raise my hand. David laid the cheque on the table, and pushed it over to me with his finger. I ignored it.

Sara said, 'Ricky, please. This might be the right way of getting rid of it.'

'Yes,' I said tersely. 'It might be. On the other hand, it's not *my* way of getting rid of it. And right now, just for a change, I feel like controlling my own destiny. That's if Mr Sears here doesn't mind.'

'Ricky!' shouted David. But I had already pulled open the back door, and was storming along to the garage for my axe. Whatever spells that chair could work, whatever hallucinations were concealed in its seat, whatever devilish bugs and beetles lived in it, I was going to take it apart at the joints. As

I crossed the driveway, I turned to that eerily smiling man-serpent's face and I thought, *right, you just wait, in one minute flat I'm going to hit you smack in the nose with a single-bit Wisconsin-pattern village-forged axe, and then we'll see who's grinning.*

I took the long-handled axe down from its rack on the wall, and swung it around as I stalked back towards the chair. I don't think I've ever been as mad at anything in my whole life, either before or since, and they could have told me the house was burning down, and I would have ignored it. I had only one compelling thought in my mind: I'm going to smash that chair.

I positioned myself close, legs apart, and whistled that axe around my head. The chair stood silent and tall and dark, the doomed damned figures still tumbling on their never-ending journey down to Sub-Hell, the vipers still rising venomously from the man-serpent's scalp, the pythons twisting their way around the arms.

Don't think I wasn't conscious that within that black-leather seat some kind of huge woodlouse was probably nestling – and don't think that it didn't frighten me, because it did. But I was shaking with rage at what that chair had done to me and my family, and the Devil himself could have been inside of that chair and I still wouldn't have held back.

I took a hefty, two-handed swing at the man-serpent's head. The axe chipped it smartly in the forehead, and cleaved its cheek. *Now we'll see who's controlling things around here*, I thought to myself, in a turmoil of temper. *Now we'll see who's damned to destruction.*

The screaming was so high-pitched that at first I couldn't make out what it was. I was leaning back with my axe for a second blow across the chair's cresting-rail when I suddenly heard Sara shouting, 'Jonathan! Jonathan!' and David burst out through the screen door and yelled at me hoarsely and urgently, 'Stop! For the love of God, stop!'

I went as cold as winter. I let the axe slide from my hands, and topple sideways on to the asphalt. Jonathan. So that was it. And I looked at that mahogany face on the chair and it was gloating at me.

'*You see,*' it whispered, somewhere inside of my head.

Then I was running towards the house. Hurling open the door, and taking the stairs two and three at a time. I ran down the corridor to Jonathan's bedroom, and stopped in horror.

Jonathan, my son, was lying on his bed with his head smothered in blood. His pillow was already soaked crimson, and there were queries and periods and exclamation-points of blood all the way up the wallpaper. There was a deep, savage cut all the way down his left cheek, and through the blood that welled out of it I could see the whiteness of his cheekbone. The cut had missed his left eye by less than a quarter of an inch.

Sara was already ripping up his sheets to bandage his wounds. She said flatly, 'Call an ambulance. That's all.'

I pushed my way through to our bedroom and picked up the phone. While I was dialling the emergency number, David came into the room and stood watching me.

I looked at him. 'Take the chair,' I said, without emotion. 'Stow it in the back of your car and take it.'

'Ricky –' he began.

'*Take it!*' I raged at him.

He hesitated; then lifted his hand in one of those discreet English waves, and left. I didn't hear his Rolls-Royce leave because I was too busy giving instructions to the ambulance service.

I went back to Jonathan's room. Sara had bandaged him up as best she could, but he seemed to have gone into shock, his eyes rolled up into his head, his little fingers clutching the bedspread as if he were afraid of falling.

'I told David to take the chair and get the hell out,' I said, quietly.

Sara didn't answer. She was kneeling beside the bed, her dress splattered in blood, stroking Jonathan's left hand over and over and over again, as if she thought he would die if she ever stopped.

'It was the axe, wasn't it?' I said. 'That was what David meant about regretting it.'

Sara looked up at me but didn't say anything at all. I didn't know if she was really blaming me for what had happened or not. But she didn't need to act so damned remote. I already felt as if I had struck Jonathan myself, and in a weird way I had.

I felt tears welling up in my eyes. I was so damned tired and so damned scared that I didn't know what to do. Yesterday morning, the most complicated problem in our family life had been choosing whether to go to Sea World or the Wild-Animal Park for our Sunday-afternoon trip. Now it seemed as if my family and my life were falling apart – shaken and shaken at the foundations by a wantonly destructive force that had come into our lives from nowhere at all.

I heard Jonathan whimper. Then I heard the sound of the ambulance siren whooping and scribbling up the driveway; and if nothing else, I knew that help was on the way.

They took him into intensive care at the Holy Sisters of Mercy Hospital in San Diego; and while Sara and I sat outside in the waiting-room, exhausted and frayed and scarcely speaking to each other, Jonathan lay white and silent on his bed, the left side of his face heavily bandaged, a nasogastric tube taped to his right nostril, and electrode leads in his arms.

Out of the waiting-room window, I could see for miles over Mission Bay, with its tall white yachts and its patches of lagoon-blue water. Far to the left, the silvery jets were landing at San Diego airport, and beyond that I could just make out the curved tracery of the Coronado bridge. It was five in the afternoon, and the heat was beginning to die. A river of cars poured northwards on the freeway, their windows catching the sun.

'He's going to be scarred,' said Sara, flatly.

I looked at her. 'A little,' I replied. 'He can have most of the mark eradicated by surgery.'

'It will still be there.'

I wasn't going to argue with her. Whatever I said, it was going to be wrong. I leaned on the window-sill and watched the sun gradually sink towards the sea.

The waiting-room door opened and a doctor came in, carrying a clipboard. He was small, like a gopher, and his white coat seemed to be three sizes too large for him. He smelled of aftershave and medical alcohol.

'Mr and Mrs Delatolla?'

'That's right. Do you have any news of Jonathan?'

'Well . . . please sit down . . .'

'I'd rather stand, thank you,' I told him.

'Okay, have it your way. But the news I have for you is kind of mixed.'

'Mixed?'

'Part excellent, and part not-so-excellent. The excellent part is that the wound is clean, and we've been able to close it very successfully. There hasn't been any substantial loss of blood, although we've given him a pint to help him keep his strength up.'

'What's the not-so-excellent part?' asked Sara, in a wavering voice.

'The not-so-excellent part is that Jonathan appears to have gone into deep shock. Much deeper than we'd normally expect, even with a severe facial injury.'

'You mean he's in a coma?' I asked.

The doctor nodded. 'It's not altogether uncommon with head injuries, but we're surprised that his coma is so deep. There was no apparent damage to the brain tissues, and all his vital signs are normal. Even his breathing is normal, whereas a comatose patient usually breathes in a noticeably stertorous manner.'

'Do you think he's going to stay in a coma for long?' I wanted to know.

The doctor made a *moue*. 'It's impossible to say at this moment in time. We're continuing to monitor his reflexes and his respiration, and we don't have any indications yet that he's in any imminent danger of vital failure, but we're going to have to make several thorough tests before we can determine exactly what's wrong.'

'When you say "vital failure",' put in Sara, 'does that mean death?'

The doctor held his clipboard tight against his chest. 'Not one hundred per cent,' he said, keeping his eyes averted. 'We do have means of resuscitation, depending on the cause of vital failure. But you mustn't get ahead of the game, Mrs Delatolla.

Your son's healthy, and in fine general condition, and what he needs most of all is two supportive, optimistic parents who can really help him to pull through.'

'Yes,' said Sara, softly.

The doctor left us, and we sat in the waiting-room as the light died and the fluorescent tubes flickered on. The stream of cars on Interstate 5 became a thick flow of red corpuscles through the dark body of the night.

Sara came up behind me and leaned her cheek against my shoulder. I could see our faces reflected in the window, and the reflection reminded me strangely of one of our wedding photographs. Instead of the gaudy flowers of Sara's garden in Pasadena, however, the background was as black as Monday night, and that was all.

'I'm sorry,' said Sara, 'I know it wasn't your fault. I know you were only trying to protect us.'

'David did warn me,' I said. My throat felt dry.

'He didn't tell you what might happen. You couldn't have guessed. I'm sorry I've been so mean about it.'

I put my arm around her and held her close. 'I can understand how you felt.'

She touched my lips with her fingertips. 'Angry, more than anything,' she whispered.

'Did they ask you how it happened?' I said.

She nodded. 'I told them he was playing with your axe. He hit himself by mistake.'

I looked at her closely. 'You said that? Even when you felt that it was all my fault?'

'What was I going to tell them? That you were trying to chop up a chair in the garden, and chopped up your son instead? This thing's brought us enough misery without having the police involved, or our neighbours thinking we're child-killers.'

'I guess you're right. Thanks for being so sane.' I kissed her, and then I asked, 'Do you want some coffee? There's a machine down the hall.'

'Tea, if they have it. Black, no sugar.'

I dug around in the pockets of my jeans and came up with

86

three quarters and a nickel. Then I opened the waiting-room door and walked along the corridor on squeaking sneakers until I reached the coffee machine. There was a choice of coffee, hot chocolate, minestrone soup, or out of order. I dropped in a quarter and pressed the button for coffee.

As I stood waiting for the plastic cup to fill up, I saw a small white figure pass across the end of the corridor. By the time I'd focused, it had gone. But somehow I had the disturbing feeling that it was Jonathan. I didn't quite know why, any more than I can explain why an earth tremor always feels exactly like an earth tremor, and nothing else, but my conviction was so sudden and so strong that I started walking fast along the corridor, and then running, and by the time I reached the corner I was pelting along at full tilt.

I collided with a Mexican woman wheeling a trolley of fresh laundry, but then I was running again, my sneakers slapping loudly on the floor, my vision a jumble of doors, walls, fluorescent ceiling-lights.

I caught sight of him right at the very end of the corridor as he turned the next corner. I only glimpsed the back of his tousled hair, and his white operating robe, but now I was sure. I yelled out, 'Jonathan! Jonathan, stop!' and a black nursing sister popped her head out of an office door and stared at me in amazement.

At the next corner, I stopped, gasping for breath. Jonathan had only been walking, and yet he seemed to have vanished down a 200-foot corridor without a trace. I started to jog along the shiny waxed tiles, glancing to left and right whenever I passed an open door, and peeping quickly into every window that wasn't covered by drapes. A whey-faced old lady scowled back at me from her bed, and I found myself giving her a foolish grin by way of apology.

Soon, I came to the very end of the corridor. There was nothing there but a window which looked out over the hospital parking lot, and a pair of grey-painted doors marked 'Emergency Exit'. I sat on the window-ledge for a moment, trying to catch my breath.

Then, I heard it. The *snick* sound of a closing door. If I'd been running, I never would have picked it up. But now it echoed along the polished corridor with tell-tale clarity.

Softly, cautiously, I retraced my steps. Somewhere in the distance, a paging bell chimed *bing-bong*, and the faint garbled voice of the hospital receptionist came down the corridor like the voice of an official guide in the Carlsbad Caverns. Bored, remote, and unreal.

I reached the door marked *Laundry, 812*. I hesitated, and stood staring at it for a long time. A small unsettled sensation in the back of my mind kept telling me, *this is it, this is where your son's hiding*. And then I suddenly remembered the Mexican woman I had run into further back down the corridor. She had been pushing a trolley of fresh laundry, which must have come from here, and if any door along this corridor had been left ajar, it was most likely to be this one.

I peered in through the circular window, but it was too dark inside to make anything out. I tried the handle, and the door came open straight away.

'Jonathan?' I queried.

There was no answer. I pushed the door open a little further, and the light from the corridor angled across the floor and showed me five rows of shelves, each one neatly and tightly stacked with sheets and pillow-slips.

'Jonathan, are you in there?' I called, louder this time. I don't know why I was being so cautious. He was, after all, only my six-year-old son. But there was something about the way he had vanished so quickly along the corridor that made me feel apprehensive. That, and the fact that he was supposed to be lying in intensive care, in a coma.

I opened the door wide, until it touched the shelves of laundry right behind it. The laundry-room was only five feet square, and unless Jonathan was squeezed right into the angle of the door, or lying on one of the shelves I couldn't see, he wasn't inside it. And yet . . .

A deep, sensitive radar told me that somebody was close.

I listened. At first I couldn't hear anything, because the hospital public address system was '*paging Dr Oliver, please . . . paging Dr Oliver . . .*' But then I heard the breathing. Slow, gentle, and measured. The breathing of somebody who is trying to keep as quiet as they possibly can.

'Jonathan,' I said again.

I groped sideways and found the light switch. I switched it on, and a fluorescent panel flickered for a second and then popped into life.

'Jonathan, I can hear you,' I said. 'If you're in there someplace, you have to come out.'

Then suddenly I was gripped by the realisation that the breathing I could hear wasn't coming from the shelves, or from behind the door. *It was coming from directly above me!* I jerked my head up and what I saw made me freeze with terror.

Lying on the ceiling in a white surgical gown was the diminutive figure of a six-year-old boy. His arms were spread wide as if he were flying, or crucified. But his face wasn't Jonathan's face. It was the wooden smiling head of the man-serpent from the mahogany chair, chipped down its left cheek, but alive now, and staring at me with malevolent satisfaction. The vipers that grew from his scalp were slowly waving and undulating, like seaweed on a sullen wave.

'It's you,' I managed to choke out. My larynx felt as if it was being squeezed in a cider-press.

'*It will always be me,*' smiled the man-serpent. His eyes were blank and grained with wood, but his eyelids rolled over them when he blinked as if they were real eyes. '*Until you accept what I have to give you, it will always be me.*'

'You hurt my son,' I told him.

'*Every time you hurt me, you will always inflict pain on yourself or your family,*' the man-serpent said. His voice was husky and echoing, and didn't seem to be synchronised with his lips. It was like talking to some kind of frightening ventriloquist's dummy.

'Then what can I do to get rid of you?' I asked.

'*You will never get rid of me. Not until you accept what I have to give you.*'

'What about Henry Grant? Did he accept what you were offering?'

'*Henry Grant would rather have died. So, he did.*'

'And what about me?'

'*You would rather survive. For your own sake, and for the sake of your wife and son.*'

'And my dog? What harm did he do you?'

Up above me, the man-serpent dreamily grinned. He didn't appear to be fastened to the ceiling, or even touching it. Instead, he was floating horizontally an inch or two below it. I couldn't believe what I was seeing, but there he was, two feet above my head. I could have reached up and touched him.

'*Your dog was your familiar. I, too, need a familiar — and mine is the trilobite. It can only come to life through the sacrifice of my owner's closest animal companion, and that is exactly what happened. My trilobite is as faithful to me as your dog was to you. More venomous, perhaps. But faithful.*'

Gradually, jerkily, the fluorescent light in the laundry-room was beginning to dim.

'Listen,' I said, 'supposing I reject your offer? Supposing I tell you to go to hell?'

'*You cannot,*' whispered the man-serpent.

'But supposing I do? Supposing I won't do anything you want me to? Supposing I break you to pieces?'

'*You saw what happened before.*'

'Then I shall call a priest, God damn you, and I shall have you exorcised. I shall have all the strongest spells of the Father, and the Son, and the Holy Ghost, all bound around you until you *choke.*'

The laundry-room was almost dark now. All I could see of the figure on the ceiling was the whiteness of its robes and a blueish luminosity around its eyes and its jaws.

'I repudiate you,' I said, as forcefully as I could. 'I repudiate everything you are, and everything you've done, and everything you ever plan to do.'

There was a moment of utter tension. It was like the moment before the first flash of lightning in an electric storm, when everything goes silent. Then there was a consuming roar, and the whole laundry-room burst into flames. I was thrown back against the other side of the corridor, my hands and face scorched, and I twisted my ankle.

Through the open door, I saw sheets and towels blazing furiously, and fragments of charred linen whirling up to the ceiling. It was like a furnace in there, and the flames were already licking around the door frame and scorching the paint on the corridor wall.

I limped painfully along to the nearest fire-bell, and smashed the glass with my knuckle.

5 — Explorings

We stayed at the Holy Sisters of Mercy all night, dozing uncomfortably on the foam-cushioned sofas in the waiting-room. I told Sara what had happened in the laundry-room, but nobody else. As far as the doctors and nurses were concerned, I had been taking a stroll along the corridor to stretch my legs when I had smelled something burning. They thought I was a minor hero – losing half of my right eyebrow in an attempt to close the laundry-room door and stop the fire from spreading.

They didn't realise that what had burned that night was my whole future happiness, my last hope that it was possible for my family to escape from the damning influence of that terrible chair.

In the morning, as we sipped scalding coffee and ate two unappetising lemon Danishes, Dr Gopher came in with his clipboard and sat down opposite us, hiking up the leg of his pants to reveal a wrinkled maroon sock.

'I'm happy to tell you that Jonathan's condition is stable,' he said. 'The wound's healing well, and apart from the fact that he's still unconscious, all his reflexes are fine. He's responding to all of the external stimuli to which any healthy but comatose person could be expected to respond. We're still keeping a very attentive eye on him, of course, but we have an expectation that he may come out of the coma later today.'

Sara let out a sigh of relief.

'I don't want to raise your hopes prematurely,' Dr Gopher added quickly, raising one of his fingers. 'You may have to accept the fact that he won't come around for two or three days. But, on the whole, we're more optimistic than pessimistic.'

'Thank you, Doctor,' I said. 'My wife's going to stay here for the rest of the morning, just in case he comes round sooner. I'm going off to get us a change of clothes.'

'Yes, I'm sorry you had to sleep here,' said Dr Gopher. 'Usually, we have a couple of rooms free for parents to stay, but we're pretty full at the moment. Kawasaki disease, burns, broken limbs. It's vacation time, of course. Always our busiest time on the pediatric floor.'

'I just want to thank you for everything you've done,' I told him.

'Well, that's appreciated,' said Dr Gopher, 'but *I* ought to be thanking you. If you hadn't spotted that fire, there wouldn't have been any pediatric wing left to *get* busy.'

We both stood up. 'We'll do everything we possibly can,' Dr Gopher told us, and left the waiting-room.

I reached over and stroked Sara's cheek with my fingers.

'Are you going now?' she asked me.

'I guess I'd better. What do you want me to bring you?'

'Anything, so long as it's clean. How about my green blouse and my white skirt with the sash? And clean panties, of course. And a toothbrush. My teeth feel like they're growing fur.'

'Sure,' I said. 'Anything to eat?'

She shook her head. 'There'll be plenty of time to eat when Jonathan wakes up.'

I kissed her, and went to the door. She said, 'Ricky?'

'What is it?'

'That – *thing* you saw last night. You warned it that you were going to have it exorcised.'

'I was trying to challenge it, that was all. Exorcism was the first challenging thought that came into my head.'

'You don't think it might be worth your talking to Father Corso?'

'Father Corso? You can just imagine what *he'd* say. "Mr Delatolla, modern theology has no place for physical manifestations of negative values. You're probably externalising a psycho-religious conflict by superimposing the positive-negative interface on to an inanimate object, to wit, your chair."'

Sara couldn't help smiling. Father Corso was very enthusiastic, and often very perceptive, but he was heavily into the sort of Catholicism that sounded good at Southern

California cocktail parties. Bill, my assistant, called him 'Saint Jacuzzi'.

'You could try, though, couldn't you?' asked Sara. 'Even if he can't help us directly, he might have some relevant ideas.'

I gave her a tired nod. 'I'll ask him. He'll probably have me certified and locked up, but I'll ask him. I won't be away more than a couple of hours. Try calling me at the house if there's any news of Jonathan.'

'Okay, my darling. I love you.'

I left the hospital and caught a cab back to Rancho Santa Fe. It was another one of those hot, hazy mornings, and by the time the cab drew up in my driveway, I felt like taking an ice-cold, ten-minute shower. I paid the driver and stiffly climbed out.

Hortensia opened the door for me. 'How's Jonathan?' she asked. 'I've been worrying myself sick.'

'He's still unconscious, Hortensia, but the doctors say he's getting better. They hope he's going to wake up some time today.'

'That was such a shock, Mr Delatolla. And all of those bad things happening . . .'

I looked at her. 'You know what's been happening here?'

'I see for myself, Mr Delatolla. That monster-thing what killed poor Sheraton. I see for myself, out of the window. And what happened to them pictures.'

I frowned. 'What pictures? What are you talking about?'

Hortensia blew out her cheeks. 'Uh-oh. You haven't seen them pictures yet? I swear to you it's black magic. Devil's doing.'

'Show me,' I said.

She waddled ahead of me along the corridor, twirling her feather-duster like a drum-majorette's baton. She took me into the living-room, and then planted herself in front of my Copley painting of the mariner being rescued from the shark.

'There,' she said, dramatically. 'You see if that isn't devil's doing.'

I stared at the painting with mounting dread. The original composition had shown the mariner lying on his back in the sea, naked, while a boat-load of rescuers fought off a huge white-bellied shark. Now, the boat appeared to be further away from the mariner, and the faces of the rescuers had changed expression from grim determination to frustrated horror. The shark, with its mouth open wide to reveal rows of ferocious teeth, was closer to the mariner than before, and it was clear to anyone looking at the painting that it was going to reach him minutes before his friends could row near enough to beat it off.

After two hundred years, it looked as if Copley's mariner was at last going to be devoured by his grinning nemesis.

Without waiting for Hortensia to lead the way, I crossed the living-room and looked at the Gilbert Stuart. The serious-faced colonial gentleman hadn't altered; but in the thicket of woods which formed the background of the painting, a dark and barely distinguishable shape had appeared. It looked as if it was wearing a tall pointed hood, and I was uncomfortably reminded of the beast in the story *The Casting of The Runes.*

'Well, Hortensia,' I said. 'I'm quite surprised you didn't quit.'

She clasped her hands together. 'I don't have papers, Mr Delatolla. Where could I go?'

'But if you had papers?'

She crossed herself. 'God protects his children, Mr Delatolla.'

'Well,' I said, 'let's hope so.'

I went upstairs, while Hortensia went back to the kitchen. In our bedroom, I collected all the clean clothes we needed, and packed them into a zip-up TWA bag. Then I undressed, and went into the bathroom to take a shower. In the large mirror over the vanity basin, I appeared as a pale haggard stranger, with a day's growth of beard and an angry zit on my left temple. I stepped into the yellow-tiled shower, closed the door, and turned on the water. For ten full minutes, I stood with my eyes shut, leaning against the side of the shower, letting the cool water splash all over me. I don't think I've ever enjoyed a shower as much in my life.

When I walked back into the bedroom, however, towelling

my hair dry and dabbing my face, I had the distinct feeling that a subtle change had occurred while I was in the shower. I looked around the room, but everything seemed to be just as it was. The airline bag on the bed, my crumpled clothes still lying on the floor. The top drawer in Sara's bureau a couple of inches open, with the lacy edge of a pair of peach-coloured panties still showing. My car keys on top of the bedside table.

I circled slowly around, drying myself more abstractedly, and trying to work out what it was that was so different.

'Hortensia,' I called out. 'Did you touch anything in here?'

There was no reply. She was probably out in the yard. I sat down on the end of the bed, and I could see myself in Sara's dressing-table mirror now, frowning and alone. I looked like a character in a German expressionist painting, probably entitled *Fürchtbarkeit*, fearfulness.

I pulled on a clean pair of cotton jeans, and a blue chequered shirt. While I was buttoning up the cuffs, I went to the open door again and called, 'Hortensia? You there?'

There was still no answer. I shrugged, and went back to find myself a pair of socks.

Quite suddenly, the telephone started ringing. It gave me a jolt for a second or two, because I wasn't expecting anybody to call except Sara. I'd already told Bill to handle any queries down at the antiques store by himself. He might make one or two mistakes on pricing, or sell something that I'd been saving for a favoured customer, but there was no way that I was going to be able to cope with business problems until Jonathan came round.

I picked up the phone and wedged it under my chin as I fastened my right cuff.

'Delatolla.'

'Mr Delatolla? This is Nurse Evans at the hospital. Your wife asked me to call you.'

'Is everything okay? How's Jonathan?'

'His condition hasn't changed. Your wife's in with him now, trying to get him to respond to the sound of her voice.'

'Well, you can tell her I'll be right back.'

'That's what I was calling about, sir.'

'I beg your pardon?'

'Your wife was anxious to know where you'd gone. She's been calling you all day, but getting no reply.'

'I haven't gone anywhere. I've been at home for the past ten minutes, taking a shower and getting us a change of clothes. That's all.'

'All right, sir. I understand.'

I was just about to put the phone down, when I suddenly realised what the nurse had said.

'Just a minute – ' I asked her, 'did you say "all day"?'

'I'm sorry?'

'You said my wife's been calling me *all day*.'

'Yes, Mr Delatolla. She has.'

'But it's only ten in the morning.'

'Sir?'

'I said it's only ten in the morning. How can my wife have been calling me all day when it's still only ten in the morning?'

There was a long silence. Then, very cautiously, Nurse Evans said, 'I'm sorry, sir. I think you must be making a mistake. It's eight minutes of five in the afternoon.'

I turned slowly around. My wristwatch was lying on the bed, only a couple of feet away. I reached over and picked it up and it read 4.49. Then I looked at the brass carriage clock on top of the bedroom bureau and I saw that it showed the same time.

That was what had been so different when I had come out of the shower. Not the room itself, nor anything in it. It was the quality of light that had changed, and the direction of the shadows. Instead of being delineated by the sharp bright light of a California morning, the room was now suffused in hazy afternoon gold.

Nurse Evans said, 'Is that all, Mr Delatolla? Mr Delatolla?'

'Yes,' I told her, quietly. 'Just be kind enough to tell my wife that I'll be back at the hospital within a half-hour.'

'Very good, sir.'

I laid down the phone. I felt swimmy and detached, as if I were suffering from jet-lag. Somehow, a whole day had passed me by while I was taking a shower. The clock had jumped by trickery, and another seven or eight hours of my life had vanished beyond recall. I went to the dressing-table and stared at myself in silence. The influence of the chair was stealing my life away, and I didn't even know how, or why.

No wonder Hortensia hadn't answered when I called. She must have gone home some hours before.

I picked up the phone and called Bill at the antiques store. 'Bill? It's Ricky.'

'Oh, hi, Ricky. Will you excuse me one moment? That's right, sir, it's genuine Georgian silver. That's right, George III. Or maybe George IV. Well, I know, but they *were* related, weren't they? So I guess their spoons must have had a lot in common, too.'

I rubbed my eyes. Usually, Bill's attempts to show off his knowledge of antiques really amused me. He once told a customer that the cushioned cresting-rail of a *prie-dieu* chair must have been put there for kibitzers to lean on while the chair's occupant was playing cards. But today, I wasn't in the mood for anything light-hearted. My son was lying in a coma, and I'd just been robbed of a whole morning and afternoon of my life.

'I've been trying to get you,' said Bill, after his customer had left. 'I know you told me not to call, but Sara rang up a couple of times and asked me if you were round here at the store; and then Mr Sears came in, and wanted to speak to you urgently.'

'Mr Sears? Did he say what he had on his mind?'

'It was something to do with the chair, he told me. But he didn't say which chair.'

I raked my fingers through my wet hair. 'That's okay, Bill. I know which chair. Maybe I'll be able to call at Presidio Place. Are there any other messages?'

'Mrs Greenbaum came in about the dumb waiter.'

'Did she nibble?'

'She's still interested, but I think we're going to have to come down a couple of hundred.'

'I already came down three.'

'Well, I told her I'd talk to you, and see what we could do.'

'Bill,' I replied, 'you have such a way with eighty-year-old ladies. You missed your vocation. You should have run a retirement home.'

'Are you going back to the hospital now?' asked Bill.

'As soon as I've locked up the house.'

'There's, uh . . . there's nothing *wrong* is there?'

'What do you mean?'

'Between you and Sara. I mean, I don't like to stick my nose in where it isn't wanted, but she was real worried about you today. It's not like you to take off and not tell her where you're going. She was real worried.'

I stood up. 'Bill,' I said, 'I appreciate your interest. But everything's fine between Sara and me. We're just experiencing a few domestic problems, that's all. No marriage break-up, no traumas. Just a few problems.'

'Okay, I'm glad to hear it. Can I expect you around the store tomorrow?'

'Maybe for five minutes. It depends how Jonathan's responding.'

'I'll say a prayer for him, you know?'

'Thanks, Bill.'

I put down the phone. I hesitated for a moment, and then I took the San Diego telephone book out of the bedside table and riffled through it until I found the number for Presidio Place. I pecked out the number with the end of my ballpen and waited while it rang.

'Presidio Place.'

'Hi. I'm trying to contact Mr David Sears. He's staying with someone at the Place. I'm afraid I don't know whom.'

'Hold on. I think he's with Mr Eads. Yes, that's right, Mr Eads. You want me to try the number?'

The switchboard girl rang and rang and rang but there was no reply. In the end, I said, 'Thanks all the same, but forget it,' and hung up. I stood for a while in the shadows of our late-afternoon bedroom, and wondered what the hell had happened to David. We hadn't parted yesterday on particularly friendly terms, but I didn't like to think that he'd been hurt. Even worse, I didn't like to think that the chair had somehow escaped him.

I took the airline bag and went downstairs. In the living-room, my paintings hadn't changed any further – not that I could distinguish, anyway. Maybe the hooded figure in the background of the Gilbert Stuart portrait was a fraction clearer, a fraction more prominent. But that was probably nothing more than my imagination.

On the way out, I stopped by the library door. It was ajar, only about an inch, but enough for me to be able to see the side of my desk and the sunlight falling across the rows of books. I pushed it open wider, and it creaked introspectively on its hinges, like an old man disturbed in a dream.

The library, apart from its regular furniture, was empty. No chair. No surprises. I found myself letting out a puff of relief.

I went outside, locked the screen door behind me, and crossed the driveway to my wagon. High up above me, the sky was already beginning to fade to the colour of blue flag flowers.

They showed me through to the room where Jonathan was lying, and I stood at the end of his bed looking at his bandaged face and his one visible eye, and I thought to myself, *why*, God? Why did it have to be him? *I* did all the damage, and yet I escaped unscathed. Why is it always the innocent people who get hurt the most?

Sara was sitting at the bedside looking white-faced and utterly exhausted. She cupped her chin in her hands and stared up at me as if she'd heard that I'd been caught *in flagrante delicto* with another woman.

'Where have you been?' she asked me, making no attempt to conceal the acid in her voice.

'I went home for some clean clothes,' I told her. 'I showered, and then I came out of the shower, and – '

'Ricky, I've been waiting for you all day! I've been going out of my *mind* with worry! I've called you again and again, and nobody knew where you were! I've been sitting here all on my own trying to coax Jonathan out of his coma, without any word, without any support, while you've been – well,

God knows where you've been. I don't really want to know.'

'Sara, listen,' I replied. 'As far as I'm concerned, I've only been away for two hours. You remember what happened on Sunday night – how the night simply disappeared? Well, that's what happened today.'

'How could it have done?'

'What do you mean, how could it have done? How the hell do I know? I don't know where Sunday night went and I don't know where today went. But it went. I spent ten minutes in the shower and when I came out, it was afternoon.'

She slowly lowered her hands and sat up straight. 'You're not fooling me?' she asked. 'The day actually disappeared?'

I nodded, with exaggerated emphasis. 'The day actually disappeared. One minute it was morning, the next it was late afternoon. I don't know how it happened, but it did. What do you really suppose I was doing for seven hours? Playing around with some woman while Jonathan's lying in hospital?'

She reached out her hand for me across the red hospital blanket. 'I'm sorry. I was frightened for you, that's all. I didn't mean to sound bitchy.'

'I don't blame you, Sara, for Christ's sake.'

I came around the bed and kissed her. Then we both looked at Jonathan, who was lying on his pillow so still and white that he could have been dead. Only the tell-tale heartbeat which pulsed across the screen of the electro-cardiograph equipment told us that our son was still alive. A steady *beep-beep-beep* to record the tenuous survival of that life which I had first heard when I pressed my ear to Sara's stomach, six years and six months ago.

We had lost one child already. I prayed to Our Lady that we wouldn't lose Jonathan, too. He was too precious, too important. He was everything good that Sara and I had brought to our marriage, the best of both of us, and most of all, he was himself.

'The nurse told me you'd been talking to him,' I said.

Sara said, 'Yes. Most of the day.'

'And no response?'

She shook her head. 'I even tried singing, but it didn't do any good.

'You think a song might get through to him?'

'I don't know,' she said. 'It's been successful before . . . or so Dr Gopher told me. Sometimes coma patients start to come around when they hear one of their favourite records.'

I leaned over Jonathan's bed, and stared at his face for a long time. My son, where are you now? What are you dreaming, behind that single closed eye? I was so near that I could almost have kissed him, but he was so far away from me that I couldn't tell if he was ever going to be able to come back.

I cleared my throat, and sang:

> *'Johnny shall have a new bonnet,*
> *Johnny shall go to the fair,*
> *And Johnny shall have a new ribbon,*
> *To tie up his bonny blond hair.'*

My voice was husky, wavering, off-key. It's hard to sing and swallow back your tears at the same time. When I looked across at Sara she was openly weeping.

I turned back to Jonathan. He hadn't stirred. I sang the nursery-rhyme again, but there was no sign that my singing had penetrated his private dream, or touched his sleeping memory.

'What do the doctors say?' I asked Sara.

'They still don't know,' she said, tiredly. 'He's in good physical shape, and they can't find anything wrong with his brain. No contusions, no infection. One of the specialists said it's almost like he's hypnotised. As if he can't wake up until someone gives him the right command.'

I bit at my knuckle. 'If this coma is anything to do with that damned chair . . .'

'The chair's gone now, hasn't it?'

I said, 'Yes, as far as I know. It wasn't in the house. But if it could take seven hours out of my life . . . maybe its influence is still around.'

'Did you talk to Father Corso?'

'I didn't have time. As soon as I found out that it was nearly five o'clock, I rushed straight back here.'

'You *will* talk to him, though?'

I stared at Jonathan, lost in his coma. 'Yes, I'll talk to him. I'll try anything. I'll even try an exorcism if you think it'll do any good.'

'I don't know what the doctors would think.'

I walked around the bed. 'I don't give a damn what the doctors would think. The doctors didn't see Sheraton. The doctors didn't see the leaves falling off the trees.'

Sara touched Jonathan's arm, and stroked the back of his curled-up fingers. Outside in the hospital corridor, the paging bell rang, and a garbled voice asked for *one cardiac resuscitation pack, urgent please, to 911.* Somebody else was fighting for their life.

Dr Gopher came in. 'Would you mind leaving Jonathan for a short while?' he asked us. 'We have some more tests to run.'

'What do you think about his chances now?' I asked him. 'Are the odds any better than they were this morning? Or are they worse?'

Dr Gopher shrugged. 'I'm not a bookmaker, Mr Delatolla. I'm a specialist in pediatric brain problems.'

'What tests?' I wanted to know.

'I need to make sure that there's no pressure on the brain that our first tests may have overlooked. I also need to analyse the spinal fluid. I can't overlook any possible causes. You may like to know that I've asked Detroit's Neural Research Centre for all the information they have on infantile coma, and that the Susskind Foundation have already sent us all of their latest findings on concussion. We're doing everything we can.'

I looked at Jonathan lying on his high hospital bed, surrounded by drip-stands and tubes. 'I hope it's enough,' I said, in a tone that wasn't meant to sound harsh, but just came out that way.

Dr Gopher lowered his clipboard. 'I hope so, too, Mr Delatolla. Believe me.'

While Sara showered and changed, I sat in the waiting-room

and flicked through *National Geographic* magazines, and old copies of *Los Angeles*. I liked the small ads in *Los Angeles*, particularly the classification 'None Of The Above'. Somebody was offering party entertainment by 'The Unknown Gypsies Kumpania . . . unique, outrageous, and dramatically different' and another company could provide singing telegrams by 'Frank The Giant Singing Hot Dog'.

I was practically asleep when the waiting-room door opened and David Sears came lurching in. He was looking sweaty and dishevelled, and he'd taken off his striped necktie and crammed it into his breast pocket. He sat down heavily on the chair next to me, and searched around in his coat for cigarettes.

'My God,' he said, lighting up, and taking down a deep draught of smoke. 'I thought I was never going to make it.'

'What's going on?' I asked him. 'Did you get rid of the chair?'

He shook his head. 'The chair almost got rid of me. It's far more powerful than I ever realised.'

'Where is it now?'

'I haven't a clue. I've been looking for it everywhere. I've even been around to your house, trying to see through the windows. I got moved on by a security guard. He damn near arrested me.'

I watched him closely. The cigarette began to calm him down, and soon he was steady enough to sit up straight, mop the sweat from his face with a handkerchief, and tug his cuffs.

'Well?' I asked him. 'How did you lose it?'

'I'm not entirely sure. I was going to take it to Los Angeles airport, have it crated up, and fly it back to England on tomorrow afternoon's plane. But I was only a mile or so past San Juan Capistrano when I started to get the most ridiculous sensations. I kept feeling that I was bleeding all down my back – as if I was sitting in a welter of my own blood. I actually pulled off the road to make sure that I was all right. Then, when I started driving again, I became convinced that I was afflicted with leprosy, that my ankles were coming away in chunks inside of my socks, and that the flesh was actually falling off my bones. I stopped again, and this time, when I looked in the back of the car, the chair had gone.'

I tossed down my magazine. 'It looks like we haven't carried out the proper sales ritual, then, doesn't it?' I asked him. 'What did you call it, a runic transaction?'

He sucked at his cigarette so violently that it burned down almost a half-inch in one hot inhalation. Then, with smoke spurting out of his nostrils, he said, 'That's right. A conveyance of sale in the ancient manner of the runes.'

'How's it done? Do you happen to know?'

'I haven't the faintest idea. But somebody must know.'

'Who?'

'Old man Jessop. Otherwise, how did *he* get rid of the chair?'

I blinked at him. 'You really think we can go up to old man Jessop and ask him how to carry out a runic sales transaction?'

'Why not? He owned the chair for fifteen years, and all it ever brought him was money. He must know how to handle it.'

'Well, I guess you're right,' I said, thoughtfully. 'The Jessops sure did seem to get nothing but luck.'

'It probably depends on your inclinations,' David remarked. 'If you're an unscrupulous old tightwad like Jessop, then you and the chair are very probably going to get along. But if you're at all moral . . . if you actually believe in God, and stay faithful to your wife, and try not to tread on ants when you walk along your garden path . . . *then* I think you've got yourself more trouble than you can handle.'

I thought of what the floating figure had whispered to me in the laundry-room. '*You will never get rid of me. Not until you accept what I have to give you.*'

'I've been thinking about exorcism,' I told David, rather bashfully.

'Exorcism? You can't do that. Besides, it's nothing more than ecclesiastical mumbo-jumbo. Waving candles about and spraying Holy water and reciting some of the sillier pieces in the Bible.'

'David,' I insisted, 'we have to do something. That chair has hurt my son, and now he's lying in a coma, and the doctors don't even know when he's going to wake up. That's if he ever *does* wake up. Exorcism isn't going to be any less effective than taking lumbar punctures and singing songs.'

'Well, I suppose not,' said David, 'but I did hear that someone had tried to exorcise the chair before.'

'Oh yes, who?'

'I don't exactly know who. One of the chair's previous owners. As soon as it began to play unpleasant tricks on him, he called on a priest and they went through the whole procedure . . . you know, "yield to me by the Sacred Virgin Mary who gave Her womb" and all that stuff.'

'What happened?'

David lit a fresh cigarette from the glowing butt of the first. 'I don't think they realised that the chair is not *in itself* an evil spirit. The chair in itself is nothing more than a passageway through which evil spirits can pass from the nether-world into the real world. A nexus, as I said before.'

He paused, and then he said, 'The owner of the chair, and the priest who had agreed to perform the exorcism – both were found the following day by neighbours. The neck of one had been twisted around the neck of the other, so that they formed a sort of two-headed monster. They were both dead, of course, of shock and strangulation.'

I sat back. 'Listen, David,' I said firmly, 'are you coming clean with me about this chair? Every time you talk about it you seem to be able to remember just a little bit more pertinent information. Are you hiding something?'

'Why should I hide anything?'

'Now you're answering a question with a question.'

David looked at me, thoughtfully and unswervingly, for almost a whole minute. Then he leaned forward and tapped the ash off his cigarette into the stand-up ashtray.

'I do know quite a bit about the chair, I must admit. There are certain gaps in my knowledge . . . certain vital gaps . . . but I suppose you could say that I know more about it than anybody who hasn't actually owned it.'

I cleared my throat. 'What I want to know is if there's

anything at all in the history of that chair that could help me to save Jonathan. The rest of it can go hang.'

David shook his head. 'I wish there were. But the chair seems to behave differently towards different people, according to what they want from it. And according to how much they want to keep it.'

'*I* don't want to keep it at all.'

'I know you don't,' said David. 'That's probably why it's treating you so badly. And although I can't be sure, that's probably why Jonathan's gone into a coma. He's a hostage, or at least his mind is. Because as long as he's unconscious, you're always going to be interested in the chair. The chair wants your attention.'

'But why? How can a chair want attention? And what for?'

'I just don't know. I have a kind of weak theory, based on what I know of the chair's history, but it's been impossible to verify.'

'Well, weak or not, let's hear it.'

'If you really want to,' said David. 'You see . . . whenever somebody comes into possession of the chair . . . they always seem to do extraordinarily well at whatever business they might be in. With the Earl of Beckenham, of course, it was gambling. With the Jessops, it was aviation. As I've said before, I don't know who all of the owners of the chair have been, but my banker friend Williams made an absolute fortune. And about two years ago I came across a rather circumstantial account by a nineteenth-century magazine writer who visited the home of Charles Dickens, and described a curious carved chair with the face of a male Gorgon.'

'So the chair helps people to make a success of their lives.'

'That's right. If you allowed it to, it would probably help you make a resounding success out of yours.'

I massaged the back of my neck. My muscles were as tight as spinet wires. 'If it wants to help me,' I asked David, 'why is it acting so goddamned malevolent? Why did it kill Sheraton? Why did it blight all the trees around my home? Why has it taken Jonathan?'

'I don't know the answers to all of your questions,' said

David. 'But my guess is that the chair is trying to make you surrender. It's trying to show you how powerful it is, and that it's no use trying to fight against it. Wouldn't you think so?'

'Well, maybe you're right,' I admitted, reluctantly. 'But it all sounds pretty screwy to me.'

'What the hell do you *expect*?' demanded David. 'You expect *logic*? You expect *sanity*? You're asking me to rationalise a piece of furniture that was made to the order of a corrupt eighteenth-century rake by an unbalanced eighteenth-century freak – and made for the express purpose of bringing its owner the luck of the devil. The *real* Devil, if there is such a person. For Christ's sake, Ricky, you've seen for yourself what that chair can do. It's like a magnet in the middle of a field of iron filings. It can swirl everything around it just the way it wants. Trees, dogs, pictures, hours of the day, even human destiny.'

'But *why*?' I retorted. 'I don't want it to help me in my work, or at home, or anywhere. I don't want anything from it at all, except that it should go off and leave me and my family alone. Why does it keep coming back to me? What does it want?'

'I don't know,' said David. 'It seems to want something, but I simply can't imagine what it is.'

I got up, exasperated, and paced to the window. It was dark outside now, and the night was glittering with lights. An aeroplane sank into San Diego airport like a cluster of slowly falling UFOs. I turned back to David, and said, 'Somehow, I have to get rid of that chair, for good and all. I just have to get rid of it.'

'You know that I'd take it away from you if I could.'

'You can't, though, can you? The minute you try to drive it away you start bleeding or falling to pieces.'

'Hallucinations,' said David.

'Sure they're hallucinations. But can you tolerate them? Obviously not, or you wouldn't have come scurrying back here.'

'Ricky,' insisted David. 'I want that chair. And if we can find any way of transferring ownership from you to me, then I'll do it like a shot.'

I stood over him, my hands on my hips. 'You want the chair

but the chair doesn't want you. That's the whole trouble.'

'My client wants the chair, to be slightly more accurate.'

'It doesn't matter who wants it,' I said. 'If it doesn't want to go, then it won't.'

'Supposing we go talk to old man Jessop?' David suggested.

'What difference is that going to make?'

'Well, Jessop managed to off-load the chair on to your late friend Henry Grant. So, how did Jessop do it? Why didn't the chair go back to Escondido? Maybe Jessop knows all about runic transactions. He's owned that chair for nearly fifteen years; he must know more about it than we do. Even a clue would help.'

He crushed out his cigarette as he watched me for my reaction.

'You could be right,' I said, grudgingly. 'I guess it wouldn't do us any harm if we went out to Escondido and asked him.'

'Would Sara mind if you left the hospital?'

'Not if she thought I was doing something constructive to help Jonathan. Which I hope I will be.'

'What else is there to do? Sit here and wait? You can't help Jonathan if you're sitting here.'

Sara came back from the bathroom, smelling fresh and clean, with her hair tied up in a towel.

'David,' she said. Her face fell.

I put my arm around her. 'David just got here. He tried to take the chair away, but . . . well, it wasn't any use. He got as far as San Juan Capistrano and it vanished out of his car.'

'Where is it now?' asked Sara, her face as waxy and expressionless as one of those store-window fashion models.

'I just don't know,' David admitted. 'But if you were to ask me to make an educated guess . . . I'd say it was back at your house.'

Sara sat down. 'Oh, God,' was all she could say.

'David thought that it might be worth going out to Escondido to talk to old man Jessop about it,' I explained.

'Do you think it'll do any good?' asked Sara.

'It can't do any harm,' said David.

Sara held her hand over her mouth as if to prevent herself

from saying anything more. I could see the hurt in her eyes, and the fear too, but there wasn't anything I could do to help her. Not unless I managed to purge our house and our family life of that hideous chair, for ever.

'I'll try to be quick as I can,' I told Sara. 'Barring accidents, or time warps, I should be back here before ten.'

She nodded, without taking her hand away from her mouth.

I bent over and kissed her forehead. 'I love you,' I said, simply, and she closed her eyes in acknowledgement of that simple fact, and to show that my feelings were returned.

The nurses allowed me to take one quick look at Jonathan before I left. David waited in the corridor, his hands clasped behind his back like the Duke of Edinburgh, clearing his throat from time to time as if he were about to make a speech. He was the first Englishman I'd ever gotten anything like close to, and I must say it was a curious and educational experience. It was like playing a game in which your opponent knew the rules, but you didn't, and so you had to pick it up as you went along just by watching him. Quite often I couldn't work out if he'd made a genuine move to improve our relationship, or if he was only being polite.

Jonathan hadn't stirred. His one visible eye was still closed, his small fingers still clasped the blankets. I stood over him for a few minutes, and then looked up at the nurses.

'Any change? Any signs at all?'

One of the nurses sympathetically shook her head.

I gently touched Jonathan's forehead with my fingertips, and sang:

> *'Johnny shall have a new bonnet,*
> *Johnny shall go to the fair,*
> *And Johnny shall have a new ribbon,*
> *To tie up his bonny blond hair.'*

There was no response. I stayed where I was for a moment, bent over him, and then I stood straight.

A voice inside of my head, echoing and metallic, said, *'You shall never have him back. Not as long as you resist me.'*

I stared at Jonathan. 'I won't resist you,' I said.

'*Ah, that's easy for you to say now. But I have heard you swear to be rid of me. Once I release the child, you will try to destroy me.*'

'I won't. That's my solemn promise. I'll stake my life on it.'

'*Your life is worth nothing.*'

'Then what do you want? You keep attacking me, you keep turning my whole world upside-down, but you won't tell me what you want!'

'Mr Delatolla – ' said one of the nurses. 'Mr Delatolla, please – '

'You've taken my son, you've scared my wife half to death, you've killed my dog. Tell me what you want!'

'*Can't you guess? You've had long enough now. Can't you guess?*'

One of the nurses wrenched at my sleeve, and tried to twist me away from the bed. I shook her off, and she fell with a clatter against the metal trolley of swabs and oxygen equipment.

'*Tell me what you want!*' I screamed at Jonathan. '*Tell – me – what – you – want!*'

'*Can't you guesssssssss?*'

The other nurse had managed to pull the door open now, and she beckoned silently but furiously to two passing orderlies. I was still screeching at Jonathan when they came into the room, two big men with muscles like lifeguards and sweatbands around their hair, and I only realised what was happening when they squashed my arms behind my back into a sinew-cracking full nelson. Then they forced me to teeter out of the room on tiptoe, and out into the corridor.

'Okay, friend, what's the big fuss?' asked one of them, in that slow courteous way that people use when they're quite confident that they can break both your legs without even breathing hard.

David came up and said, 'I say, is everything all right? Ricky, are you sure you're all right?'

'He's the father of that little boy in there,' explained one of the nurses. 'I guess he just got kind of upset.'

'That your kid in there?' the other orderly asked me. I nodded, dumbly.

'Okay,' said the orderly. 'But keep it down, huh? These

ladies are trying to do the best they can. No point in giving them a hard time.'

'I wasn't – ' I began, but then I gave it up. Arguing with hospital orderlies, cops, airline stewards, and Disneyland staff always gets you wound up into a ball for no purpose. They're trained to be calmly offensive to you, and to make you appear to everyone else around you like an apoplectic maniac.

'I'm sorry,' I said. 'I guess I was overwrought.'

'I'm afraid you'll have to have special permission from the doctor to come visit your son again,' said one of the nurses, through her nose.

'I said I'm sorry,' I repeated, more doggedly.

David and I walked the length of the corridor in silence until we reached the elevator.

'Are you all right, old boy?' David asked me. His voice was full of genuine concern.

I leaned against the wall, and nodded. 'I'm okay. I heard the voice of that man-serpent again, that's all.'

'I thought that was it. It was the way you were shouting, for no apparent reason. I thought you were trying to rouse Jonathan at first, until I realised what you were saying.'

The elevator arrived, and the doors opened with a soft chime. We stepped inside, and it dropped down to the next floor, where three nurses and two interns crowded in. David and I shuffled to the rear of the elevator, and down it went again.

We were passing the sixth floor when I happened to look at the polished stainless-steel doors in front of us. Everybody in the elevator was facing forward, and so their faces were all reflected in the smeary metal. There were two black girls, one quite pretty, and an intern with bushy hair and a bald patch.

But as I looked at the next reflection in the line, I felt my skin creep with cold. The face that smiled at me out of the stainless-steel elevator door was that of the man-serpent on the Devil's chair.

6—Alarmings

We drove out to Escondido with the radio tuned to KOGO 6 Radio News. I just wanted to hear something normal, something real. I just wanted to know that the world was still going on outside of my house at Rancho Santa Fe and the Hospital of the Sisters of Mercy.

David said, 'You're sure you saw that face? You're not letting your anxiety run riot?'

I glanced across at him stonily.

'Well,' he said, 'I still believe we ought to challenge everything we see and experience. Otherwise our own minds are going to start working against us, too. One panic leads to another.'

I flicked my eyes at the rear-view mirror, and depressed my lane-change signal to overtake a rattling bus crowded with Mexican roadworkers. The dark freeway rose ahead of us towards the cutting at Del Mar, and then dipped down again, an endless river of red lights.

Back at the hospital, the elevator doors had rumbled open almost as soon as I saw the man-serpent's face, and the nurses and interns had all pushed their way out into the lobby before I was able to make up my mind which of them had taken on the demon's features. Even if I'd caught up with the right intern, and stopped him, I probably would have found that he was quite normal and ordinary and didn't have the faintest idea what I was babbling about. I'd already allowed the chair to make a fool out of me in Jonathan's room. I didn't want to be banned from the hospital altogether.

'I'm going to drive back to the house after we've seen Jessop,' I said. 'I want to see if the chair's made its way there ... or whether it's decided to leave us alone for a while.'

'It won't leave you alone,' said David. 'Until you confront it, and deal with it according to the proper rituals, it won't ever leave you alone.'

'Now you're beginning to sound like the chair yourself.'

'Is that what it told you?'

I nodded. 'It won't release Jonathan out of his coma, and it won't allow me to get rid of it, not until I accept what it has to offer.'

'And you still can't work out what it is that it's offering?'

'I can't even begin to guess. Mind you, I haven't really been trying. That chair is so damned evil, I can't think what it could possibly do for me that wouldn't be illegal, or immoral, or downright homicidal.'

David thought for a while. 'You want to be rich, don't you?' he asked me.

'I'd like to be slightly wealthier, but then who wouldn't? I don't actually have a burning desire to be a zillionaire.'

'Is there any antique you've ever wanted to own? Some fabulous piece that you could never hope to lay your hands on?'

I shrugged. 'I've always wanted the "Diana and Minerva" commode in Harewood House in England. Do you know that Chippendale charged less than two hundred and ten dollars for it? But, you know, I can live without it.'

'What about women? Is there a woman you covet?'

'Yes. My wife. I'm in love with her, as corny as it may sound.'

'Is there something you want for your son?'

'Apart from his recovery, only health, and happiness. I don't even want him to become a plastic surgeon.'

David adjusted the wide white cuffs of his shirt. They were English-style, doubled-over, with mother-of-pearl cuff-links. He smelled slightly of tobacco, perspiration, and cologne.

'Do you have any religious or spiritual desires?' he wanted to know. 'I knew one fellow at university who would have given his right arm to meet John the Baptist.'

I took the sharply sloping ramp that led off the freeway on to the Escondido road. As I pulled up at the stop light at the bottom of the ramp, I said to David, 'What's with all these questions? I don't want the chair, or anything to do with it, and that's all there is to it. I don't have any unfulfilled ambitions. I don't have any outrageous desires. I'm happy. All I want is for that goddamned piece of black-hearted furniture to get out of my life.'

'I'm trying to help,' insisted David. 'If you could think what it is that the chair is so eager to have you accept, then you might be halfway to getting rid of it.'

The lights changed to green. 'I'm damned if I know,' I said, testily, as I shifted the Impala into Drive.

It took us another thirty-five minutes to reach Escondido. The road is well-surfaced and wide, but it winds in leisurely loops through the hills and around the mountains, and we were stuck for ten minutes behind a dawdling Winnebago, and for another five minutes behind a milk truck.

At last, on the outskirts of Escondido, we came to the narrow black-topped turning marked *Jessop*. The turning led nowhere else but up to the Jessop residence – a grandiose Gothic house whose dark spires we could already discern through the chokeberries and manzanita.

'I just hope he doesn't kick us out on our ass,' I remarked, as I steered the wagon up the driveway. A sign by the roadside warned 'This Estate Patrolled by Dobermans'.

We came at last to a high pair of wrought-iron gates, firmly locked against us. On the left-hand gatepost was a stainless-steel plate with an intercom button and a speaker. I put down my window and pressed the button twice. There was a warm evening smell in the air, dust and oranges and chaparral. David drummed his fingers nervously on the top of the dash.

I was just about to press the button again when a croaky woman's voice said, 'Yes? Who is it?'

It sounded like the same woman I had spoken to on Sunday – the woman who had denied that the Jessops had ever owned a carved mahogany chair. I turned to David, but he pointed to the intercom, and said, 'Go ahead. Tell them the truth.'

'Erm – it's Mr Richard Delatolla here, ma'am – and Mr David Sears – we're both antique dealers.'

'Do you have an appointment?'

'Well, I regret not. But we have to see Mr Jessop as a matter of urgency. It's a matter of life or death.'

'Oh, is it?' croaked the voice. 'Well, I'm afraid that Mr Jessop is unwell. He can't see anybody, no matter how urgent it is.'

There was a burp and a click, and the intercom was obviously shut off. I pressed the button again, and then twice more.

'What do you want?' demanded the woman.

'I have to see Mr Jessop,' I repeated. 'There's a small boy lying critically ill in hospital, and only Mr Jessop can – '

'Mr Jessop already pays hundreds of thousands of dollars to charity. He does not make personal donations.'

'I'm not asking for money. I've come about the chair.'

There was a crackling pause. Then the woman said slowly, 'The chair? Which chair?'

'The chair I called about on Sunday. The chair which you told me you'd never owned. The chair with the man-serpent's face on the top of it.'

'I'm afraid I don't know what you're talking about. I don't know anything about a chair.'

'You can't pretend any more, ma'am. I have absolute proof that the chair once belonged to Mr Sam Jessop, and that he sold it to a Mr Henry Grant.'

'Don't be ridiculous,' the woman snapped. 'There was never any documentation at all.'

'*I* know there wasn't,' I replied. 'But if Mr Jessop never owned the chair, how come *you* knew there wasn't?'

I distinctly heard the woman say '*Damn*' to herself.

'Well, then,' I said, 'do we get in to see Mr Jessop, or don't we?'

'Certainly not. He's sick. He's not seeing anybody.'

David leaned across the car in front of me, and said clearly, 'I think it would be wise to let us in, Mrs Jessop. That is Mrs Jessop, isn't it?'

'Yes it is, and what on earth makes you think that letting two perfect strangers into our house would be wise, especially after dark?'

'It would be wise,' said David, 'because if you turn us away, we'll make absolutely sure that you get your chair back again. No delivery charge, either.'

I started to say something, but David put his finger to his lips and stopped me. We both waited, listening to the faint crackling of static from the intercom. Eventually, Mrs Jessop said, 'Very well. But I will only let you in on one condition. That you don't harass my husband, and that you leave when I require you to.'

'That's two conditions,' I said.

'Perhaps it is,' she snapped back. 'And I may very well think of more before you reach the house.'

There was a metallic shuddering sound, and the wrought-iron gates gradually swung open. I started the wagon up again, and we drove through the dark trees towards the house, up a steep and curving gravel drive that eventually levelled off and widened into a parking area. There were two cars already parked beside the low brick wall that bordered the house – a black Fleetwood sedan and an old but highly-polished Chrysler Windsor.

The house itself was extraordinary. I had only ever seen it from a distance, from a vantage point on the Ramona road. But close to, I realised for the first time how enormous it was, with sheer walls that rose sixty or seventy feet like red-brick cliffs. The windows were tall and arched, with leaded panes, and the gutterings and rooftops were decorated with gargoyles and pottery flowers and crests. There were balconies and spires and odd dormer windows everywhere, and from the highest roof a large cast-iron weather-vane flew like a medieval banner.

'Castle Dracula,' I remarked, as I climbed out of the wagon and slammed the door.

'It's an interesting place, isn't it?' said David. 'It was originally built by Drummond Thody, who financed part of the Santa Fe Railroad. He was inspired by St Pancras Station in London, I believe.'

We crunched across the gravel until we reached the steps that led up to the baronial front door. One of the doors was already open, and in the dim orange light from the hallway a Mexican manservant in a black tuxedo was waiting for us.

'Good evening, gentlemen,' he said, without any noticeable hint of welcome or respect. 'Would you step this way, please?'

He walked in front of us with the stiff-backed swagger of a man who had enjoyed his years of military service more than any other time in his whole life. 'Fort Ord?' I asked, to the back of his well-oiled head. He didn't seem to think that was funny, because he didn't reply, and when he showed us into the living-room, he stared at me as if he was considering me for knife-throwing practice.

The hall had been echoing and huge, a parquet mausoleum; but the living-room was hung with rich plum-coloured velvet drapes, and decorated with fresh-cut orchids, and there was a glitter of silver and gilt and varnish about it which made it luxurious and comfortable. As David and I crossed the Ardebil carpet, which itself must have been worth nearly half a million dollars, I noticed in the corner a particularly fine inlaid Sheraton serpentine-fronted sideboard for which I would have given half the contents of my shop.

There was a log fire burning in the massive stone fireplace, despite the warmth of the evening, and sitting beside it in a tall-backed leather armchair was Sam Jessop. Not the Sam Jessop I knew from magazine and newspaper pictures – the stern, ruddy-faced Californian with the pugnacious jawline and bristling eyebrows. This was a ghost of Sam Jessop, old and pale and sick, with all the appearance of a half-collapsed pig's bladder. His liver-spotted hands hung on to the arms of his chair as if they were all that were preventing him from dwindling away to nothing on his seat-cushion. He wore a camel-coloured robe and brown velvet slippers with SJ embroidered on them.

Beside Sam Jessop stood a tall and reedy old lady, in a purple dress and strings of pearls. She must have been eighty-five, but she had perfect facial bones, and half a century ago she was probably the most beautiful woman in Southern California.

There was only one ornament in the whole room which gave any kind of clue how the Jessops had made their money. On the mantelpiece, gleaming in the firelight, was a chromium-plated model of a guided missile.

I held my hand out. 'Mrs Jessop,' I said. 'My name's Ricky Delatolla. I'm very impressed with your house.'

She ignored my hand, and indicated with a cursory nod of her head a small sofa on the other side of the fireplace. 'Won't you sit down?' she asked. 'You'll have to speak rather loudly, I'm afraid. My husband doesn't hear too well. And don't tax him too much, will you? He has Bright's disease.'

'I'm sorry to hear that, Mr Jessop,' I said. 'I have a son who's lying in hospital right now, in a coma.'

Jessop stared at me with eyes as impenetrable as pebbles. 'Well,' he said, in a thick voice, 'the Grim Reaper gets us all, one time or another, sooner or later.'

'Mr Jessop,' I said, at the top of my voice, 'I don't like to bother you when you're not feeling good, but I think you may be able to help me save my son's life.'

'How can I do that, may I ask?' enquired Mr Jessop. 'I don't even know your son.'

'No, but you have some knowledge of what brought his coma on.'

'I'm not a doctor, Mr Dela-whatever-your-name-is.'

'Tolla. Delatolla. No – I know you're not a doctor, sir. But you did used to own a chair . . . a dark mahogany chair . . . with carvings all over it and a kind of a face on the cresting-rail.'

Sam Jessop's expression remained confused and incomprehensible, like a crumpled handkerchief.

'What of it?' he asked.

'Well, it may sound ridiculous, Mr Jessop, but I believe that chair has an aura about it that brought on my son's coma.'

'You're right,' said Jessop.

'You mean I'm right about the aura?'

'No, you're right about it sounding ridiculous.'

'Mr Jessop – '

The old man bent his head forward. 'Mr Delatolla, I don't know why you're wasting your time. I used to own that chair, certainly. It's a very special chair. But the particular properties with which it is imbued are not for the likes of you. What did you say you were? A salesman?'

'I'm an antiques dealer.'

'Well, even worse. What do antiques dealers know about furniture?'

He gave three wheezy coughs, which I took to be an attempted laugh. I didn't join in, and neither did David.

David said, 'My friend here is only interested in knowing how to get rid of the chair, Mr Jessop. He doesn't want anything from it. He just wants it out of his life.'

Jessop sucked at his gums. 'Well . . . that's not at all easy. Giving up that chair is like giving up morphine. I had to take morphine once, you know, just after the First World War. I went through hell on earth trying to shake it. Hell on earth.'

Mrs Jessop, who had remained standing by her husband's side, now walked haughtily across to the other side of the room, and sat down on a spindly gilded chair. But the way she held her head up, like a watchful buzzard, showed that she still considered herself to be in control of the conversation.

'I'll tell you about that chair . . .' said Sam Jessop. 'Before I bought that chair I used to be a man of nothing more than moderate means. We lived in Leucadia in those days, in a beach house that wasn't worth more than three or four hundred thousand. I liked to collect fine things, though . . . always did . . . always had good taste for fine things . . .'

'I used to know the man who owned the chair before you,' put in David. 'He was an English banker, wasn't he? A man called Williams.'

'That's correct,' Sam Jessop nodded. 'I met him at an auction at Sotheby's, in London, and we went for a bottle of wine afterwards, and talked furniture. I always liked good furniture. My daddy was a cabinet-maker, and his father before him was a cabinet-maker. I guess I was only rebelling when I went into aeronautics, and sometimes I wish I hadn't. But it's kind of late to worry about that now.'

'Did Williams offer you the chair?' I asked him.

'Yes, he did. He said I could buy it for two thousand pounds.'

'That wasn't too much, considering its history.'

'It depends whether you think its history is a good history or a bad history.'

'What do *you* think it is?' David asked him.

Old man Jessop shrugged his bony shoulders. 'There are those who can handle the forces, and those who can't. But even for those who can, there's usually a price to pay.'

'You're being very unspecific,' I said. I was growing impatient. 'When you talk about forces, what forces exactly do you mean? Is there any way of controlling them?'

Sam Jessop sniffed, a dry thump in the back of his nasal cavity. 'Boy,' he told me, raising one bony finger for emphasis, but still clutching on to the arm of his chair. 'Boy, do you think for one moment that a human being, no matter how strong, could have shoved a stopper into Mount St Helen's?'

'So the forces are pretty powerful. Is that what you're saying?'

'Pretty powerful? You just think of that one volcano! And then you think of all the power that the Devil can muster, which is a hundred hundred times more devastating. That chair you're talking about . . . that chair that's worrying you so much . . . that chair is the *throne* of this world's aggregated wrongfulness! Do you understand what I mean, Mr Delatolla? The force which that chair was designed and built to raise up out of the darkest reaches of the universe – the force which that chair can summon into being, is cataclysmic! And horrifying, too, beyond belief!'

I leaned forward. 'Do you really mean the chair can raise the Devil? Is that what you're telling me?'

Sam Jessop cupped his hand over his ear. 'I can't hear you. What did you say? Devil?'

'You said *Devil*!' I shouted. 'Do you really mean Satan? That chair can raise Satan?'

The old man sat back. 'Oh, come on now. Satan! You young people don't even know what the world is all about. When I say Devil, I don't mean a fellow with horns and a tail and a toasting-fork. That kind of imagery – that's for scaring children into eating their cream-of-wheat. When I say Devil . . . I mean the psychic epicentre of all those cold, negative, hostile, and malevolent influences which exist in our universe. The Devil, if you want to describe exactly what He is, is like a

Black Hole, only He's moral and spiritual as well as physical. As you approach Him . . . you are drawn into Him by total gravity, total attraction, and there isn't *any* means of escape.'

'He hasn't attracted me yet,' I said. 'Not physically, not any way at all.'

Sam Jessop wiped spittle from his lips with a large handkerchief. 'Well,' he said, 'you're probably a contented man. Difficult to tempt. But I might as well tell you that if you continue to keep that chair around, it will get you in the end. One day, you'll want something from it, and then it'll get you.'

'Did it get *you*?' I asked him.

He looked away. The firelight sparkled in his eyes, giving him a spurious appearance of brightness and life.

'I'm a very sick man, Mr Delatolla,' he said. 'I've had my share of the Devil's bounty.'

Mrs Jessop stood up. 'I think you gentlemen have asked my husband enough, thank you.'

'Please,' I said, 'I have to know some details.'

'Details?' asked old man Jessop. 'The details are even more sordid than the grand design.'

'Don't tire yourself any more, Sam,' Mrs Jessop pleaded.

'No, no,' he said. 'If Mr Delatolla wants details, I can give him details. If Mr Delatolla doesn't mind frightening absurdities, and things that might attack him in the night . . . then, who am I to say that he shouldn't be introduced to them?'

While Mrs Jessop watched me unforgivingly, I asked Sam Jessop, 'Tell me something – when you first bought the chair from Mr Sears's friend – how did you get it away from him?'

Sam Jessop frowned. 'By van, if I remember, and then by steamer.'

'You didn't have any trouble with it? It didn't try to go back to Mr Williams by itself?'

He shook his head.

I turned to David. 'I thought you said there had to be some kind of runic transaction. Some special ritual of sale.'

'That's only what I heard,' said David.

Sam Jessop said carefully, 'You're partly correct. If you're going to pass the chair on to somebody else . . . then certain conditions have to be fulfilled.'

'Like what? What conditions? Please, I have to know.'

'Sam,' said Mrs Jessop, in a warning voice.

Sam Jessop looked uncomfortable. 'Well . . .' he said, turning his head this way and that, 'they vary . . . the conditions vary . . .'

'*How* do they vary? I mean, how did you manage to pass the chair on to Henry Grant, and then on to me? What did you actually do? Specifically?'

Mrs Jessop said coldly, 'He can't tell you.'

'Can't he speak for himself?' I retorted.

'He's a sick man. He has acute glomureonephritis. He has to rest, and keep warm, and avoid unnecessary excitement.'

'Mrs Jessop, I'm quite aware of that,' I said, controlling myself as tightly as I could. 'But my son is lying in a coma that could be fatal, and unless I know how to get rid of that damned chair, he's probably going to die. He's six years old! Six! Doesn't that mean anything to you?'

Mrs Jessop pursed her lips. 'I'm sorry about your son,' she said, very quietly. 'If I thought that Sam could help you, then I would gladly let him speak. But when he told you that the conditions of sale always vary, he was quite right. The chair itself is the only authority when it comes to deciding where it shall go next, and how. You must wait and see what signs you get from the chair. What Sam had to do . . . well, I expect it will be different for you. I'm sure it will.'

David uncrossed his legs and unfolded his arms. I'd learned enough about his English mannerisms to know that this meant he was getting serious.

'As a matter of record,' he asked, sharply, 'what *did* Sam have to do?'

Sam Jessop lowered his head on to his chest. His breathing was difficult and laboured.

Mrs Jessop said, 'I'm afraid it's private.'

'Did he sell his soul?' asked David.

'Don't be facetious,' snapped Mrs Jessop.

'Did he sell his collection of Impressionists?'

'I'm afraid you'll have to leave,' said Mrs Jessop, and tugged at the braided bell-pull beside the fireplace.

'Did he sell his Picasso?'

'For God's sake,' Mrs Jessop shouted at him, in her throaty voice.

David stood up. He looked suddenly very grave. 'Yes,' he said to Mrs Jessop, 'for God's sake. We all hope, for God's sake, that you haven't prevented your husband from saying something vital to my friend here which might have saved the life of his son.'

The Mexican manservant appeared in the doorway, his face as impassive as a Mayan mask.

'Good night, gentlemen,' said Mrs Jessop.

'Martin,' mumbled old Sam Jessop. 'My poor Martin.'

I looked at him, and then interrogatively at Mrs Jessop.

'Martin's our son,' said Mrs Jessop. 'He's away in Europe right now, and I'm afraid that Sam misses him.'

'I see,' I said. 'I guess we all have our problems.'

We left Sam Jessop by his flickering log fire, and followed the sullen manservant back through the hall. Then we were outside again, in the warmth of an Escondido evening, and still no nearer to solving the frightening mystery of the chair.

'What do you think?' I asked David, as we crossed the gravel.

'I'm not sure,' he mused. 'I get the feeling that old Jessop has an urge to confess something, or at the very least to explain himself. But whatever he's done to get rid of that chair, it's pretty drastic. You notice how prickly Mrs Jessop got when I started pressing him to say what it was.'

'Who told you about the runic business?' I asked him, slamming the wagon door shut.

'That was in a paper I read in the British Museum. There was a very short passage about the Earl of Beckenham's chair, and it said that it could only be successfully sold by an agreement that involved the writing of certain runes.'

'That was all?'

'I'm afraid so.'

'Was your friend Williams in good health when he sold the chair to Jessop?'

'As far as I know.'

'Does your client know how difficult it's going to be for you to get the chair?'

David said nothing.

'What's he going to do if you can't get it?' I asked.

David turned away from me. 'Ricky,' he said. 'I really can't discuss it. It's confidential.'

'How can anything involving you and me and this damned chair be confidential? Jonathan's unconscious, and all of a sudden you're worried about your professional ethics.'

'The identity of my client has no bearing on Jonathan at all. If you knew who it was, it still wouldn't make the slightest difference.'

'And I'm supposed to trust you?' I said, as I piloted the wagon down the steep driveway in the dark.

'Whether you trust me or not is entirely up to you,' said David.

'Well, I don't trust you,' I told him. 'But the miserable fact is that you're all I've got.'

'Charmed,' said David, and pressed in the cigarette-lighter on the dashboard so that he could smoke.

The outside lights under the eaves of my house were all shining when we drew up in the driveway. They were controlled by a time-switch, and automatically came on at dusk. The windows, however, were all dark, and the house had a strangely abandoned appearance, as if it were no longer a home, but merely a stage-setting for some unfathomable California nightmare.

I climbed out of the car. It was colder now, and there was a faint wind breathing through the bare branches of the eucalyptus trees. David and I walked to the front door, and he stood watching me expressionlessly as I took out my keys and unlocked it.

'What are you going to do if it's here?' he asked me.

'I don't know,' I said. And the truth was that I didn't. I

was worn out, and dispirited, and just about ready to give up.

We entered the house, and walked along the corridor to the living-room.

'Well, it's not in *here*,' said David.

'If it's anywhere, it's in the library,' I told him. I went to the library door, and opened it. I switched on the lights.

To my surprise, the chair wasn't there. I peered cautiously around the door. I even went over and prodded the velvet drapes. But apart from my own desk, my antique globe, and my own two chairs, the library was empty.

David appeared in the doorway. 'Not here either?' he asked.

I shook my head. 'I can't understand it. If it didn't come back here after it vanished out of your car . . . then where did it go?'

'Perhaps you shouldn't let that worry you,' said David. 'As long as it's gone, it's gone.'

'But its *influence* hasn't gone. It's still keeping Jonathan in a coma. And it's still turning my life upside-down. So wherever it is, it can't be that far away.'

I went across to my desk and dialled the hospital on the telephone. After a whole array of buzzes and clicks, I was connected with Sara. She sounded as tired as I felt.

'Where are you now?' she asked me.

'At home. I'm checking to see if the chair came back here.'

'Did you have any luck with old man Jessop?'

'I'm not sure. He said one or two things . . . kind of generalised comments . . . and I'm still trying to work them out.'

'Jonathan's still the same.'

'I guessed he was. Has Dr Gopher had the results of his tests yet?'

'One or two of them,' she said. 'There's no pressure on the brain, and the spinal fluid is clear. They're still trying to analyse his electro-cardiograph records to see if he's suffered some sort of trauma. So all we can do is pray.'

'I know.'

There was a momentary pause, and then Sara said, 'Is the chair . . . did it come back home?'

'I haven't seen it so far. But I haven't checked upstairs.'

'What if it isn't there?'

'It must be someplace nearby. It wants something from us, right? And that means it must be staying in the area. Maybe not here, in the house. But close.'

Sara said, 'You sound tired.'

'No more than you.'

'I'm going to get some sleep in a minute. One of the nurses has found me a spare room. Why don't you stay at the house until the morning? There isn't going to be any news tonight.'

'Are you sure of that?'

'Dr Gopher told me. He said there wasn't any expectation of Jonathan waking up yet. They're going to try some more electrical stimulus tomorrow.'

I washed my face with my hand. 'I could use some sleep. You promise to call me, though, the minute anything happens?'

'You know I will.'

'Okay, then,' I said. 'Sleep well. And remember I love you.'

'I love you, too.'

David had gone through to the living-room, and when I walked in he was squatting in front of the fire, clearing the ashes.

'If we're staying,' he said, 'I thought a blaze might be cheerful.'

'Do you want a drink?' I asked him.

'Scotch, if you have it. Neat.'

'Neat?'

'Sorry. Straight up, in American.'

I poured him a couple of fingers of Cutty Sark, and opened a Billy beer for myself. One of my friends who knew that I had gravitated away from the Republicans towards the Democrats had bought me a whole case of Billy Carter's special brew as a mocking gift.

'Have you seen what's happened to my paintings?' I asked David.

'What do you mean?'

'Come take a look,' I said.

127

David got up from the hearth and followed me to the opposite wall, where the Copley shark painting hung. I couldn't be certain, but it looked to me as if the shark was even nearer to the floundering mariner than last time, and the boatload of rescuers was even further away.

'That's extraordinary,' David breathed.

'It's more than extraordinary,' I said. 'It's grotesque. Can you imagine what's going to happen inside of that picture unless I manage to get rid of the chair? That man's going to be ripped apart.'

I took David's arm and led him across to the Gilbert Stuart. Now, the hooded beast in the thicket had become even more distinct than ever, and there was no question about its sinister intentions. It appeared to me that the black-suited colonial gentleman in the picture had sensed what was happening behind him, and had slightly turned. His eyes, too, seemed to have widened, as if he were experiencing the first creeping suspicions of fear. '*Because he knows a frightful fiend doth close behind him tread . . .*'

'Well?' I asked David.

He gave the Gilbert Stuart one last look and then turned away. 'It seems to me that what's happening to those pictures is that they're being affected by the Devil. The Devil as Sam Jessop defined Him . . . the psychic epicentre of everything cold, evil, and negative. These paintings are turning into the very reverse of themselves . . . Instead of the mariner being saved, he is lost . . . and instead of that colonial gentleman being the king of his local sandbox, he is being threatened by some kind of sinister and frightening manifestation.'

He went back to the fire, and stacked on a pyramid of split logs.

'I'm afraid we're up against something monstrously powerful,' he said, without looking at me. 'And I'm afraid we're going to have to face it on our own.'

I poured out the drinks while David lit up the fire, and we sat for an hour or two talking about furniture and business. Every now and then I found myself glancing up at the two large paintings on the wall, just in case the shark had started to savage the mariner, or the hooded beast had crept closer to Gilbert Stuart's colonial gentleman, but the pictures stayed as they were, and short of destroying them, there was nothing I could do to alter the slow and hideous destinies which were unfolding in front of my eyes.

The force of the Devil was at work, and as old man Jessop had said, what human being could stopper up Mount St Helen's?

At a few minutes after eleven, we went up to bed. I showed David through to the guest room, with its rose-patterned wallpaper and its faux-bamboo bed, and then I tiredly went along to our own bedroom two doors down the corridor. I was yawning as I opened the door and switched on the lights.

Then I froze. I thought that I had cried out loud for a moment, but I realised almost immediately afterwards that I hadn't. The only sound that had come from my throat was a gasp of strangled breath.

The chair was standing at the end of my bed. Tall, polished, and dark. And the face of the man-serpent was looking at me with a new expression – an expression of evil relish, as if it knew that it would soon be getting what it wanted.

'David,' I called, in a voice that was far too hushed for him to hear.

I took a step backwards, but the bedroom door flew shut behind me, and when I tugged at the decorated brass handle, it refused to turn.

'*David!*' I shouted. '*David!*'

There was no answer. He had probably closed his own bedroom door as well. I turned back and stared at the chair in horrified fascination.

'What do you want?' I demanded. 'Just tell me what the hell you want and you can have it.'

'*You are not ready yet,*' whispered the chair. The voice seemed to echo from the drapes and the furnishings all around me.

'Ready?' I asked. 'What do you mean by ready? I'm totally ready. You tell me what you want, and I'll give it to you. Just let my son out of his coma, and leave my family alone.'

'*All these demands, and yet nothing for yourself.*'

'I don't want anything for myself.'

'*That's why you're not ready. But, you will be.*'

I circled around the back of the chair, and by some nerve-racking process, the curved face on the front of the chair seemed to rotate right around so that it was staring at me wherever I went. I paced nervously backwards and forwards, shooting anxious glances at the chair from time to time like a cooped-up madman looking at his jailors.

'All right,' I said, remembering the questions that David had asked me in the car, 'I want you to make me rich.'

'*That is not a true desire. You are content already with what you have.*'

'I want another woman. A sexy, voluptuous woman. I want ten women. I want them all right now, here, on this bed.'

'*You have no such wish.*'

'Who says I have no such wish? Suddenly, I do. I want to be wealthy and I want women. What's the matter with you? Don't you have the power to do it? Or are you all sham?'

'*I am no sham. But for you, money and women are not crucial needs. When the time comes, you will be crawling across the floor to beg me for what you want. That is the only way.*'

'Did Williams beg you?'

'*Of course.*'

'What did Williams beg for?'

'*Williams begged for release from his jealousy and his torment. And I gave it to him.*'

'What did Sam Jessop beg for?'

'*Sam Jessop begged for the opposite of what you will beg for.*'

'I don't understand. How do you know what I'm going to beg for?'

'*I know it well. I have known it for longer than you could ever imagine.*'

'All right, then,' I said, 'if Sam Jessop begged for the opposite of what I'm going to be begging for, what will *I* beg for?'

'*You will know, and understand, when the time comes.*'

I continued to stalk furiously and nervously around the bedroom, slapping at the walls and the furniture with my hands, jittery and almost out of control. That whispering voice was as frigid and frightening as hell itself, and somehow I knew that the riddles it spoke were true. The day was going to come when I was going to need something so desperately and so abjectly that I was going to cling on to the legs of that chair and plead with it to give me what I wanted.

But what? What was I ever going to want so badly that I was prepared to crawl to some demonic piece of furniture?

'What do you expect me to do now?' I asked the chair.

'*I expect you to sleep.*'

'With you in the room, staring at me?'

'*You need to rest. Your destiny requires it.*'

'My destiny? What the hell do you know about my destiny?'

'*I am your destiny.*'

I sat down on the edge of the bed. My pulse-rate must have been way over 100, and I felt as if I were teetering on the edge of some vertiginous girder, sixty storeys above the street. I couldn't even think straight any more. The presence of that devilish chair seemed to mix up my mind so that the thoughts cut in and out like a radio being turned from station to station. 'What happens if Jonathan – can't possibly sleep – even try to escape but – can't get rid of the chair – can't – '

Then, I sensed a vibration in the air. Very low and subtle, like the rumble of a very distant aeroplane. I turned, and the chair appeared to be wavering, and losing definition. Then, with the soft *whoomph* of a collapsing vacuum, it disappeared.

At the same time, with a definitive click, the door-handle turned, and the bedroom door swung open by itself.

I got up from the bed, and searched the room with the over-elaborate intentness of a half-wit. I lifted up the drapes, looked under the bed, even opened the drawers of Sara's dressing-table. But there was nothing there. No chair, no satanic manifestations, no nothing.

I went into the bathroom and stared at myself in the mirror.

'Ricky Delatolla,' I breathed. 'What the hell is it that you're going to want so bad?'

I didn't answer. I didn't know.

My reflection splashed his face with water, brushed his

teeth, and swilled out his mouth with Scope. Then he switched off the bathroom light and let me go to bed.

I've always hated sleeping alone, no matter how much I complain about Sara's jiggling and joggling, and the way she always tugs the comforter off me. I read for a while, *The World Almanac and Book of Facts,* in a circle of solitary light, and I learned that 690 million people speak Mandarin, while only 230 million people speak English. Mind you, only two million people speak Samar-Leyte.

After twenty minutes or so, I put the book down, and switched off my bedside light. I lay back on the pillow, staring at the ceiling, and listened to the sounds of a Southern California night. An owl in the distant eucalyptus. The rustle of squirrels. And that sad wind that blows from the mountains at night towards the sea.

My fear of the chair had become, over the past two days, almost a normal state of existence. Nothing had ever scared me so much in my life before, and I knew that if I survived, nothing would ever scare me so much again. I could face a mugger, or a mad dog, or a riptide off the beach, because none of those dangers threatened my human integrity. I could face up to them, and struggle, and even if I lost out, I could go down fighting.

The threat of the Devil's chair, though, was different. The threat of the Devil's chair was that I was going to have to crawl, and beg, and lose all of my spirit. That was what scared me, the idea of being reduced to a grovelling creature who would do anything, absolutely anything, to escape whatever fear it was that the chair could arouse.

I was still awake half an hour later when I thought I heard a slight furrowing sound. I opened my eyes wide, and raised my head, and listened. I was so silent and so tense that I could even hear the blood rushing through the veins in my ears.

'Who's that?' I said, in a loud, false voice. 'Is there anyone there?'

There was nothing but silence. But then I thought I saw a dark oval shape rush across the white shaggy rug and disappear behind the end of the bed.

I could just see my face in the shadowy mirror of Sara's dressing-table. It was a white mask of utter fear. Slowly, as carefully as I could, I drew my feet up from the end of the bed, and retreated backwards so that I was sitting on the pillow with my back against the headboard. There was something down on the floor at the bottom of my bed and I thought I knew what it was.

I groped for the lightswitch, but my hand caught the edge of the shade and knocked the lamp off the bedside table on to the floor. The rug was very soft, but I heard the bulb break against the metal side-support of the shade. Now there was nothing but me, the darkness, and whatever was concealing itself at the end of the bed.

'*David!*' I called. '*David!*'

I should have vaulted out of bed and made a break for the door; but some intuitive feeling warned me that my feet were bare, and that it was a good ten paces to the door, and that whatever was waiting for me was far faster and far more predatory than I was. Maybe it was better to stay up on the bed, out of harm's way.

But then, I heard a scratching noise, as if scaly insect claws were pulling at the sheets. *And, to my horror, the comforter at the end of the bed bulged up, and shifted jerkily with the movements of the creature that was concealed underneath it.* I let out a low, shuddering, 'Oh, no. For Christ's sake. Oh, no.'

The bulge in the comforter hesitated for a moment. I stayed where I was, paralysed. Then it made a sudden rush across the bed towards me, and even though I leaped back, striking my head against the bedside table, the Devil's dark trilobite scurried out from under the sheets and ran right up my bare thigh towards my groin, heavy and jointed and prickly with earwig legs.

I screamed. I rolled over twice, slapping at it with my hands. Then I felt a sharp sting as it bit me right inside the curve of my leg, next to my balls.

Still screeching, still panting, I seized the creature's writhing, muscular body in both hands, and pressed my thumbs relentlessly into the thinner shell that protected its belly. I heard the shell crunch, like a soft-shell crab, and my hands were suddenly full of broken pieces of crustaceous material, and wet slime.

I rolled over again, and managed to dislodge the insect's fangs from my skin. Then I scrambled to my feet, holding it up in front of me, while it twisted and wriggled backwards and forwards, and its poisonous-looking rear pincers lashed at my unprotected forearms. The damned thing was so strong and so vicious that I could hardly hold it, and I knew that if I couldn't think how to kill it soon, it was going to wrestle its way free and attack me again. Already, my groin was beginning to feel cold and numb, and the backs of my hands were smothered in blood.

Limping, cursing, struggling from one side of the corridor to the other, I carried the trilobite along to the head of the stairs, and then down to the living-room. It grazed me twice with its tail, and I could feel an unpleasant prickling sensation in my arteries, as if I had been injected with metallic salts.

The fire was still glowing red-hot in the hearth, although it had burned quite low since we had gone upstairs to bed. It would have to do.

The trilobite fought even more viciously as I approached the fireplace. But I managed to hold it against the stone mantelpiece for a fraction of a second with my left hand alone, while I grabbed the poker with my right. I shoved the poker deep into the rippling embers of the fire, and then secured my grip on the insect again with both hands.

Again and again and again the trilobite wrenched its articulated body from side to side, but I managed to pray and to hang on. Maybe it had lost some of its strength from being crushed. Maybe I was just too determined for it. But it didn't take long for the end of the poker to glow bright red, speckled with white fiery sparks, and then I knew I had beaten it.

Pressing the creature hard against the stonework with my left forearm, I seized the red-hot poker, drew it back, and then thrust it right into the insect's jointed head.

There was a sharp sizzling noise, and a smell like burnt varnish. The insect gave such a violent muscular spasm that I dropped it, and it fell on to the hearth with a horrible clattering noise. I jumped away from it, my nerves thrilled with fright, and for a moment I thought it was going to come scuttling after me again.

Instead, it rolled and unrolled itself around the hearth in mindless reflexive agony. Sometimes it twisted itself right into the hottest part of the fire; but then it jerked its way out again, its scales covered with powdery ashes, its legs singed and crippled.

I heard a step on the stairs, and turned. It was David, halfway down, in nothing but his long-tailed English dress shirt, and his socks.

'My God,' he said, 'what's happening?'

I pointed with a trembling poker to the squirming trilobite in the fireplace.

'I've killed it,' I said.

'You've done *what*?'

'I've killed it. I stuck it in the brain with this.' I held up the poker and I knew there were tears in my eyes.

David came down the rest of the stairs, and cautiously approached the hearth. The insect was giving one or two last jerks. Then it lay still.

'Do you think you should have done?' David asked me.

'David, it *attacked* me. I was lying in bed and it made a rush for my legs. In fact, it practically bit my balls off.'

David looked at me seriously. 'You don't think that perhaps the chair is going to take its revenge on you for this?'

'Maybe it is, maybe it isn't. What else was I supposed to do? Lie there like a sucker and let it eat me up alive?'

'I don't know,' said David. 'But the point is that you haven't really killed it.'

'It's dead, isn't it?'

'This particular manifestation of it is dead, of course. But it's a familiar of the Devil. It never really dies. And what worries me is how the chair is going to arrange its next revival.'

I was shaking. Cold, naked, and stung by the trilobite's venom.

'I think I need a drink,' I said, in a hoarse voice.

'Of course,' said David, going over to the drinks cabinet. 'But you're going to have to think about this. You're going to have to be doubly careful.'

'How's that?' I said. I dropped the poker back into the hearth.

David sucked in his breath. 'Last time, the creature was born out of your pet dog. What's it going to be born out of next time? Your wife? Your son? You?'

He handed me a whisky and I drank the whole glassful in one gulp.

'I'm going to talk to my priest,' I said, flatly. 'If I need anyone's help right now, it's God's.'

7—Exorcisings

After I'd washed the scratches on my arms and groin and sprayed them with Medi-Quik, I tugged on my dark blue velvet bathrobe and went downstairs to the library to call Father Corso. There was no sign of the chair anywhere, but I had the strongest of feelings that it was somewhere close. There was something in the air, like the irritating reverberation of a tuning-fork, or a bitter odour that you couldn't quite place.

David had borrowed a green robe from the guest bathroom, and was sitting edgily by the fire with a glass of whisky. As I came down the stairs, he said, 'You're sure you're doing the right thing?'

I walked straight through to the library without stopping. 'No,' I told him, as he followed me through the door and across to my desk. 'I'm not at all sure that I'm doing the right thing. But I'm not at all sure that I'm doing the *wrong* thing, either. Are you?'

'I don't know. I just think you ought to be careful.'

I opened my black telephone book and found Father Corso's number. 'So far,' I told David, punching out the digits, 'being careful has lost me my dog, taken my son away from me, totally disrupted my life, and scared the living daylights out of me. It's practically got me killed. Maybe it's time I stopped being careful, and fought back.'

The phone rang for a long time in Father Corso's house before it was picked up. A rumpled-sounding voice said, 'Corso.'

'Father Corso? I'm sorry to call you so late. It's Ricky Delatolla.'

'Ricky? What time is it?'

'I'm not sure. David, what time is it?'

'A quarter to one.'

'Did you hear that, Father Corso?' I asked him. 'It's a quarter of one.'

'Well, Ricky, what is it that needs to be discussed at a quarter of one? Nothing's wrong, is it?'

I took a deep breath. 'As a matter of fact, there is. I want you to perform an exorcism for me.'

This remark was followed by a silence so long that I thought Father Corso might have put the phone down. But I could hear him breathing, in a steady, thoughtful rhythm, and eventually he said, 'You're not drunk, are you, Ricky?'

'No,' I told him. 'I really wish I were.'

'You know what I feel about demons and mystical manifestations, don't you, Ricky? As far as I'm concerned, they're really not part of the modern religious situation. The devils we're facing today are all the psychological mismatches between personal aspirations and eco-sociological strictures.'

'Father Corso, I wish, just once in a while, you'd speak English. I need your help with a demonic presence. I don't care what you call it. A psychological mismatch, whatever. But it's here in my house and it's scaring me to death, and it has to be gotten rid of.'

'You want *me* to chase out an evil spirit?'

'Who else is there?' I screamed at him. 'You want me to call a plumber?'

'Ricky, please,' said Father Corso, hastily. 'There's no need to get hysterical. Now, just tell me what kind of – well, what kind of evil spirit you think you've got there.'

'Father Corso,' I said, 'I have the Devil's chair. The throne of Satan himself. It's in my house, and it's wrecking my life. Jonathan's down at the Hospital of the Sisters of Mercy in a coma, my dog's been slaughtered by a giant insect, and I've only just managed to fight off that same insect myself.'

There was another pause. Then Father Corso said, 'Are you serious about this?'

'Do you think I'd call you at one in the morning to make a joke about it?'

'Very well,' Father Corso told me. His voice sounded

shocked. 'Just stay there – stay at home – and I'll be right round.'

'You'll hurry, won't you?' I asked him.

I put the phone down. David was standing by the globe, steadily propelling it around and around so that it softly rumbled on its mounting.

'He's coming?' he asked.

I nodded. 'He still doesn't believe me. But he will when he gets here. Let's hope he knows how to perform an exorcism. It's not the kind of thing they tend to teach them at Catholic seminaries these days. They seem to be more interested in Jung and the collective unconscious, and nude encounters.'

David slowed the globe with his fingers, and stopped it precisely with the prime meridian uppermost. 'Greenwich,' he said. 'A fine observatory, a sloping hillside, trees, and the River Thames. I used to walk there with Jennifer, years ago.'

'Jennifer was your wife?'

He tightened his mouth in assent. It was plain that he didn't really want to talk about it.

'Extraordinary, that all of those peaceful walks should eventually lead me here,' he reflected. 'That's the oddity of life for you, isn't it?'

'Sure,' I said. 'How's your drink?'

'I could probably manage another. How about you?'

'I'll have another whisky.'

We went into the living-room and waited for Father Corso. The crisp and curled-up body of the trilobite was still lying beside the hearth, but it seemed greyer and smaller now. Most things do in death, including people. I remember seeing my father lying in his coffin in that mortician's parlour in Anaheim in 1958, and how delicate he looked. There was nothing left of the hearty, slap-dash plasterer; nothing left of the father who used to swing me up on his shoulders and give me rides around the yard. Nothing left but a small, diminished image, as unlike Joseph Delatolla as a photograph taken in the wrong light.

David said, 'Maybe we should go and look for the chair. Your priest will want to see it, won't he?'

'I'm not looking for it unless he's there. I want to be armed, you understand? Even if it's only with a bible and a crucifix and a vial of Holy water.'

'You call that armed?'

'I don't know. I'm not particularly superstitious. But axes and saws aren't going to help, are they? That chair responds to violence with more violence, and right below the belt, too.'

David circled the tip of his finger around his glass, so that it made a high-pitched droning noise. 'It's strange that you should have been attacked by that insect,' he said.

'Tell me something that isn't strange around here.'

'No – what I mean is that the chair obviously wants something from you. And since it does, why did it have its creature go after you like that?'

'Who knows, for Christ's sake? You can't rationalise a what-d'you-call-it. A moral and spiritual Black Hole.'

'Perhaps it was just trying to frighten you into taking some positive action,' David suggested. 'Trying to guide you towards that moment when you're going to have to ask it for something.'

'Well, what did I do? I called my local priest. Why should the chair want me to call my local priest?'

David's finger paused on the rim of his glass. 'I'm not sure,' he said. 'But I just get a feeling that we're being manipulated.'

It wasn't long before I saw the lights of Father Corso's car swivel across the kitchen ceiling. I put down my drink and went to the front door to welcome him in. He slammed the door of his shiny black Rabbit and came across the driveway with an expansive wave of his long inelegant arm.

'Thank you for coming, Father,' I greeted him.

'I couldn't very well refuse, could I?' Father Corso smiled. 'It's not every night of the week that one of your congregation offers to demolish every theological concept you ever held to be valid and true. So, lead on.'

Father Corso was tall, loose-jointed, and physically awkward. He was good-looking if you had a thing for men with black curly hair and dark circles under their eyes. Sara had once described him as looking like Lenny Bruce, after three days on the rack.

David stood up as Father Corso came in, and switched his whisky from his right to his left hand. I said, 'Father Corso, this is David Sears. An antique dealer from Britain.'

Father Corso shook his hand. 'And a Protestant, no doubt?' he smiled.

David smiled rather sourly in return.

'Where is your devil then, Ricky?' asked Father Corso. 'If I am going to carry out an exorcism, I must have a devil to exorcise.'

I pointed towards the hearth. 'There's part of the evidence. The Devil's familiar. It attacked me this evening and I killed it. Or at least I killed that particular incarnation of it,' I said, looking across at David.

Father Corso went across to the hearth and knelt down. He prodded the insect's body with the poker, and it rolled over like an overdone prawn cracker.

'Well,' said Father Corso, 'this is certainly a frightening creature. But there is nothing to suggest that it is actually an agent of Satan.'

'Sit down, Father,' I told him. 'Let me tell you the whole story from the beginning.'

Father Corso looked at the Baccarat decanter on the table. 'A small glass of that might help to stimulate my attentiveness,' he said.

'*That whisky priest*,' quoted David, under his breath.

Father Corso turned to him, with one dark eyebrow raised. 'Ah,' he smiled. 'You've read *The Power and the Glory* too. Good book. Rather too British for my taste.'

David didn't answer, but crossed his legs and sat back with a rather childish show of aloofness. I hadn't actually realised how sectarian English people could be. But then I guess that any nation that can create the Rolls-Royce, and send their children to schools where the boys still have to wear top-hats, and spend hundreds of thousands of dollars each year on sustaining a non-elected Head of State, just for the snob value

– I guess a nation like that can be chauvinistic about anything.

Carefully, as if I were giving evidence in a court of law, I explained to Father Corso everything that had happened since Henry Grant's first appearance in my driveway. He listened to me without saying a word, occasionally sipping at his Cutty Sark, or stroking at his cheek with his long bony finger.

When I'd finished, he said, 'You should have come to me before.'

'Sara wanted me to. But I didn't think you'd believe me.'

'I'm not sure whether I do. You're talking about the Devil, Ricky, and the Devil is a concept that went out of theological thinking along with half of those phoney saints like St Harriet the Hysterical. There isn't any way that a modern priest can cope with the actual religious needs of the people around him if he believes in demons. I should carry out exorcisms for post-natal depression, or pre-menstrual tension, or job psychosis?'

David got up and helped himself to more whisky without offering any to Father Corso. I glanced up at him, but I wasn't going to start an argument. We were all tired, and doubtful, and fraught.

'Something's going on here, Father,' I said. 'Whatever name you put to it, it's evil and it's dangerous, and it has to be destroyed.'

'I agree with you. There's a very negative situation here. But before we take any action we have to identify what the nature of the negative pressures is. Otherwise, any attempts to deal with them may be as harmful as the pressures themselves. *You* think your chair is the Devil's throne. Mr Sears here believes it's a kind of a nexus, through which malevolent influences can pass between this world and the nether-world. From what you've told me, however, I've begun to entertain a theory myself that the symbolic images on the chair – the demon-like faces – have become a focus for some very strong negative feelings within you yourself. Like, it's not actually the *chair* which is the source of the negative situation, it's *you*.'

'Me?' I asked him, in disbelief. 'What negative feelings do I have? I'm the least negative person I know.'

'Well, that's often a characteristic of negative feelings. You don't know you have them.'

'But, for Christ's sake, Father, I'm a happy man. Or at least I was until this chair arrived in my life.'

Father Corso raised his hand, partly as a warning that I shouldn't break the third commandment, and partly as one of those Biblical gestures that priests always unconsciously adopt when they're just about to disagree with you. Verily, I say unto you.

'A happy man – a man who is contented with his domestic life-style, his career achievement, and all the ongoing characteristics of his social and intellectual environment – a man like that is frequently most susceptible to deep emotions of destructiveness and frustration. If you want to use an old Biblical phrase – '

'I wish you would,' David interrupted, with a bored tone of Protestant impatience.

'If you want to use an old Biblical phrase,' Father Corso repeated, undeterred, 'you could say that it is an essential human characteristic to *strive*. And if you have nothing left to strive for, then, quite simply, all those positive energies within you turn around inside of you and build up as negative charge. You, Ricky, may have built up such a charge . . . and all it took was the Satanic appearance of that chair for your negative charge to be catalysed into physical reality.'

I turned to the hearth. 'You mean I created that bug out of my own imagination? That creature came out of my head?'

'That's exactly it. It's like a very powerful and lasting form of psychic ectoplasm.'

David set his glass down on the table with a sharp, punctuating tap.

'In my opinion, Father, it's more like a very powerful and lasting form of modern theological bullshit.'

'You can think what you like,' said Father Corso. 'But if we don't consider every possibility, we may inadvertently release forces that are far more damaging to Ricky and his family than whatever they've suffered already.'

'Oh, yes?' asked David, sarcastically. 'And what can you

think of that's far more damaging than the death of Mr Delatolla's dog, and the imprisoning of his son in a coma?'

At that moment, before Father Corso could answer, I looked across the room and there it stood. Up against the wall, just where a tidy maid might have placed it. The chair itself, carved with snakes and doomed souls. And I thought for one clear and logical split-second that David had probably been right: and that the chair had wanted me to invite Father Corso here, for some purpose that I couldn't even begin to understand.

'Father,' I said, in a hushed voice. 'The chair.'

And I nodded towards the wall behind him the way a bidder nods at an auction. Don't look now, but it's there.

Father Corso slowly turned around. 'That's it?' he asked me. 'That wasn't standing there when I came in.'

'Well, of course it wasn't,' said David. 'We decided to frighten you, so we arranged for a friend of ours to get up in the middle of the night, sneak into the kitchen, and place it there when you weren't looking.'

'You don't have to be so hostile,' Father Corso retorted. 'I'm just trying to do my best under what you must admit are pretty mystical circumstances.'

'For somebody whose vocation it is to act as an envoy for an invisible deity, and a two-thousand-year-old woman who conceived the son of that invisible deity without any identifiable means of impregnation, I'd say your understanding of the mystical must be rather confused.'

'Do you want me to help or not?' snapped Father Corso.

'I don't think you have any choice,' David told him, laconically.

Father Corso hesitated, swallowed the rest of his whisky, and then stood up. He advanced on the chair while both David and I sat where we were. He stood in front of it for a while, peering at it narrowly, and then he reached out and touched the man-serpent's cheek.

'It's wood,' he announced.

'Of course it's wood,' said David. 'That's what makes it so alarming.'

144

Father Corso ran his hand over the carved vipers that made up the man-serpent's hair, and down the intricately-sculptured splat. Then, very quickly, he pressed the black leather seat cushion.

He came back to the middle of the room. 'It seems like a perfectly ordinary chair to me.'

'I assure you it isn't,' I told him. 'You want another glass of whisky?'

'No, no thank you. You said it talks?'

'That's right,' I nodded. 'It talks, and it threatens.'

There was a long silence. Father Corso stood looking at the chair and David and I sat looking at Father Corso.

Eventually, Father Corso said, 'This is a little embarrassing. But I want to try one of the very oldest tests for evil spirits.'

'I know that one,' said David. 'You invite them to tea, and if they refuse to eat hot-cross buns, you know that they must be disciples of the Devil.'

'Please!' barked Father Corso, in suppressed rage. 'I'm trying to do whatever I can, and you're not making it any easier.'

'I'm not *trying* to make it any easier,' said David. He stood up, and poured himself another drink. 'I'm trying to make you understand that if you don't believe that this is the Devil's chair, then you're doing nothing but fooling yourself and endangering Mr Delatolla.'

'This isn't the sixteenth century!' said Father Corso, hotly.

David pointed to the chair with a rigid arm. 'Tell that to the Devil. Don't try telling it to me.'

Father Corso took a breath. 'You have some kind of special interest in this, don't you, Mr Sears? Some interest quite apart from acquiring the chair for a client of yours?'

'I've already told you what my interest is,' said David. He swallowed another mouthful of whisky, and shuddered.

'Well, I don't believe you,' said Father Corso. 'I may be the envoy of an invisible deity, and a sacred Virgin, but I'm not stupid, and I'm not gullible.'

'Of course not,' David replied, turning his back. 'You're just unbearably fashionable.'

Father Corso looked at me in exasperation. But I did nothing more than nod towards the chair again, and say, 'Go ahead. Test it.'

Father Corso approached the chair again, unbuttoned his coat, and reached into the inside pocket. He took out a silver crucifix, about five inches long, and a glass bottle of water.

David kept his back turned as Father Corso crossed himself, and then drew the sign of the cross in the air over the chair.

'If the Devil is concealed within you, I command Him to manifest Himself,' said Father Corso. 'If the Devil is hiding inside of you, I command Him to appear.'

'I suppose you think a Jungian analyst with a pointed beard is going to pop out of nowhere and confirm your theory of negative situations,' put in David, caustically.

Father Corso ignored him. He had a carefully-memorised ritual to perform, and it was obvious now that he was trying to build up and sustain an aura of his own – what I can only call a force-field of Catholic strength. I had never seen it attempted before, and I don't suppose that Father Corso had ever had occasion to try, but it was remarkable to watch. No matter how trendily he usually talked – regardless of Christian interfaces and ongoing socio-theological dialogues – he was drawing now from the fundamental and traditional powers of his belief.

'I adjure thee . . . if spirit you are . . . to go out. God the Father, in His name, leave our presence. God the Son, in His name, make thy departure. God the Holy Ghost, in His name, quit this place.'

With a sweeping stroke of his arm, Father Corso splashed the Devil's chair with Holy water, first one way and then the other, in the sign of the cross.

'Tremble and flee, O impious one, for it is God who commands thee. Tremble and flee, O impious one, for it is I who command thee. Yield to me, to my desire by Jesus of Nazareth who gave His soul. Yield to me, to my desire by sacred Virgin Mary who gave Her womb.'

It was difficult to hear at first, but gradually it grew louder. A deep, irresistible hum, like a high-voltage generator. The

146

same hum that I'd heard before. Father Corso must have heard it too, for his voice became suddenly more strident.

'By the blessed angels from whom thou fell . . . I demand thee be on thy way.'

I stood up, and crossed the room to stand right beside him. He was breathless, as if he'd just been doing twenty push-ups, or jogging around the block.

'Do you know what it is?' I asked him. 'Do you have any idea at all?'

He didn't look at me. His cheeks were anointed with sweat, and he was shaking like an alcoholic with the horrors.

'It's something,' he said, in a choked voice. 'There's some influence there . . . something very . . .'

He took two or three deep breaths. Then he said, 'It's come here . . . for a purpose . . . it wants something . . .'

'Do you still think it's me? Is it really me that's creating these influences?'

'I can't – I can't really say – I – I'm having a hard job holding it.'

I took his arm, and gripped him tight. 'Let it go,' I told him. 'If it's taking control of you, let it go.'

'I'm not – I'm not too sure that I can.'

'Come on, Father. Just let it go. It tried to get hold of me once, remember, and all I did was reject it. Come on, Father, let go.'

David, with an alarmed expression, quickly put down his drink and came over to help me.

'What's happened?' he asked. 'What's the matter with him?'

'I don't know. He started to go through the exorcism ritual. At least, that's what it sounded like. Then all of a sudden he said he couldn't hold it any more. Look at him. He looks like he's having an epileptic fit.'

Father Corso threw his head back. His neck was knotted with tightened sinews and veins. His teeth were clenched, and his eyes were bulging out of their sockets.

'Negative – charge – ' he said hoarsely.

I looked towards the chair. The face of the man-serpent was

staring as fixedly as ever. And where the drops of Holy water had sprinkled across the seat and the woodwork, steam was rising. The Holy water was gradually being boiled away.

'Let's get him out of here,' I urged David. 'He's going to get himself hurt if he stays any longer.'

But it was too late. It had probably been too late the moment that Father Corso had agreed to come over and help. The priest was abruptly and violently shaken in our hands like a rag doll being worried by a fierce dog, and he let out a grunt of pain and desperation.

'Can't – hold – it!' he screamed. 'Can't – hold – it!'

Bright red blood gushed from between his lips. He had been gritting his teeth so tight that he had bitten right through his tongue. And blood sprang from between his fingers, where his nails had dug in agony into his palms.

'Get him out!' I yelled at David. 'Get him out!'

We both tried to make a grab for Father Corso's arms, but they windmilled around as if they were on stiff frenetic hinges, and we were knocked away.

'Oh, God!' screeched Father Corso. 'Oh, Holy Mother, save me!'

I took a couple of steps back, and then charged at the priest in a flying football-tackle. But as my shoulder collided with his hip-bone, I felt him being plucked out of my grasp with all the speed and all the violence of a subway train hurtling out of a station. He was tossed clear across the room, and slammed up against the opposite wall with a thunderous crack that must have broken most of his ribs.

'Save me!' he gibbered. 'Save me!'

He was hurtled back across the room, and collided with the side of the chimney-breast. Blood sprayed up the wall, and I saw a broken arm-bone thrust itself right through the skin of his elbow.

'Save – me – save – me – save – !' he shrieked. But the Devil had him now, and the Devil was determined to destroy him.

Helplessly, David and I watched as Father Corso was smashed from wall to wall. He tumbled and flew as if he were being thrown in a hideous and sadistic wrestling-match. It rained blood, and there was nothing we could do but stand there in that grisly shower and witness Father Corso's brutal death like spectators at a macabre prize-fight. I looked at David and there were splashes of blood all over his shirt, and across his forehead, and he was staring in horrified fascination at the priest's flying body, as numb and as disbelieving as I was.

Father Corso was still whimpering and begging and screaming for help when he was dragged by forces that we couldn't see towards the fire. The embers had all crumbled away now, but the white ashes were still hot enough to sear meat on, or char a fresh-cut log. His eyes were swollen and bruised from their violent battering, but he was able to see where the Devil was pulling him, and he let out a moan of despair that, months later, still gave me nightmares.

I rushed towards him, and tried to tug him away from the fire, but I was knocked back by an invisible blow that felt like a fierce gust of wind.

For one moment, Father Corso knelt up straight in front of the fire, his broken hands clasped together in a mockery of prayer. He couldn't have been holding his hands up there himself, because both his arms were broken in several places, and the pain that 'prayer' must have cost him was un-imaginable. But the Devil was reminding him of the price of trusting in God.

David, behind me, whispered, 'He can't . . .'

Gradually, impossibly, Father Corso bent forward over the ashes of the fire. Soon, his bare face was only six or seven inches away from it, and I could see the skin on his cheeks puckering and twisting in the heat. He was trying to cry out, trying to breathe, but the heat above the ashes was so fierce that he couldn't manage anything except a high, terrified panting.

Then, with ugly finality, his face was pushed right into the hottest part of the hearth. He fought for a few seconds, and I couldn't even begin to think what agony he was having to endure. But then he keeled over sideways, his face mercifully hidden by the side of my armchair, and it was clear that he was dead.

David stood up. He reached for a cigarette, lit it, and let out a long expressive breath.

'Now we know,' he said, with bitter conviction.

'Now we know what?'

'Now we know why the trilobite attacked you. The chair wanted you to call for Father Corso, with the specific intention of killing him in front of your eyes.'

'But *why*?'

'It's impossible to say, exactly. I'm not a mystic. But my guess is that the chair wanted to demonstrate that it can't be defeated or dismissed, even by the ritual of exorcism.'

'And what good could that possibly do?' I asked him.

David puffed at his cigarette. 'The chair wants you to do something for it. In order to manoeuvre you into a position where you're willing to help it out, it has to show you that there are no possible alternatives. Exorcism was going to be your last resort, wasn't it? Well, now the chair has made quite certain that you don't have *any* resorts at all.'

I walked around the sofa and stared at the chair with utter hostility and loathing. It took all of my self-discipline not to pick it up and smash it to pieces. But, for all I knew, I would have been smashing Jonathan to pieces at the same time, or Sara, and I wasn't going to give old man Jessop's demonic chair the pleasure of doing that.

'I've never hated anything in my life before,' I told David. 'But, by God, I hate this chair.'

'I think it wants you to,' David replied. 'So that when you have to grovel for its help on your hands and knees, it will be able to remind you, and make you eat your hatred, word by word.'

I turned around, although I could still feel the man-serpent's eyes on me. 'Get me another drink,' I said. 'Then we'd better work out what we're going to tell the police about Father Corso.'

Three hours later, just as the sky was beginning to pale, we drove out along the winding road that leads from Rancho Santa Fe to the Pacific Ocean, David a few feet in front of my

Impala in Father Corso's Volkswagen Rabbit, and both of us driving without lights.

We reached a sharp left-hand curve in the road. On one side, there was a rough brake of bamboo. On the other, a forty-foot drop down reddish, eroded banks, and then a tangle of chokeberries. I flashed David once with my headlights, and he drew in to the side. I drew the Impala up behind him.

'Are you okay?' I asked him, leaving my wagon and walking along the edge of the road to join him. The morning air was sharp and crisp, and I shivered in my short-sleeved shirt.

David was tugging Father Corso's body into the driver's seat, and trying to jam his stiffened feet on to the pedals. As I came up, I tried not to look at Father Corso's face.

'That's one drive I won't forget in a hurry,' said David. He stood straight, and wiped the cold sweat from his forehead with the back of his shirtsleeve.

'You're sure this is going to work?' I asked him.

'My dear boy, you can never be sure of anything,' he said. 'But the engine's hot, and I shall cut the fuel line, and I shall be very surprised if the car doesn't catch fire. Now, why don't you turn your wagon around, and reverse into it, so you won't get any incriminating dents on your front bumper.'

'You're so expert at this, anybody would swear you'd done it before,' I remarked.

He wiped his hands distastefully on the sides of his pants. 'I'm simply using my head. That's why my parents mortgaged themselves up to the neck to send me to Lancing.'

I went back to the Impala, and three-point-turned it on bouncing springs so that it was facing back towards Rancho Santa Fe. Then I waited with the engine running while David reached into Father Corso's black Rabbit and turned the key. He also took the precaution of shifting the manual gearbox into top, so that it would look as if Father Corso had been driving along the road at a high speed. He wedged the clutch down with the priest's death-rigid left leg, and then slammed the door.

'Right,' he said, climbing into the wagon. 'Back it up and let's see what happens.'

Carefully, I backed the wagon up until my rear bumper was touching the rear bumper of the Rabbit. Then I bipped the gas pedal, and pushed the little Volkswagen inexorably through the bushes at the edge of the road, and over the rough stones that bordered the steep crumbling canyon.

'It's going,' David told me. 'It's going.'

I gave the gas pedal one more nudge, and then the Rabbit tilted, swayed, and disappeared. We heard a creaking, tearing, crashing sound, and the noise of a whole barrage of branches breaking. Then, there was silence, and darkness.

'It's not going to blow,' I said, anxiously.

We both opened our doors, ready to step out and take a look. But then we heard a deep, rumbling *whoomph*, and a ball of garish orange fire rolled up into the air, and the Rabbit started to burn furiously.

'Let's go,' said David, quietly. I shifted the wagon into second, and drove slowly back on to the highway. Then I engaged Drive, and we sped off towards Rancho Santa Fe as fast as the twisting road would allow.

'Well?' I asked. 'Do you think the police will take it on its face value?'

'Probably. He was a priest, wasn't he, with no personal enemies? The very worst they'll think is that he was accidentally pushed over by a hit-and-run driver. And if they think that, they'll be looking for cars with damage to the front, or the fenders. Personally, I believe they'll put it down to accidental death. Priests and menopausal women are notoriously poor insurance risks.'

I steered the Impala round a tight hairpin, and the tyres complained in unison, like a Sunday-meeting choir. 'You don't think we should have simply told the truth?'

'The *truth*, dear boy? What is the truth? The truth is that you called up a Roman Catholic priest in the middle of the night and asked him to come to your home. The next thing anybody knows, the poor man has been brutally assaulted and killed. And the only people in the house with him at the time were you and me. *That*, dear boy, is the truth. And I can't see any jury in the world giving even a minute's credence to some story about a malevolent chair, can you?'

'No,' I said. 'I guess you're right.'

'Of course I'm right. Anyway, what difference does it make? We both know damn well that we didn't kill him ourselves. All we've done is give a dignified cremation to a mutilated body. And there's no law against that, moral or otherwise.'

I glanced across at him. His face was sweaty and strained in the reflected green lights from the dashboard. 'I believe there's a California statute against do-it-yourself burials,' I said.

David smiled grimly. 'Let's try to deal with this chair first. Then we can worry about statutes.'

Later in the morning, we drove back into San Diego. David collected his Rolls-Royce in the hospital parking-lot, and went off to Presidio Place to shower and change, with a promise that he would telephone me after lunch. I went up to the eighth floor to see how Jonathan was getting on.

He was still lying unconscious on his bed, although the dressings on his face had been changed, and now I could see both of his eyes. Sara was sitting sleepily beside him, a discarded copy of *Sunset* on the floor beside her, and Dr Gopher was busy in the corner of the room with a series of antibiotic injections.

'Hi, darling,' I said, kissing Sara on the forehead. 'How's it been?'

'No change,' she said, in a weary voice. 'It's just like he's asleep and he won't wake up.'

I leaned over Jonathan's bed and stared at him for almost a minute. Inside of my head, I was trying to compel him to wake up. Wake up, Jonathan, please. Wake up!

But he continued to lie still and pale, his hair tousled on the pillow, and all I could do was step away from the bed, sad and frustrated, and leave him to his endless dreaming.

. 'Dr Gopher,' I said. The doctor looked up from his bottles of antibiotics, and frowned.

'My name's Dr Rosen,' he said. Fortunately, I don't think he realised that I'd gotten into the habit of talking to Sara about him as Dr Gopher just because he looked like one.

'I'm sorry. I – mixed you up with someone else.'

'You want to know how your son is?' the doctor asked me.

'Is there any improvement?'

'No, no improvement. But no deterioration, either. His body is functioning perfectly normally in all respects – respiration, heartbeat, digestive functions, everything. If he wasn't comatose, I'd say that he was an extremely healthy young man.'

'Are you going to try any more stimulus tests?'

'Oh, sure. Your wife will tell you that we tried a new programme of stimulation last night. Stroboscopic lights, music, minor electrical shocks, a whole battery of different stimuli. So far, of course, we haven't had any response. But I'm sure that we will.'

I said to Sara, 'How about coming out for some lunch? We can leave the number of the restaurant with the switchboard here.'

She stood up. 'I think I'd like that. I haven't really eaten properly for two days. Then maybe we could go home for the rest of the afternoon, and come back tonight.'

I hesitated, thinking about the chair. Then I said, 'Sure, why not? It'll give you a break.'

We were walking down the hospital corridor when a short squat man with fierce black hair and glasses came jogging along after us. 'Mr Delatolla?' he puffed. 'I'm glad I've caught you.'

'Oh, yes?'

He thumbed through a sheaf of papers he was carrying, and tugged one sheet out for me. 'I'm the hospital treasurer, sir. John Jarman. I wanted to give you your charges up to date.'

I took the bill and glanced down it. Private room, $500 a day; auxiliary room for one night, $125; medical supplies, $756; professional charges, $950; nursing charges, $320; commissary charges, $78.50.

'I'll bring you a cheque when I come back to the hospital tonight,' I said. 'That's unless you charge interest by the hour.'

'Tonight will be fine, Mr Delatolla.'

It was a vivid, glaring day, with only a single cloud close to the western horizon. I took Sara to a northern Italian restaurant called the Old Trieste, in Clairemont close to San Diego's Old Town. The Old Trieste is more like a New York restaurant than a California restaurant, with dark leather booths where lovers and veeps can meet in quiet and private. We drank a bottle of fresh dry Corvo, and ate veal Fiorentino. We didn't talk much.

'Do you really want to go back to the house?' I asked Sara.

'The chair's there?' she said.

I nodded.

'I can't go on running away from it,' she said. 'I've got to face up to it some time. Both of us have.'

'If I knew what it wanted, at least I could get it all over with,' I said, laying down my knife and fork.

'I still think we ought to call in Father Corso,' said Sara.

I took a small sip of wine, and lowered my eyes. 'Yes,' I agreed. 'Maybe we could.'

I looked up again, and Sara was staring at me curiously.

'Is that it?' she wanted to know. 'Just "maybe we could"?'

'What else do you want me to say?'

'I'm not sure. But you sounded funny. Don't you think that Father Corso could give us some advice? There has to be somebody in the church who knows about things like this. Maybe he could put us in touch with them.'

I tried to look as non-committal as possible.

'Well, *say* something,' Sara demanded. 'Do you think we ought to talk to Father Corso or not?'

I glanced at the people eating in the next booth. They were busy arguing about the Navy Hospital in Balboa Park, and I didn't think they were going to take much notice of anything I was saying. So quietly, I said to Sara, 'I already talked to Father Corso. Last night.'

'You did? And what did he say?'

'He came over to the house.'

'He believed you?'

'Not at first. But then he saw the chair for himself.'

'So what did he do? Ricky, tell me!'

I pressed my fingers to my forehead. I felt as if I had a migraine coming on. 'He tried to exorcise the chair. At least, that's what it seemed like. He was reciting some kind of stuff about God commanding thee, and thou art dismissed, and quit this place. Stuff like that.'

Sara reached across the table and held my wrist. 'So what happened?'

I couldn't look at her. I knew that Father Corso's death wasn't my fault, but I still felt responsible because I'd called him up to the house when I *knew*, or at least I should have known, that an attempted exorcism was exactly what the chair had wanted.

'The chair – killed him. Threw him around the room as if he didn't weigh anything more than Jonathan's Raggedy Andy. Then it pushed his face right into the fire.'

'Oh, my God,' said Sara. 'Why didn't you tell me this before?'

'I didn't want to upset you more than you're upset already.'

'But what have you done? Have you told the police that he's dead?'

I looked quickly at the next booth to make sure that none of the diners there was half-listening. Then I said, 'We couldn't. It looked just like we'd beaten him up ourselves. They would have locked us up on a first-degree homicide charge.'

'So what have you done?'

'We arranged an accident. We pushed Father Corso's car off the road, and it burned out.'

'Whose idea was that?'

'What does it matter?'

'I don't know.'

'Well, it was my idea. David helped me. So, in the eyes of the law, we're both as guilty as all hell.'

Sara looked as if she were about to cry, but she remained dry-eyed. She had cried enough tears for Jonathan, and there was nothing left. By the look of her, she was beginning to feel the same numbness that a constant condition of fright and despair had already brought over me. You can't stay in high key all the time. You just run out of adrenalin, and strength.

'Can you pour me some more wine, please?' Sara asked. 'Then I think I'd like to go back to the house.'

'You're sure?'

'Positive. That chair's already torn my life to pieces. It's not going to keep me out of my own home.'

8—Threatenings

Before we drove back to Rancho Santa Fe, I decided to call by Presidio Place and tell David where we were going. I had tried to telephone him from the restaurant, but his line had been constantly busy.

Presidio Place is one of those expensive private adult communities, set in a landscaped park with artificial lakes and carefully-planted willows and tennis courts. No children, no dogs, no beach-bums, and nobody with a less-than-substantial income. I'm surprised they even allow Democrats.

I left the San Diego Freeway at the Mission Valley Freeway turn-off, and then turned off left again on to Hotel Circle and Fashion Valley Road. The afternoon was growing dusty and hot, and I had the air-conditioning in the wagon turned down to cold.

I parked the Impala in one of the condominium's under-ground parking areas, and then we walked across the wide paved courtyard around the swimming-pool until we reached the entrance to the apartment where David was staying. Beside the pool, a hugely fat man was sitting on a sun-lounger with a cigar clenched between his teeth and a copy of *The Wall Street Journal* spread over his belly like a tent.

We came to the door marked discreetly *Eads*. I pressed the doorbell and heard a distant chime. Then David's voice called, 'Just a moment!'

After a minute or two, David opened the door and invited us in with a bow. He had showered and shaved, and dressed himself in a blue shirt, dark blue cravat, and cavalry-twill pants. He looked so English he looked like an American trying to look English. 'Come on in,' he said. 'Ted Eads is away this afternoon, which is a pity . . . but come on in and help yourself to his cocktail cabinet. Sara – it's so good to see you. How's Jonathan?'

'The same,' said Sara, flatly. 'No worse, but no better.'

We walked along a corridor lined with expensive modern paintings — two Barnett Newmans and a Morris Louis — and then found ourselves ankle-deep in a cream-coloured shag-pile carpet that seemed to stretch away on all sides for almost a quarter of an acre. It was one of those condos you see on the cover of glossy magazines — all chrome Italian tables and frondy ferns and little throwaway touches like Giacometti sculptures used as bookends. Outside of the tinted windows, there was a view of Mission Bay, blue and hazy, with rows of sailboats and palm trees. Silent air-conditioning and humidity control kept the inside of the apartment at seventy degrees, and dry.

'Not a bad little *pied-à-terre*,' I remarked, picking up a gold-and-emerald turtle and peering into its ruby eyes. 'What does Mr Ted Eads do for a living? Print his own money?'

'He's a banker. Something to do with financing construction projects in Central America. He only lives here for three or four weeks of the year. He also owns a Tudor mansion in England, a small château in France, and three floors of that new condominium in Manhattan.'

'Is that all?'

I went to the cocktail cabinet, which was a converted French secretaire, crested by an ormolu clock. All the drinks were in matching antique crystal decanters, with silver labels hung around them on chains.

'Do you want a drink, Sara?' I asked her.

'Just a Campari, please.'

I mixed the drinks. 'I must say, David, this place is almost unbearably ostentatious. *Almost* unbearably ostentatious, but not quite.'

'It does lack a certain cosiness,' David admitted. 'But would you forgive me for a moment? I have to make a couple more telephone calls to New York before close of business.'

'Go ahead,' I told him. 'We'll just wait here and luxuriate.'

We sat side by side on an Italian settee upholstered in soft white kid. The opulent atmosphere made us fall silent, and we drank our drinks as if we were distant and unpopular relatives who had dropped in unannounced. David disappeared into a room at the far end of the living area which I took to be a study, because I could just see the edge of a gilded desk, and a row of books. Every now and then, I heard his clipped English voice raised in a laugh, or level off into a long persuasive monologue.

I was swilling the last of my whisky around with the ice in the bottom of my glass when there was a soft warbling noise from a mahogany box on the table beside me. Sara looked at my surprised expression and grinned. 'It's a phone, dummy. Answer it.'

I unlocked the box with the gold key that protruded from it, and lifted out a gold-plated telephone with a mahogany handle. 'Ritzy,' I remarked, and then said, 'Hallo? Can I help you?'

A curiously familiar voice on the other end of the line said, 'Is Mr Sears there? Mr David Sears?'

'I'm afraid he's on the other line right now. Can I take a message, or ask him to call you back?'

'Well . . . I don't think so,' said the voice.

'Can I ask who's calling?'

'No, don't worry. Listen – just tell him that it's all fixed up for the day after tomorrow.'

I frowned. 'It's all fixed up? Will he know what that's supposed to mean?'

'Oh, yes. Tell him the carrier arrives at Escondido a little after ten.'

'The carrier? Okay. I've got it.'

The caller put down the phone, and I was left with a gold-plated, mahogany-trimmed, and very dead receiver.

'That was odd,' I said.

'What was odd about it?' asked Sara.

'I don't know . . . but I have the distinct feeling that I've talked to that guy before.'

'You have? Well, maybe you have. Did he sound young or old?'

'It was hard to tell. Thirtyish, I think. But his voice was kind of muffled . . . like he was holding the phone funny, or maybe he had a handkerchief over the mouthpiece.'

'Why should he want to do that?'

'Search me.'

At that moment, David came out of the study, scratching the back of his head with his ballpen and squinting at a heap of papers that he was carrying.

'You know something,' he said, abstractedly, 'I really thought the recession was going to help us . . . encourage people to invest their money in antique furniture . . . but it seems like they're spending as hard as ever.'

'There was a call for you,' I said.

He looked up. 'Oh, yes? Leave a message?'

'Only some kind of code that I couldn't understand.'

He was reading his papers again, and he suddenly blinked at me and said, 'Code? Sorry?'

'The message your caller left was couched in cryptic language. That's what I'm trying to say.'

'Well?' asked David, rather impatiently. 'What was it?'

'Your caller said that it was all fixed up for the day after tomorrow, and that the carrier arrives at Escondido a little after ten.'

David stared at me. 'Ah,' he said. 'Did he?'

'Yes. Those exact words.'

'He didn't say anything else? Nothing about a starting time?'

I slowly shook my head. 'Nope. Nothing about a starting time. Just that it was all fixed up, and that the carrier arrives at a little after ten. He said you'd understand what he meant.'

'Yes, well I do,' said David. 'Partly.'

I pushed my hands into my pants pockets and strolled through the shaggy cream rug to the window. Outside, a large silvery helicopter was circling over Mission Bay like a dragonfly. The helicopter was quite close, but inside the apartment it was utterly silent. Silent enough for me to be able to hear David breathing slightly more quickly than usual.

'Only partly?' I asked him.

He gave an ambiguous, flurried gesture that seemed to mean, well, it doesn't actually matter, and in any case I don't particularly want to talk about it.

'You could always go ask him to explain himself in more detail,' I said.

'Oh, well, that's not possible, really,' David said quickly. 'As a matter of fact he was calling from rather a long way away.'

'I wouldn't call Escondido too far to go,' I replied, dryly.

'Escondido?'

'That's where he was calling from, wasn't it? I recognised his voice. He was trying to disguise it, I think, but I've only talked to one man who sounded anything like that recently, and that was Sam Jessop.'

David looked at me with an expression that I couldn't begin to understand. For a moment so fast that I almost missed it, what the Germans call an *Augenblick*, all his upper-crust self-control appeared to slip, and what I saw instead was an untidy kaleidoscope of fright, worry, and ruthlessness.

Then he turned away, and went to the French secretaire to pour himself a full tumbler of whisky. As the decanter clinked against the glass, Sara looked at me wide-eyed, but I reassured her with a small shake of my hand.

'Well?' I demanded. 'It's true, isn't it? You knew Sam Jessop long before last night.'

'Does it make any difference?'

'Of course it makes a difference! If you knew Sam Jessop before yesterday, then you must have known him for a reason. And the only reason that would have led to you both pretending in front of me that you'd never met each other before – the only possible reason is that goddamned chair.'

'I hate to send your little theory crashing down in flames,' said David, sitting down on a chrome-and-canvas chair and crossing his legs, 'but the verifiable truth is that I had never met Sam Jessop before last night, nor talked to him, nor had anything to do with him whatsoever.'

'Then who was that on the phone? It sounded too much like Jessop to be anybody else.'

'Well, that's where you're right, old boy. It *was* Jessop – but not Sam Jessop. It was his son, Martin.'

'You know Martin Jessop? But how?'

'How does one ever get to know anybody? I met Ted Eads through my friend Williams in England, and I met Martin Jessop through Ted Eads. Ted put up a great deal of the money that Martin has been spending on uprating the Jessop cruise missile.'

'This is getting too complicated for me,' I told him.

David untied his cravat, as if he felt suddenly hot. 'Do you really want to hear the truth?' he asked me. 'The reason why I came looking for the Devil's chair, and the reason why I've stuck around for so long and done so much to lay my hands on it?'

Sara said quietly, 'I don't think it's a question of *wanting* to hear the truth, David. I think it's a question of *having* to. Our whole lives are at stake, especially Jonathan's, and if you're holding anything back from us then you'll be guilty of Jonathan's death, just as surely as if you'd gone up to the hospital with a gun and shot him.'

David was silent for a while, staring at the rug. Then he said, 'Very well. I didn't want to tell you any of this until much later, but I suppose now is as good a time as any. Believe me, I wasn't doing anything to hurt you. I was simply trying to do my job, the job that I was assigned to do, and to protect you from some facts that you may not be able to face. I was also trying to get something for myself, but I'll tell you about that in a moment.'

I checked the clock over the secretaire. It was five past three. 'I'll just call the hospital and tell them where we are,' I said. 'Then you can unburden your bosom for as long as you want.'

I rang the Hospital of the Sisters of Mercy and left a message for Dr Rosen, *née* Gopher. Then I fixed myself another drink and sat down next to Sara to listen to David's explanation.

'I first heard about the chair in England, when my friend Williams bought it at a private auction in Gloucestershire,' said David. 'He only went to the auction out of curiosity, because there was a rather lurid story connected with the sale of the house and its contents. Apparently, the house had belonged to a very wealthy and successful British carmaker – there *were* such creatures in those days! – one of those inspired engineers who used to build handmade sports cars in which wealthy young men could kill themselves with rather more panache than usual.

'Well – the carmaker had a bit of a reputation for womanising – and it was fairly common knowledge that his wife hated him for it, and did everything she could to embarrass him. Eventually, she threatened him with divorce, which could have meant the loss of his house, his treasured collection of paintings and furniture, and possibly even the closure of his carmaking business.

'Within a week, though, his wife was found in a restored sixteenth-century flour-mill in the grounds of the house, crushed into a pulp between the millstones. The carmaker was arrested, of course, and remanded in custody, but – he managed to evade justice.'

There was a silence. Neither of us asked, 'How?'

David gave a brief and painful little smile at our hostility towards him. 'He evaded justice by cutting his wrists when he was in Strangeways prison,' he said. 'And that was why the house and all of its contents were up for auction.'

'Did your friend Williams know anything about the chair's reputation?' I asked David.

'Not at first,' he said. 'But soon after he'd bought it, and taken it back to his house in Woking, in Surrey, he became conscious of its aura. Odd things started to happen around the house. Dishes were inexplicably broken, and his wife boiled her hand by holding it in a saucepan of bubbling potatoes for over a minute. His cat died, although he never told me how. Presumably in the same terrible way that your dog was killed. And it was after these incidents that he came to me and asked me to look into the chair's history. What I found out, I've already told you.'

'You said your friend Williams became very successful,' I said.

'That's right, he did. I'm not quite sure how, but at some stage of the proceedings he came to terms with the chair, and the chair began to help him. He pulled off two incredible mergers in the City of London, and he made over a million pounds sterling on some deal with Nigeria that was so complicated that the Department of Trade are still trying to unravel how he did it. He also found himself a mistress . . . and a very beautiful girl she was too.'

'So what he wanted was money and women . . . and the chair gave them to him.'

David nodded. 'For a while, he was one of the most sought-after dinner-guests, one of the ten wealthiest and most stimulating men in the country. But then, at the very height of his achievement, he was involved in a car crash, and he lost the use of his right leg, and badly scarred his face. He hardly ever went out in public any more. He became bitter and cantankerous. What was worse, his mistress, whom he had grown to love almost fanatically, began to see another man, and although she still clung on to Williams for his money, it was quite obvious to him that she didn't love him any more.

'To begin with, Williams didn't know the identity of his mistress's new lover; and the lover, taking advantage of this fact, approached Williams in a roundabout manner and attempted to acquire the Devil's chair from him . . . so that he, too, might be as rich and successful as Williams, and attract Williams's mistress away from him for good.

'Williams, who had grown to believe that his financial talents were so superior that he no longer needed the chair, agreed to the sale. But no matter how often the chair was taken away from his house and delivered to the house of his mistress's lover, it always returned . . . just as it keeps on returning to your house.'

'Did Williams ever find out who the lover was?' asked Sara.

David nodded. 'Oh, yes. Because Williams's moods and his behaviour grew so bad that his mistress eventually left him, and married her new lover. Williams was eaten up with jealousy, and tried everything from legal action to kidnapping to get her back. He became so twisted up about her that he was sent for a while to Cane Hill sanatorium outside of London, which is a mental hospital. As it turned out, however, neither he nor her lover got her in the end. The day after Williams came out of the sanatorium, his onetime mistress was at home, helping her maid prepare an evening meal, when a pan of oil caught fire on the stove, and somehow the blazing fat was splashed all over her. She died of her burns within an hour.'

There was no mistaking the tremble in David's voice, nor the glisten of tears in his eyes. He leaned forward in his chair, holding his whisky glass in both hands, and he took a deep breath to recapture his English equilibrium.

'The lover was *you*, wasn't it?' I asked. 'And Williams's mistress was the girl who became your wife?'

'That's right,' said David, snappily. He tossed back the rest of his drink. 'All damned bad luck, really.'

'Did you try to buy the chair from Williams a second time, after your wife was dead?' asked Sara.

'There wasn't any point, was there? At least, I didn't think so at the time. And besides, I was beginning to suspect what one of the principal conditions for getting rid of the chair happened to be, and I didn't like it.'

'You mean – every time the chair was passed on – somebody died?'

'Somebody *had* to die. Like a sacrifice.'

'And that's why you didn't want to tell us this before?'

David nodded. 'As far as I know, the only way in which you will ever shake that chair off is for one of you to die.'

I was silent for a long time. I looked at David and David looked back at me. Then I said, 'What about Sam Jessop? How did he get rid of the chair? Nobody died in the Jessop family that I know of. Nobody even close.'

'Sam Jessop . . . made an arrangement,' said David.

'What arrangement?'

'Listen, Ricky, I've already told you more than I intended to. I can't betray a professional confidence.'

'What arrangement?' I barked at him.

'I can't tell you.'

I stood up, walked across the room to a huge red-and-white abstract by Mark Rothko, and raised my fist in front of it.

'So help me, David, if you don't tell me what I want to know, I'm going to punch this painting full of holes.'

David half stood up in his chair. 'That's a Rothko,' he said, in a drained voice. 'That's worth – well, damn it, I don't even *know* how much it's worth. That's how much it's worth.'

'My son's life is worth more than any painting, David.'

David sat down again. 'You're making this very difficult,' he said.

'*I'm* making this difficult? *You've* told nothing but lies and half-truths since I first met you.'

'I had a professional confidence to respect.'

'I don't give nuts for your professional confidence,' I said, acidly. 'Tell me what arrangement Sam Jessop made.'

'Well . . . this is only second-hand . . . from Martin . . . and Martin got it from his mother.'

'For Christ's sake, David.'

'Very well,' said David, soberly. 'It seems that the price of seeking your heart's desire from the devil's chair is that you get physically and mentally burned up much more quickly than you would if you made your way through life normally. Remember the Earl of Beckenham, who died at the age of fifty-four? That wasn't particularly young in those days, I grant you, but it wasn't particularly old, either. Then there was Charles Dickens, who was said to have owned the chair for a while. His health deteriorated appallingly. And I recently saw an old British press photograph of the chap who crushed his wife in the flour-mill, the car manufacturer. He was only forty, according to the news story, but you would have taken him for a man of sixty.

'The same thing happened to Sam Jessop. He acquired great success and even greater wealth when he bought the Devil's chair. In only a few years, he managed to build Jessop's into the third most profitable aerospace corporation in the world. But, he also acquired Bright's disease. And that's why he made the arrangement.'

David got up to pour himself another drink, but I said clearly, 'No more, David. Not until you've finished telling us.'

David hesitated, looked at his empty glass, and then

shrugged and sat down again. 'Very well. The arrangement that Sam Jessop made was simple. He stipulated that he should live for at least another ten years; and that he should immediately be able to dispose of the chair without it coming back to him. I think he'd tried to sell it once or twice in the past, but it just wouldn't leave.'

'But what did the chair demand in return? It didn't let him have all that for nothing.'

'No. It didn't. It demanded the life of his son.'

I frowned at David incredulously. 'Are you seriously trying to tell me that Sam Jessop asked the chair for ten years of life as a sick cripple, and that in exchange he was prepared to see his son killed? His only son?'

'That's the way it was.'

'I don't believe you. No father would possibly – '

'You're wrong,' David interrupted me. 'Some fathers would, and have. Sam Jessop never got on particularly well with Martin. He's always been a stubborn, unlovable, domineering man, and even before he came across the Devil's chair he believed he had a divine right to do whatever he damned well liked. The Devil's chair made him worse. As Martin told me – when Sam Jessop was struggling, he was obnoxious; but when he was rich, he was intolerable. Besides that, you have to realise that Sam made a classic error in his agreement with the chair. He asked for ten years of life, but he forgot to specify *healthy* life. So what he's faced with is ten years of suffering from acute Bright's disease. When he offered his son's life, he thought he was going to get a very much better bargain than he actually did.'

Sara shook her head. 'Whatever kind of bargain he got, good or bad, how on earth could he have sacrificed his own son?'

David lifted his hands to show that he didn't really understand Sam Jessop's sense of morality any more than we did.

'If *you* know that Sam Jessop has arranged to give his son's life to the Devil,' I said, 'then surely Martin Jessop knows it, too.'

'Oh, yes. It was his mother who told him, actually. She never liked Martin very much, either. But when she found out what Sam had done, she couldn't keep quiet about it. Martin was in Hamburg at the time, and his mother called him up and told him all about it.'

'How did he react?'

'How would *you* have reacted, if your father had done it to *you*? First of all he didn't believe it. But during his college years he'd seen enough of the Devil's chair to convince him that it had some kind of influence in the house. And so, gradually, he realised that what his mother had told him was actually true, and that his own father had sold his life in exchange for his own.'

'This couldn't have happened very long ago,' said Sara.

'No, it didn't. Only ten days ago. But as soon as he knew, Martin telephoned me and told me to make every effort to get hold of the chair, so that he could try to reverse the deal, or maybe qualify it in some way. Then he took the risk of flying back to California, and he arrived on Monday.'

'What's this carrier he talked about on the phone? And what's going to be ready the day after tomorrow?'

'That's nothing.'

'David,' I warned him. 'I want to know everything – *everything* – or else I'm going to vandalise this apartment like you wouldn't believe.'

'I can't tell you, Ricky. It's crucial to Martin's life. Right now, he's hiding away in a beach house at La Jolla, making sure that he doesn't go anywhere near anything dangerous, like knives or electric plugs or automobiles. He's pretty sure that the chair is going to try to kill him when he's flying his private Cessna . . . it'll look more like a genuine accident that way . . . but he's not taking any risks.'

'David,' I said, with menacing softness, 'every single detail of what's going on here is my business. Jonathan makes it my business. And unless you tell me what's happening, I'm going to crucify this whole deal. I mean, don't you think old man Jessop would like to hear what you're trying to pull?'

'You wouldn't. A sick old man, for the sake of a bright young guy like Martin?'

'You're talking like a fascist now.'

'The deal includes more than a sick old man, Ricky. I told you earlier that there was something in it for me. Well, there is. Jennifer.'

'Your wife? I thought she was dead.'

David looked at me with sorrowful eyes. 'She is. But apparently it's possible . . . provided one offers the chair enough in return . . . to have a loved one restored. Whole and healthy, I might add. Not mutilated, or burned. Whole and healthy.'

'And what, if you don't mind my asking, is "enough"?'

David spoke very quickly and abruptly, so British and hurried that I could hardly understand what he was saying. 'Martin – as you probably know – is senior vice-president in charge of guided weapons at his father's factory in Phoenix, Arizona. He has the authority to test the new cruise missile however and whenever he decides it's necessary. He is not, obviously, allowed to test nuclear warheads, not without US Air Force supervision. But he can use a conventional warhead with the force of quite a few hundred pounds of high explosive.'

He paused, and then he quickly continued, 'The day after tomorrow, an interdenominational religious conference assembles at the Los Angeles Convention Centre. We believe that if we can get the chair by tomorrow, and make the necessary transactions with it, we can offer it a high bodycount at the Convention Centre in exchange for Martin's life, and for Jennifer's revival.'

Sara and I looked at each other – each of us searching for some kind of reality. Did David actually believe that his dead wife would be returned to him, just as she was the minute before she was splashed with fiery cooking-oil? Did Martin Jessop actually have the gall to consider that his own life was worth more than hundreds of dead and injured worshippers at the Los Angeles Convention Centre?

And worst of all, how did they propose to get hold of the

chair by tomorrow, when the only possible way was for me or one of my family to die?

I said to David, 'I hope you understand that what you're contemplating is total madness. And I hope you understand that I can stop you. Occult murders are one thing. The police will never believe that anyone could be hurt by a chair. But if you and Martin Jessop try to launch a cruise missile at Los Angeles, then we've got something else altogether. We've got conspiracy to commit a mass homicide, and a damned great deadly weapon to prove it; and I can call the police and have you stopped.'

'I did take a small precaution,' said David.

'A precaution? What precaution?'

'When we carried Father Corso out of the house, I unfastened his crucifix. It's hidden in your house somewhere, and it's still stained with Father Corso's blood. If you try to pressure me, Ricky, then just remember that I've got a very effective way of pressuring you back. And, as you say, the police will never believe that anyone could be hurt by a chair.'

'You expect me to believe that?'

David nodded. 'You should. Because I can always prove it to you in the most inconvenient way.'

'I can implicate you, too.'

'How? It was your house. You don't have any way of proving I was there. I washed all the drinks glasses, remember?'

'Are you really as cold-blooded as you seem to be?' I asked him.

He looked me straight in the eye. 'Ricky,' he replied, 'I want my Jennifer back. I know it seems crazy to you. I know that you think I'm morally wrong. But as far as Jennifer is concerned, my vision is completely distorted. I admit it. And you could talk to me till dawn, and still not be able to persuade me that the lives of a few Christian worshippers, all of whom will be instantly received in the Bosom of Heaven, can in any way be compared to the life of the most beautiful girl who ever lived, and who was once my wife.'

I finished my drink. Then I stood up, and offered my hand to Sara to help her up, too.

'All right, David,' I said. 'If that's the way you feel about it. But just remember there's one small snag. You don't have the chair yet, and unless you have the chair you can't make any kind of a deal with it. So, until that religious conference is over, I'm not letting you lay one single finger on it, no matter how much of a bad time it's giving me.'

David smiled. 'It's all futile, you know, all this bravado. You have all the odds stacked against you. Martin Jessop is wealthy enough to have any one of you dealt with quickly and unobtrusively, and the moment one of you is dead, we can take the chair with impunity. Apart from that, the chair itself may well destroy you, and then we won't have to bother.'

'I'm not giving up yet,' I snapped.

'You will,' grinned David.

We left him where he was, sitting in his chair with a large glass of whisky in his hand, swinging his leg and smiling at us. It was past four o'clock now, still sunny and hot, but the shadows were beginning to lengthen across the pathways and gardens of Presidio Place. We clattered quickly down the concrete stairs to the underground car park, and drove out into the sunshine again with a squeal of tyres.

'What are we going to do now?' asked Sara. She was looking tired and shocked, and I expect I was looking the same.

'We're going to go home first, and get that chair.'

'What do you mean?'

'I mean that if David's serious, and he and Martin Jessop *do* want the chair that badly, then I'd rather have it right beside us where he can't get at it. From now on, we're all going to stick together like a tight little family. You, and me, and Jonathan, and that goddamned hideous piece of furniture.'

We drove back to the house. The day was growing cooler now, and the garden was strangely filled with purple-throated humming-birds. We stood watching them fluttering around the bushes for a moment as if they were an omen of misfortune, and then we went inside to collect the chair.

The chair was waiting for us in the living-room. It seemed taller than before, darker, even more threatening. The man-serpent almost seemed to be welcoming us back with a smile of unholy satisfaction. It may have been my own imagination, playing tricks on me, because now I knew the terrifying price I was going to have to pay to get rid of it. Sara knew too, although she hadn't said anything during the drive out from San Diego.

I couldn't let the chair take Jonathan, and I certainly wasn't going to let it take Sara. So the only way I was going to be able to rid my family of that horrific chair was to sacrifice *myself*. Maybe not now, maybe not for years. It would depend what kind of uneasy relationship the chair and I could work out between us. Certainly I would have to start using its evil powers in one way or another, if only to keep it busy and content, and to direct its malevolence away from me and my family.

We stood staring at the chair for a long time, hand in hand.

'I wonder why Henry Grant chose to leave it with us,' said Sara.

I shrugged. 'I don't suppose we'll ever find out. Maybe we were the nearest antique dealers he could find. We're listed in the California Antique Dealers' Register, you know – home address and all.'

'He must have been in a terrible panic to get rid of it.'

'I expect he was. Although he must have had *some* idea of what the chair was all about before he bought it. Remember he left a message with his office before he came down here from Santa Barbara, telling them that they mustn't accept the chair back from anyone, under any circumstances.'

'And then he died in that road accident,' said Sara.

'Accident? Maybe it wasn't an accident. Everything that happens involving this chair seems to be part of some deliberate plan. I just wish I knew what the hell the plan was.'

Sara looked around the room. There was no trace of the violence that had taken place there in the early hours of the morning, except for a damp patch on the rug where I had painstakingly washed out Father Corso's blood. The fireplace had been swept and relaid, and the crispy shell of the Devil's familiar had been buried in the garden. Still – there was a chilly and unpleasant atmosphere – and a curious smell that was alien to both of us. It was bitter, and acrid, and it gave me a taste in my mouth that reminded me of the salted-up plates of old car batteries.

On the wall, the shark in the Copley painting was only inches away from the silently screaming mariner; and the hooded figure in the Stuart portrait had begun to cross the stretch of open ground between the woods and was now only twenty or thirty feet away from the terrified colonial gentleman in black. The hooded creature's face was still invisible, but a greyish kind of tube seemed to be dangling out of the darkness of its robes.

Sara examined both paintings without saying a word. I came up behind her and laid my hands on her shoulders. 'The gradual approach of inescapable doom,' I remarked. She turned and looked at me and her eyes were bright with anxiety.

'You're going to think this all out, aren't you?' she said. 'You're not going to try any rash heroics?'

I shook my head. 'I've never been given to heroics, rash or otherwise.'

'You mean a lot to us, that's all,' said Sara. 'I know it seems as if the only way we're ever going to get rid of this chair is for one of us to die . . . but there have to be other ways. Remember David's friend Williams? He was able to get rid of the chair after his *mistress* died, David's wife. So it doesn't look as if you necessarily have to be related for the sacrifice to count.'

'So where does that leave us?' I asked her. 'Free to sacrifice someone else, so that we can stay alive?'

'I didn't mean that. Well, maybe I *did* mean it. When it comes down to the bottom line, I'm afraid that I'd prefer somebody else to die rather than one of us. Especially rather than you. I love you, and I can't help it.'

I wearily pressed my fingertips against my eyelids. 'Well, I don't know. Right now I don't have any ideas of how we're going to get rid of this chair at all. And right now we've got the problem of smuggling it into the hospital so that David can't lay his hands on it.'

'It would come right back to us even if he did.'

'Maybe it would, and maybe it wouldn't. I don't trust David a centimetre, if you want my feelings in metric. If he's willing to let loose a guided missile on a crowded convention hall, then he's willing to try any kind of deal with the Devil to wrest the chair away from us . . . and that would include bumping one of us off.'

'You really think he's serious about the missile? It sounds so far-fetched.'

'Darling,' I told her, 'he wants his Jennifer back. Fanatically. And Martin Jessop obviously has no intention of dying for the sake of his father, or for anyone else's sake, either. Okay – it could be nothing but some kind of nutty scenario that David's created in his head. But Martin Jessop *does* have access to missiles, and there *is* going to be a religious convention in Los Angeles tomorrow, and the whole thing could easily be covered up as a tragic mistake. Systems failure, computer breakdown, or something like that. They're always testing missiles out over the Pacific, or at China Lake. If one went off course, they'd have to hold an enquiry, naturally. But if Martin Jessop knows his missiles, he must have worked out a way to cover the crime up afterwards.

Sara looked away. 'It's like a nightmare,' she said. 'I keep feeling that I must be asleep, and that I'm dreaming all of this.'

I kissed her. 'Why don't you go upstairs and pack some more clothes? A couple of shirts for me, too. I'll see if I can load the chair on to the wagon.'

She glanced up the stairs. 'You're sure it's safe up there? No Devil's bugs, or anything like that?'

'If there are, scream.'

'Oh, I shall,' she promised me, fervently. 'I shall.'

When she was gone, I took a deep breath and went back across the room to face the chair. It was smiling down at me with bared fangs. *Down* at me – from almost six-and-a-half feet. It had grown nearly six inches, and the confusion of damned souls who plummeted down the length of its splat now seemed to have been stretched, like characters by El Greco. I was aware of a wavering in the air all around it, like the rippling of heat over a charcoal barbecue.

'*Listen,*' it whispered, somewhere in the recesses of my cortex.

'Listen to what? To more lies?'

'*I know of the arrangement for the slaying of Christian souls.*'

I looked at it carefully. 'You know about that? How?'

'*The thoughts of the man called Sears are transparent.*'

'So? What about it?'

'*I have been thinking it over, and the arrangement is an interesting one.*'

'Well, I'm sure it is. To someone who likes torturing innocent priests and threatening young children, the idea of blowing up a few hundred religious pilgrims must seem like a regular beanfeast.'

'*Your bravado is childish.*'

'So people keep telling me.'

'*In any event . . . the priest called Corso was not innocent . . . I cannot harm the innocent . . . only those who have sinned. And you would be surprised how gravely your Father Corso had sinned . . .*'

I wiped sweat away from my face with my handkerchief. Even though the living-room was cold, I felt as if I were burning up. Almost malarial.

'I'm taking you down to the hospital,' I said. 'Whatever I happen to feel about you, I don't want you stolen or damaged.'

'*Wait, listen –*'

I grasped the chair's arms. They rolled and slithered in my hands, but I kept hold of them.

'I don't want to listen,' I said. 'I'm not even sure if you're really talking or not. More likely, I'm going out of my mind.'

'*The agreement interests me,*' insisted the chair. '*It interests me enough to let you survive.*'

'What do you mean?'

'*I am usually passed from hand to hand by means of a ritual sacrifice. One of my owner's loved ones has to die. That is part of my destiny . . . part of the conditions which were laid down when I was first created*

. . . *but I do not necessarily have to insist on a sacrifice if another arrangement can be reached.*'

I straightened up. 'What are you trying to tell me? That you won't harm any of us? Not me, nor Sara, nor Jonathan? Is that what you're trying to tell me?'

'*The agreement envisaged by the man called Jessop would bring me more than a hundred souls in one day. A ritual sacrifice in your family would bring me only one.*'

I was trembling now, partly with fear and partly with excitement. For the first time since Sunday, I actually saw a way of getting off the hook – of getting rid of the chair without any more pain or death or horror. At least, not in my house . . . not in my family.

'*I will suggest a bargain with you . . .*' whispered the chair. '*If you take me now and give me to the man called Sears, I will release you from your ritual obligations, and awaken your son from his sleep.*'

'Is that a promise?'

'*That is more than a promise. It is a solemn guarantee. We will draw up the papers in the ways of old, in magic runes, and we shall sign them with living memory.*'

Sara appeared at the top of the stairs. She said, 'Are you talking to someone?' but I raised my hand to show her that I wanted her to be quiet for a moment. She stood and watched me in fascination and horror.

'You'll have to give me time,' I asked the chair.

'*I will give you no time at all. You will have to decide now. Your decision will not be any the less drastic for being postponed.*'

'What if I don't agree to give you to Sears?'

'*Then I shall demand your son's life. Even now, he dreams in the cold vestibules of hell . . . he is close to me already . . . it would be a matter of snuffing out a candle that is already burning low . . . that is all.*'

'You can't take Jonathan. He's only six years old. He hasn't even lived yet.'

'*I have made my decision. I shall take your son.*'

'I won't allow it. Take me instead.'

'*Your life is a grey remnant compared with that of your son.*'

'You can't take him!' I shouted. 'You can take me now if

you want to – right now, right this second! But you're not going to take Jonathan!'

'*How much do you want me to take your life?*' asked the chair.

I was terrified now. My whole system was bursting with adrenalin, and I knew that within a matter of seconds I could actually be killed. It was like sitting in the passenger seat of a car that has gone wildly out of control, watching a concrete rampart come blurring and sliding towards you. You think: Jesus, I'm going to die.

'I don't want you to take Jonathan, that's all.'

'*How much do you want me to take your life?*'

'Totally, if you have to take it.'

'*Do you beg me to take it?*'

'I beg you.'

'*Get down on your knees and beg me.*'

Shaking, I bent my knees and knelt in front of the chair. 'I beg you to take my life,' I said, with a throat crammed with fur.

'*You fool,*' gloated the chair. '*Why should I take your life when I could have a choice young life like that of your son?*'

'Take my life!' I shouted desperately. 'Kill me! Just get it over with and leave my family alone!'

I bent double, my forehead pressed against the floor. My fists were clenched and my teeth were gritted and all I was trying to do inside of my mind was blank out anything and everything – fear, love, happiness, pain, humiliation – so that when the chair took me I would be nothing but a human cipher. Mindless, thoughtless, gone.

I heard Sara running down the stairs. She grabbed hold of me and tried to raise my head up.

'Take me!' I yelled to the chair.

'No!' shrieked Sara. 'No, Ricky, you can't! Ricky, for the love of God, don't!'

I knelt up, trembling, and she held me tight in her arms. 'Ricky, you mustn't. I couldn't bear it.'

'It wants to take Jonathan,' I told her, croakily.

'But just now . . . when I was listening to you from upstairs . . . . you were saying something about it not hurting *any* of us.'

178

I stared at her intently. 'It won't. It won't touch a hair on our heads. Just so long as we deliver it to David.'

'Then we'll deliver it to David.'

'If we deliver it to David, then David will let the missile loose. That's what the chair *wants*. More bloodshed, more death, more sacrifices. It said that human sacrifices are part of its destiny.'

'You don't know any of those people at the convention,' Sara pleaded with me. 'They could be anybody. Anybody at all. Why should you give up your life for people you don't even know? You didn't *ask* to have the chair left here, did you? Why should you accept the responsibility for a fate you didn't choose?'

'People are always having to accept the responsibility for fates they didn't choose,' I said, although with less conviction than I had before. 'It's part of what makes people human, instead of animals.'

'So David Sears and Martin Jessop can behave like animals, and you have to suffer for it? Not just you – Jonathan and me, too. Is that it?'

'Sara, hundreds of people are going to die unless someone does something to change this situation. And the only person who can do anything about it is me.'

'Hundreds of people are going to die in road accidents this year. You can't help it. It's not your responsibility. Hundreds of people are going to be killed by murderers and muggers. You can't help it. And even if you could – would you? Would you go in front of a firing squad if it could save the lives of everybody who was going to die in a road accident next year? You wouldn't, would you? You wouldn't even consider it.'

'But, Sara, this is different.'

'How is it different? Tell me.'

I closed my eyes. I felt as if I'd been through a full course of frontal lobotomy. 'It's different because it's real. It's different because I can actually save those people's lives.'

'Why don't you tell the police? Have them stopped?'

'Because if the chair doesn't get its ration of dead bodies, it's going to come back here looking for its ritual due.'

'Are you sure of that?'

I looked at the chair, and I didn't have to ask it directly whether it would return to Rancho Santa Fe seeking its sacrifice or not. I knew in my bones that it would. And I also knew that it would be as angry as all hell, and that would mean torture, and agony, as well as death.

'Yes,' I said. 'I'm sure.'

Sara stroked the back of my hand, as if my veins were a puzzle which she was trying to decipher.

'Well,' she said, 'what are you going to do?'

'You have no time,' whispered the chair. *'Decide now, or I will decide for you. Your son is so near to death already.'*

I stood up, and walked across the living-room. Whatever I decided, the chair would get what it wanted. Hadn't it gotten just what it had wanted out of me? It had predicted that I would crawl across the floor and beg, and I had. It had actually forced me to plead for death, and at that particular moment I had wanted death as much as Williams had wanted money, and Sam Jessop had wanted his business to grow, and as much as David Sears wanted his Jennifer back.

But the chair hadn't struck me down straight away. Although it was insisting there was no more time, it was still holding off. And the only reason it was holding off was because it thirsted for those hundreds of convention delegates more than it thirsted for me. Maybe, in that grisly preference, I had a lever, a way out. Maybe I was simply making excuses for choosing that my family and I should live. Cowardice and bravery are the most complicated emotions of all. At least they seem that way when you're scared.

'Now,' said the chair. *'Now, or never.'*

I looked down at the rug. There was still a pinkish hue there, where Father Corso's hip had burst open.

'All right,' I agreed, so quietly that Sara could hardly catch what I was saying. 'I'll take you down to David Sears as soon as we've packed our clothes.'

Three things happened then, immediately. It felt as if the room were suddenly crowded with invisible demons, drawing closer with their rustling wings. Sara, alarmed by the sensation, stood up, and held on to my arm.

Across the clear green waters of the Copley painting, blood began to spread. The shark had torn off the mariner's shoulder and part of his head, and the mariner's friends were so far away now that they could scarcely be seen. In the Stuart portrait, the hooded figure was now standing right behind the colonial gentleman, and there was an expression of intense pain on the colonial gentleman's face. Through his severe black vest, a coiled shape was emerging, like a grey-coloured tube, glistening with abdominal mucus.

Something else happened, too. Out of the crevice at the back of the chair's black-leather seat, a sheaf of parchmenty-looking paper emerged, with a soft crackling noise, and then floated across the room on an unfelt draught, sheet after tumbling sheet. Sara and I collected it up, and then tried to read what was written on it.

There was line after line of curious characters, seven pages of them in all.

'What do they mean?' asked Sara. 'I don't understand them at all.'

'They're runes,' I told her. 'The magic writing of spells, and of agreements with the Devil.'

'You really believe it's the Devil? Like, the medieval Devil?'

'The Devil was never exclusively medieval,' I said. 'He takes on whatever shape we humans care to give Him. Sam Jessop thought of him as a kind of moral Black Hole – utterly negative but also totally attractive.'

'And how do you think of Him?'

I scanned the handful of runic papers. 'Right now,' I said, 'I only have to look in the mirror.'

9,—*Bargainings*

That night, the chair was so light that I could carry it by myself with ease. I loaded it carefully into the back of the wagon, and this time, by some curious distortion of size and space, I didn't have to tie the tailgate together with cord. The chair had grown taller, and yet it fitted into the wagon much more easily.

I went back into the house, and climbed the stairs to the bedroom. Sara was combing her hair in front of the dressing-table mirror. On the bed, our airline bag was packed with fresh clothes for her.

'You may not need those,' I said. 'Provided the chair keeps its bargain.'

'I'm not going to take any chances,' said Sara. 'Right now, I don't know *who* I can trust.'

I stood behind her as she finished combing her hair, watching our faces in the mirror as if they were the faces of two people with whom we had once been acquainted, but with whom we had now lost touch. The sort of person who sends you a card at Christmas, but never writes or telephones or comes to visit.

'There has to be some way to stop them, you know,' I said, quietly.

Sara looked up at my reflection. 'I hope there is. But you're not going to stop them by sacrificing yourself, or your family. The Delatollas aren't going to make a name for themselves by being martyred.'

'I just hope that we can bear the guilt.'

'I'd prefer to face up to the guilt with a living, breathing husband – rather than spend the rest of my life as a widow with a clear conscience.'

'You're being very hard, you know.'

'I'm fighting for your life, against the lives of a whole lot of people I never even heard of. And you think that's hard?'

I shook my head. 'Not particularly. After my first demonstration of selflessness, I think I'm inclined to agree with you.'

I went to the bed and zippered up the airline bag. It was then that I noticed what had happened to the large unfinished Gustave Moreau painting over the headboard. In the centre of the bare area of canvas, someone or something had sketched an outline in charcoal. It was difficult to make out exactly what it was, but it had the rough appearance of a bull, or perhaps the head of a minotaur.

'Sara,' I said. 'Come take a look at this.'

She came over, still combing the ends of her hair, and stared at the picture closely.

'That's new,' she said. 'Was that there this morning?'

'Not that I noticed. Can you work out what it is?'

Sara gently touched the canvas with her fingertips. 'It looks like the outline of some kind of monster, with horns. The funny thing is, it fits into the composition, like this was what Moreau always intended to paint here. Look at the way the woman's shying away from it.'

We both regarded the painting for a while, each of us withdrawn in our own thoughts. Then Sara said, 'You know, it vaguely reminds me of something.'

'It looks like a bull to me.'

'Well, yes, you're right. It does look like a bull, but it reminds me of a picture in one of my college textbooks.'

'Can you think which one it was?'

'I *think* – I can't remember exactly – I *think* it was a painting by Vittore Carpaccio. He was a Venetian Renaissance painter . . . a follower of Gentile Bellini. He used to paint all kinds of ceremonies and processions in Venice. Great big crowd paintings full of boats and people.'

'And?'

'And I think I'm right in saying that it was Carpaccio who painted a very mysterious picture which was suppressed at the time. It didn't fit in with any of his other paintings, and there are lots of scholars today who still say that it wasn't his. He was supposed to have painted it in about 1496, right after he finished a terrific canvas called *The Miracle of the True Cross'*.

I looked back at the painting on our bedroom wall. 'He painted a shape like this in his mysterious picture?'

'That's right. I remember a black-and-white reproduction of it. It showed a whole crowd of mourners at a Venetian funeral, some of them stepping into black gondolas, some of them lifting their hands up to heaven in sorrow. But in the background, standing on a balcony, you can see a silhouette of this same shape . . . the bull-like head, and the man's shoulders.'

I picked up the airline bag. 'Well, maybe Moreau used What's-his-name's painting for reference. Carpaccio's.'

'I wish I could remember where that textbook was,' said Sara. 'There was an interesting piece about what the shape was, what it represented, and why the experts think Carpaccio included it.'

'You can't remember off-hand?'

Sara shook her head. 'It was too long ago. I've forgotten almost everything about the Renaissance. I don't even remember who painted *Venus, Cupid, Folly, And Time.*'

'Bronzino, as a matter of fact. But what was the book called?'

'I don't know. Something like *The Italian Renaissance.*'

'That sounds original. Maybe I should go up into the attic and look for it. All your old college books are up there.'

Sara checked her watch. 'Do you think we have time? It's getting pretty late.'

'You checked in with the hospital, didn't you?'

She nodded.

'Okay then,' I said. 'Give me five minutes up in the attic, and I'll see what I can dig up.'

Up in the attic, amongst heaps of boxes, stacks of magazines, broken squash-rackets, and Jonathan's old crib, it was stiflingly hot. I crouched my way along to the very end of the gable that overlooked the front of the house, and there were Sara's old college books, as well as a Fisher-Price camper, two sections of a fibre-glass fishing-pole, a copy of *Playboy* for May 1961, and a descant recorder. Sweating in the humidity, I rifled through the books until I found a dusty yellow volume with brown lettering on it which announced itself as *Howlett's Italian Renaissance*. I blew on it to remove the dust, and then I made my way back to the stepladder.

'Did you find it?' asked Sara.

I held it up. 'Don't you ever again accuse me of being a lousy hoarder.'

As I folded away the stepladder, Sara took the book and started to leaf through it. 'My God,' she said, 'it seems like a century ago that I studied all of this.'

'It seems like a century since that chair arrived.'

She took the book through into the bedroom and sat down at the dressing-table with it. Eventually, she said, 'Here it is. Look. *The Mysterious Funeral Guest*, attributed to Vittore Carpaccio, circa 1496–7.'

I frowned at the painting closely. It was a very small monochromatic reproduction, because the picture was only a curiosity, not an important event in the mainstream of the Venetian Renaissance. Nonetheless, the silhouette of the bull-like creature was quite clear, and there was no question at all that it bore an extraordinary resemblance to the charcoal sketching which had appeared on our unfinished Moreau.

'"*The Mysterious Funeral Guest* is an inexplicable departure by Carpaccio from his usual paintings of Venetian public events,"' read Sara. '"Although the authenticity of the painting is considered by the Accademia in Venice to be beyond question, many experts still doubt that it was painted by Carpaccio because of the number of unusual occult symbols in it, most notably the Minotaur which appears on the third-floor balcony of the building on the left-hand side. The Accademia claims that this Minotaur is *The Mysterious Funeral Guest* of the painting's title, but at least two other experts from the Museo Nazionale suggest that this beast is only an unusual shadow, and that the guest is the grand-looking gentleman stepping into the third gondola, who may very well be a member of the Medici family."'

'Anything else?' I asked Sara.

'Yes – ' she said, 'just this. "The Minotaur, however, is

mentioned in Carpaccio's diaries several times, as is a snake-demon, and it may be speculated that the artist had some interest in evil spirits and the supernatural. The Minotaur in those days was quite a common manifestation of the Devil, and he would have been attending the funeral in order to make sure that the immortal soul of the deceased found its way into his custody. An old legend that regained some currency in Renaissance times was that the Devil, after having been banished by the crucifixion of Jesus Christ, could only return to Earth in an enduring physical form if he gathered the immortal souls of a thousand thousand people, each of which had to be offered to him under the strictest conditions, and each of which had to be the soul of somebody who had died as the result of murder, suicide, or extreme pain, notably the pain of being burned alive. Carpaccio is said to have attempted suicide unsuccessfully three times, once by setting himself alight with burning oil."'

'Is that all?' I asked.

'That's all,' said Sara. 'After that it goes on to discuss the work of Piero della Francesca.'

I looked again at the minotaur-shape on our picture. Then I said, 'Supposing that Renaissance legend was right.'

'What do you mean?'

'Well – supposing it was right – and the Devil *did* have to collect a thousand thousand immortal souls before He could walk on the earth again in – what do they say there? – an enduring physical form.'

'Supposing it was? What difference would that make?'

'I'm guessing,' I said, 'but don't you think it's possible that the Devil could have decided that one way to get all the souls He needed would be to bargain for them with human beings who were still alive? Just like Faust. Give me your soul, or the soul of somebody you love, and in return you can have whatever you want. Money, success, a guided-missile contract with the Pentagon.'

Sara was silent. I sat down on the edge of the dressing-table next to her and took her hand.

'That would make sense of the chair's desire to take all the souls of those hundreds of people at the religious convention in Los Angeles tomorrow. For all we know, He's only a few score short of the thousand thousand He needs. So when that missile goes off tomorrow, we're not only going to see an urban massacre.'

I pointed to the minotaur shape on the Moreau painting. 'We're going to see *that*, too, in the flesh. The Devil returning to sit on His throne again.'

Sara looked away. 'And what will that mean?'

'I don't know. God had to send his only son Jesus Christ down to earth last time to redeem the sins of a world that was living according to the words of the Devil. It was a world of war, and cruelty, and slavery; and after the Ascension it still was. But at least Jesus had established a powerful way of fighting for human dignity and human life.'

I picked up the Renaissance book and closed it, shutting away the Devil's silhouette. 'The difference is that in the days of Jesus, men fought with nothing more dangerous than swords and spears and Greek fire. These days, we have nuclear weapons.'

'We don't have any evidence that the Devil's going to reappear, do we?' said Sara. 'You said yourself that you're only guessing.'

'Yes,' I agreed. 'I'm only guessing.'

She held my hand. 'You're not going to get any more ideas about – well, about giving yourself up?'

'I don't think so. But I still think there has to be a way out of this.'

'Let's just get the chair down to David,' Sara begged me. 'Then we can talk about it some more.'

I picked up the airline bag and slung it over my shoulder. 'I hope to God we're not playing a game we can't handle,' I said. 'You know what they say about supping with devils and long spoons.'

David was both surprised and suspicious when we arrived. He was getting dressed to go out somewhere, and his shirt tails were flapping out of the back of his pants.

'What's going on?' he asked me. 'I thought you'd decided that I was too barbarous for civilised company.'

'We've brought you the chair,' I told him, in a soft voice.

He thumbed a silver cufflink through the buttonhole in his cuff. His expression was as ambiguous as a whipped-up bowl of non-dairy topping. 'Well,' he said, 'that's as may be.'

'I didn't think you'd believe me,' I retorted. 'But I've officially drawn up a paper contract, written in runes, and sealed with living memory.'

'Sealed with living memory? What on earth does that mean?'

'I'm not too sure. But the chair assured me that it was going to take a memory out of my head and use it as a seal. Instead of blood, I suppose.'

'So where did you draw up a runic contract?'

'It appeared out of the chair. Look.'

I held it up in my hand. David stared at it for a few long seconds, and then reached out for it. I drew it away. 'It's genuine,' I said. 'You'll find out how genuine it is when we leave. The chair will stay here.'

'What made it . . . agree to leave you?' asked David, uncertainly. 'This isn't some sort of elaborate trap, is it? Because if it is – '

'It agreed to leave us on the condition that we delivered it to you,' I explained. 'It knows all about your scheme to fire a guided missile at the Los Angeles Convention Centre, and as it turns out, it approves of it. It's hungry for souls, David, and it would rather have a hundred than one or two.'

David bit his lip. He still appeared unsure. 'It will get Jennifer back for me? Unscathed?'

'You'll have to ask it. It's yours now. As soon as you help me carry it up from the car.'

'And Martin Jessop? Martin will be allowed to survive?'

'I expect so.'

David sat down. 'Well,' he said, 'I don't know what to say. This is marvellous. Martin will be absolutely delighted.'

'I thought he might be. But I don't suppose the people at the Los Angeles Convention Centre are going to feel quite as happy.'

'Don't start getting moralistic,' replied David, in a caustic tone. 'You and your wife are just as much a party to this as we are. You could have saved those pilgrims' lives, couldn't you, by sacrificing your own?'

'I could have done,' I replied. 'But there was always the risk that you would have gotten hold of the chair anyway. Heroic gestures are only worth making if they're effective.'

David took out a cigarette and lit it. He smoked for a while in silence, still looking at me, but lost in a memory. I thought I knew what the memory was, too.

'You're thinking about Jennifer?' I asked him.

He narrowed his eyes. 'She was the most beautiful girl I ever met in my life,' he said. 'The idea that I might actually be able to hold her in my arms again . . . well, it's quite devastating.'

'I'm glad you think she's worth it.'

He breathed out smoke. 'She is, Ricky. I assure you she is.'

'You'd better help me carry the chair up here,' I told him. 'I want to get back to the hospital in case Jonathan wakes up.'

'You think he's going to?'

I held up the runic contract. 'It's part of the deal. At least, it had better be.'

While Sara waited in the car, David and I carried the chair, wrapped in a blanket, up to his friend's apartment. We set it down in the centre of the room, and David unveiled it. It appeared to be taller than ever, like some grotesque ladder, and when David raised his hand up to touch the man-serpent's face with soft, reverent fingers, he could scarcely reach higher than the demon's beard.

'I want to thank you for this,' said David. 'You've really been most intelligent and considerate. When you left here this afternoon in such a temper, I was very worried that you might do something rash.'

'Like what? Like trying to save the lives of a couple of hundred unsuspecting people? How could you have thought such a thing?'

'Do we have to be enemies?' asked David. 'I thought, once Jennifer was back, we might perhaps get together for dinner . . . something like that.'

I looked him up and down with as much contempt as I could manage. It wasn't all that easy, because I felt pretty contemptuous about my own behaviour, too. But somehow the thought of going to dinner with a woman who had been resurrected at the cost of over a hundred violent deaths wasn't exactly my idea of a tasteful evening out.

'You can keep your precious zombie to yourself,' I told him. 'And apart from that, I don't ever want to see you, or that chair, ever again in my whole life. Because if I do, so help me, I'll try my darndest to get my revenge on you, and it, and I'll destroy you both.'

David cleared his throat. Then he gave me the sort of smile that company presidents give you before they tell you that you're out of a job. 'Very well,' he said. 'If that's the way you feel, then there isn't a lot I can do about it, is there? I'm sorry it all has to end like this. But it's been good to know you, and I must say you've really turned up trumps.'

'Goodbye, David,' I said, sourly.

He stood in the doorway of the condominium, watching me walk away. Behind him, down the corridor, I could see the tall and diabolical outline of the Devil's chair. From far away, it took on the appearance of a horned bull, or a minotaur. The Mystery Guest at the Funeral.

Sara was listening to a Mozart tape in the car. She hardly said a word as we drove out of the underground car park of Presidio Place and made our way back along the freeway to the Hospital of the Sisters of Mercy. In the distance, across the bay, we could see the lighted funnels of two Navy destroyers, and the dancing glitter of a helicopter. The music was Mozart's Fantasia in F Minor, and the sound of the two pianos seemed to fill the interior of the car the way the flock of humming-birds had filled our garden. At last, at long last, I felt myself beginning to relax.

Dr Rosen was waiting for us impatiently when we arrived. 'You said you would be here much earlier,' he said, tapping the face of his watch. 'I was worried that Jonathan was going to come out of his coma to find you absent.'

I took his arm. 'It was very important, Doctor, believe me. Is he actually waking up?'

'Come see for yourself.'

'Oh God,' whispered Sara. 'Please let him wake up.'

We tiptoed together into the room where Jonathan was lying. There was another specialist there, two nurses, and an intern. Jonathan was still unconscious, but Dr Rosen took out his silver propelling-pencil and pointed to the electro-cardiograph.

'Heartbeat much quicker – and look here – the electro-encephalograph is showing signs of much more responsive brain activity.'

'Could I try talking to him?' I asked.

'Sure. Go ahead. It's the best thing you could do for him right now.'

I stepped forward and leaned over Jonathan's small sleeping form. His eyes were closed, but there was far more colour in his cheeks than there had been yesterday. I had the feeling that he was right on the brink of coming back – that it would only take a little coaxing for him to open his eyes and say hello.

'Jonathan,' I called him.

His eyelids flickered.

'Jonathan.'

Again, a slight response.

'Go on,' Dr Rosen encouraged me. 'You're really beginning to get through to him now.'

Hoarsely, I sang:

> *'Johnny shall have a new bonnet,*
> *Johnny shall go to the fair,*
> *And Johnny shall have a new ribbon,*
> *To tie up his bonny blond hair.'*

Gradually, as if he were waking up from his usual afternoon rest, Jonathan opened his eyes. The silence in the hospital room was breathtaking. Even the regular *bleep – bleep – bleep* of the electro-cardiograph seemed to diminish. Jonathan looked at me sleepily and I could feel my eyes fill with tears.

Right behind me, her hand clasping my shoulder, Sara started to sob.

'Daddy?' said Jonathan, in a slurred voice. 'Mommy?'

He lifted his arms and I bent over and held him tight. He was so warm and young and defenceless, and he depended on me so much.

'You're all right,' I told him. 'Everything's going to be all right.'

'Where is this place, Daddy?' Jonathan asked, trying to focus on all the faces around him, all the gleaming chrome apparatus and all the white starched hospital coats.

'You're in hospital. You had an accident,' said Sara, a little shakily. 'You've been asleep for four whole days and three whole nights. Can you imagine that? Daddy and Mommy were worried you were going to sleep for a whole week.'

Jonathan smiled, and touched Sara's hair, and then her face. 'I've been dreaming,' he said.

'Well, you can tell us all about your dreams later,' said Sara. 'Right now we're just pleased that you're awake. Do you feel okay?'

Jonathan investigated the bandage on his left cheek. 'That's sore,' he said. 'Did I hurt myself there?'

'You fell over and cut yourself on Daddy's axe.'

We thought for a moment that Jonathan was going to say that he hadn't – but he simply nodded and smiled and half-closed his eyes again.

'I've been dreaming,' he repeated. 'I dreamed I was someplace bright and sunny.'

'At least he didn't have nightmares,' put in Dr Rosen. 'Sometimes a coma patient can have really horrendous dreams.'

'Tell us later,' I said to Jonathan. 'Now you're awake, we've got all the time in the world.'

'They said he couldn't hurt me,' said Jonathan, in a matter-of-fact way.

'Come on now, Jonathan, I think it's time for a few quick tests and some rest,' said Dr Rosen. 'Mr and Mrs Delatolla, if you'll just excuse me for one moment – '

'Daddy,' Jonathan said clearly, 'they said he couldn't hurt me. Not unto death.'

'Jonathan,' I grinned, 'please do what Dr Rosen says. I love you, and I'd love to listen to all of your dreams, but Dr Rosen wants to make sure that you're okay.'

'*He cannot hurt your son unto death,*' somebody said. A ringing, brassy sort of a voice, as if they were chiming bells at the same time.

I looked around. 'Who said that?' I asked Sara.

Sara frowned. 'Who said what?'

'Who said "He cannot hurt your son unto death"?'

'Well, wasn't that just what Jonathan said?'

'Not like *that*. That sounded like the trump of doom.'

Dr Rosen pouted at me questioningly. 'I didn't hear anything. Anybody in here hear anything?'

Everybody shook their heads. I sat on the bed and looked around at them appealingly, but none of them had heard it. I felt as if I were suddenly revealed as the village fruitcake.

'Okay,' I said. 'Maybe I'm tired, and I've got ringing in the ears. But that's what it sounded like. Bells.'

'Bats in the belfry?' one of the nurses whispered, and the other one giggled.

Dr Rosen snapped, 'That's enough,' but I couldn't help noticing that he was smiling too.

Jonathan gripped my sleeve. I turned to see what he wanted, and to my fright and amazement his eyes appeared to be on fire. They were shining at me in brilliant gold, so bright that I could hardly look at them. And there was that sound again, that bell-chiming sound, and it was ringing and reverberating through every bone in my body. It even jarred the fillings in my teeth.

'*He has been safe with us, your son,*' said the same voice as before. It was so majestic, so rich, that it gave me that cold shrinking feeling all over. I raised my hand against the dazzle of Jonathan's eyes, but nothing could blot out the overwhelming echo of that stentorian voice.

'*Is it not written in the sacred book: "Remember, I pray thee, who ever perished, being innocent?" And is it not also written that they who plough iniquity, and sow wickedness, shall reap the same?*'

'What are you trying to tell me?' I asked Jonathan. 'Jonathan – what are you trying to say?'

All around me, Sara and Dr Rosen and the rest of the hospital staff appeared to be frozen. I felt as if time had stood still; as if the room had been suspended in brilliant amber. Jonathan's lips moved, but not in exact synchronisation with the voice that blared out of his mouth. He looked like a fiery puppet, a dazzling marionette.

'He whose throne you kept in your house attempted to slay your son,' the voice rang out. *'But your son could not be killed. Even when He whose throne you kept in your house attempted to stop your son's heart beating and to numb his brain forever, your son could not be killed. Your son has been sleeping under our protection, and has always been safe. He cannot be hurt unto death by the One whose throne you kept in your house because of his innocence. He is one of Our Master's children; and Our Master will not let him die. Do you know what I am saying to you? Do you now know what you must do?*

'Our Master will not let him die.'

The ringing began to fade. Jonathan's eyes dimmed, and returned to normal. As suddenly as it had begun, the visitation was over. Dr Rosen scribbled a note on his clipboard and Sara leaned over and blew Jonathan a kiss just as if nothing had happened at all. One of the nurses dropped her pen, and out in the corridor the plangent voice of the receptionist called for 'Dr Helmuth . . . Dr Helmuth to pediatrics, please.'

'Why don't you go get yourself a cup of coffee?' suggested Dr Rosen. 'Then we can run our tests on Jonathan without any hitches. You don't mind if Mommy and Daddy go for a cup of coffee do you?' he asked Jonathan.

Jonathan shook his head. I looked at him carefully, and for a second I thought I could detect an expression in his eyes that wasn't anything to do with being six years old and sick in bed. It was too cold, too strong, and too knowing. But it vanished before I could respond to it, and then all I could do was wave Jonathan a daddy-like wave and ask him if he wanted any comics, or any toys.

'I'd just like my Evel Knievel bike, please,' he said, solemnly.

Dr Rosen smiled at me. 'That's what I call a quick recovery. You're a lucky parent, Mr Delatolla.'

'Yes,' I said. 'I think, just for once, the angels were on our side.'

Throughout the night, Jonathan's condition continued to improve. I went in to see him once or twice, and we talked for a few minutes, but I didn't see any more of those celestial flashes of brilliant light, and I didn't hear any more of those resounding voices. All the same, I had the feeling that I had been told everything I needed to know, and that in some inexplicable way we were *ready*.

Towards dawn, I curled up and went to sleep for a while on the waiting-room couch. I had a vivid dream about flying . . . about twisting and turning through the sky . . . and all the while the sun was dramatically rising from behind the clouds, throwing out shafts of golden light . . .

I was woken up by Sara bringing me a cup of coffee and a bagel. 'I'm sorry,' she said. 'I didn't know you were sleeping. I thought you might feel like some breakfast.'

I sat up, and smeared my face back into shape with my hands. 'What time is it?' I asked her.

'Seven-thirty.'

'Have you been in to see Jonathan?'

She nodded. 'He's sleeping. Dr Rosen says he's going to be fine.'

I took a sip of scalding black coffee from the styrofoam cup. 'That's good. Although I think we owe more to God than we do to Dr Rosen.'

'You're sounding very religious all of a sudden.'

'That's because everything that's happened this week has been connected with religion, one way or another. Or at least it's been connected with the historical struggle between Absolute Good and Absolute Evil.'

Sara made a face. 'You're being indecently philosophical first thing in the morning. Usually you do nothing but grunt.'

'This morning, I don't have time to grunt.'

'Because of David?'

I buttered my bagel with the bendy plastic knife that Sara had brought me. 'He's going to launch that missile at ten o'clock. That's what Martin Jessop said on the phone. And that means we have to work out what we're going to do about it, and how we're going to get Jonathan out of this hospital, all in two hours flat.'

'What?' Sara asked me.

'Listen,' I told her, 'you remember yesterday, in Jonathan's room, how I told you I heard someone talking.'

'Yes. But what of it?'

'I heard more than just one sentence. Jonathan — or rather someone who was speaking *through* Jonathan — gave me a whole explanation of what had happened.'

Sara looked at me as if I'd lost a wingnut. 'Ricky,' she said, 'it's just the strain.'

'I know what's strain and what's real, honey, and that wasn't strain.'

'But *I* didn't hear anything. How come I didn't hear anything?'

'I don't know. You didn't hear the chair either, did you? Maybe a talent for hearing occult voices runs in my family. Maybe they're like dog-whistles, that some people can hear and other people can't.'

'Maybe your family's crazy.'

I blew out my cheeks. 'Yes,' I admitted. 'Maybe we are. But this morning, over a hundred people are going to lose their lives unless I try to do something about it. And I'd rather you told me I was crazy *after* I'd tried, than before. I have to try.'

'And that means taking Jonathan out of hospital? Why?'

'Because Jonathan is the only one who can stop what's going to happen today.'

'Your voices told you that?'

'My voices, as you call them, said quite specifically that Jonathan was one of God's children . . . that he was innocent . . . and that the Devil was powerless to hurt him.'

'How can that be?' asked Sara. 'He got cut in the face, didn't he? And he went into a coma?'

'Whatever the chair tried to suggest, he was held in that

coma by some kind of agency of God, not of the Devil. It was done to protect him, to keep him out of the Devil's reach. Leastways, that's what I understood the voice to be saying.'

'Ricky, this is insane. We can't drag Jonathan out of hospital for the sake of some imaginary angels.'

'We're going to have to. You want all those people to die?'

'No, I don't. But I don't want Jonathan to die, either. And if you start using him to prove some crackpot theory about Absolute Good and Absolute Evil, and God's children, and who knows what else, then he may. Didn't David say that Martin Jessop would "deal" with us if we got in his way? Well, that's another danger, quite apart from the chair, and I won't have either you or Jonathan being exposed to it.'

'Sara,' I said, 'it's worse than just mass murder. If the Devil's been promised the souls of all those dead people at the convention centre . . . then He could have sufficient strength to be brought back to earth again. You know what it said in your college textbook.'

Sara stood up. 'I know what it said in my college textbook. It said that all that stuff was nothing more than a Renaissance legend.'

'So you're telling me that you don't believe me, and that you won't help?' I asked her.

'I didn't say I didn't believe you. I'm quite sure you *did* hear those voices. But, Ricky, we've had a terrible week. They could easily have been inside of your head, and nowhere else.'

I picked up my cup of coffee and then put it down again. 'Sara,' I said quietly, 'I'm asking for your support. Do you understand me? I know that I'm right, and whatever you think about it, I'm asking for your support. For once, please, just blindly and unquestioningly do what I say. Because right now, there's no time to argue.'

Sara came over and sat down beside me. She brushed at my tousled hair with her fingers. 'Do you really believe you heard angels?' she asked me.

'Angels, voices, I don't know. If they're calling the Devil a Black Hole these days, maybe the angels are Quasars. But I heard them all right, and they told me over and over again that

Jonathan could *not* be hurt . . . or at least, he certainly couldn't be killed.'

'How do you know you weren't hearing another voice from the Devil? You could have done, you know. He may be trying to outwit you – to take your life and Jonathan's life as well as all the others.'

I lowered my eyes. 'I've thought about that. But I think it's a risk we're just going to have to run.'

Sara took my hand. 'All right,' she said, 'I'll support you. It's against my own judgement, and against my own instincts, but if you say you truly believe it, then I'll support you. And there won't be any recriminations afterwards, either, even if it goes wrong. I know when you're really serious about something and when you're not.'

I leaned over and kissed her. 'I think we may save some lives today,' I told her.

'Well,' she said, 'let's wait and see.'

10—Sunderings

It was a quarter after nine before we were able to leave the Hospital of the Sisters of Mercy and drive out on to the northbound freeway. There was a thick ocean fog around, and everybody was driving with their headlights on, so that the landscape appeared to be that of some grey and spectral graveyard, alive with mysterious lamps. I thought of the dark outline of the minotaur, and The Mystery Guest At The Funeral.

Jonathan sat in the back of the wagon, dressed in navy-blue dungarees and a white crew-neck sweater. His knees were wrapped in a chequered travelling-blanket, and he was holding a paper bag of medicines on his lap. Dr Rosen had shouted at us all the way down one corridor and all the way up the next, trying to stop us from taking Jonathan away. But we were paying the bills, not Dr Rosen, and in the end he had given up – slamming the discharge papers down on the counter and watching us while we signed them with the veins standing out at the side of his neck.

'Caring parents, huh?' he had said, sarcastically. 'Adolf Hitler was a more caring parent. Attila the *Hun* was a more caring parent.'

He had treated Jonathan so well that I had hated to argue with him. But he hadn't been in any kind of mood to listen to excuses or flattery or anything at all, so I had simply left him standing where he was, snorting as hard as a weekend jogger, and growling to himself about fascists.

Even Sara had to admit, though, that Jonathan was in far better shape than anybody had a right to expect of a boy who had been lying in a coma for four days. This morning he was bright and perky, and he chattered all the way out of San Diego and along to Rancho Santa Fe. The cut on his cheek had almost disappeared, and he didn't have to wear anything more than a Band-Aid.

'Are we going back to the house?' he asked, as we drove around the curves of Lomas Santa Fe Road.

'Not right away,' I said, straightforwardly. 'We just have a quick visit to make to somebody in Escondido.'

'You mean the Leinmanns?'

'No, not exactly.'

'Then who?'

'You'll see when we get there.'

As we came nearer to Rancho Santa Fe, we passed the precipice where I had pushed Father Corso's Volkswagen. The blackened wreck had been taken away now, but the bushes were still scorched, and there was a black oily mark on the ground. I was probably doing nothing more than frightening myself, but that oily mark seemed to bear a haunting resemblance to the shape of the beast.

We sped past the entrance to our own driveway, and then right on to the village itself. Jonathan was singing the theme from *Star Wars* in a high-pitched voice. Pretty appropriate, I thought. And as I turned on to the Escondido road I prayed to God that what I had heard from those voices last night was true, and that there really was some force of purity that would protect us from the evil of the Devil's chair. Sara reached across the car and momentarily touched the back of my hand.

It was almost ten o'clock by the time we reached the small turn-off that led up to the Jessop house. The morning fog hadn't lifted yet, although outside of the wagon the atmosphere was uncomfortably humid. I drove up to the gates, and applied the Impala's handbrake.

'Do you think they're going to let you in, just like that?' asked Sara.

'I have a plan,' I told her. 'I've been thinking about this for most of the night.'

I reached out of the window and pressed the intercom button on the gatepost. There was a pause, and a crackle, and then the Mexican manservant said, 'Who is it?'

'It's Mr Delatolla. I was round here the other night with Mr Sears.'

'You have an appointment?'

'No, but I must talk urgently with Mr Martin Jessop.'

'Mr Martin Jessop is not at home.'

'Don't give me that. I know for a fact that he's here. He told me he would be. Now, go tell him I have to speak to him.'

Another crackle. Then, 'Wait a moment.'

Sara raised her eyebrows questioningly. I shrugged. All I was counting on now was Martin Jessop's fear that his scheme to save his life wasn't going to work out exactly the way he'd intended it to. I switched on the news station on the radio, in case there were any bulletins about the religious convention in Los Angeles.

At last, the same voice that I'd heard on the telephone in David's apartment down at Presidio Place said, 'Yes? This is Martin Jessop.'

'Mr Jessop? I'm Ricky Delatolla.'

'I've heard all about you, Mr Delatolla. I'm pleased that you came around to my way of thinking. But is anything wrong? My manservant said you wanted to talk to me pronto.'

I grabbed a map from the glove compartment, and rustled it loudly in front of the intercom. 'It's this runic contract,' I said. 'I had the runes checked over last night by a classics professor at San Diego U., and he's worried that we may all have been tricked.'

'*Tricked?* In what way?'

'Well, it seems as if we have to insist that the chair adds a clause that binds it to fulfil its contract even if the body-count in Los Angeles is lower than a certain figure; or if we have to postpone the missile-firing until tomorrow; or cancel it altogether.'

'Unh?'

'It's kind of hard to explain through an intercom,' I said.

'Okay, then. You'd better come on in. But make it quick. We're due to launch in ten minutes or so.'

'I'll hurry, Mr Jessop. Don't you worry about that.'

The gates creaked apart, and we drove into the grounds of the Jessop mansion with the feeling that we were voluntarily entering the gates of Purgatory. The trees stood silent in the mist like petrified souls, and when we turned the corner of the uphill driveway, the vast Gothic mansion loomed over us with its spires and balconies and turrets, and I couldn't suppress a shiver.

'Someone walk over your grave?' asked Sara.

Martin Jessop was waiting for us on the steps. He was a tall, well-built young man in his mid-thirties, with all the tensile strength and obvious arrogance that his father must once have possessed. He had the same square-cut face, the same starey eyes, the same abrupt nose. His hair was carefully quiffed in a style that reminded me of the Everley Brothers, and he wore an expensive old-fashioned suit with wide lapels. A little way behind him, immaculate as always, stood David Sears.

'Mr Delatolla?' said Martin Jessop. He shook my hand as forcefully as if he were adjusting my wrist with a nickel-plated wrench. 'I hope we can sort this difficulty out without any kind of delay.'

'This is my family here,' I told him. 'My wife Sara, and my son Jonathan.'

'I'm glad to see that Jonathan's recovered,' called David, in his crispest accents. I ignored him. I didn't want to lose my cool, and if I started talking to David, I knew that I would.

'You have the contract with you?' asked Martin Jessop.

I patted my coat as if the contract were in my inside pocket. In fact, I'd left it in the hospital safe for security. It was too important to all of our lives for me to risk it being snatched, or destroyed, or defaced. And, who knows, the chair may have tried to take it back.

'I'd rather discuss this someplace less open,' I said. 'That's if you don't mind.'

'Well, not at all,' said Martin Jessop. 'Why don't you come round to the back of the house? You can see the missile for yourself then.'

We all walked across the mossy flagstones that edged the house, until we reached a wide patio at the back. The patio was decorated with stone urns and a sundial, but today the pride of place was given to the chair. It stood in the centre of a star-shaped pattern of coloured bricks, and it was even taller and more ominous in its appearance than ever. It must have been at least eight feet high. And it was resonating with a deep, almost inaudible bass note – a note that reverberated through the stonework, and even through the ground we walked on.

'It's that *chair*,' said Jonathan, alarmed, and came up close to me and held my hand.

'Don't you get frightened now,' I told him, and ruffled his hair. 'You and me, we're a whole lot tougher than any old chair, aren't we?'

Martin Jessop gave me a slanted, uneasy smile. David kept his distance, his hands clasped behind his back, trying to appear both remote and interested at the same time.

Further away, at the foot of the long downhill slope of the garden, where the front driveway curved around the house and made its way to a row of stables and carriage-houses, the missile-carrier was parked. I don't think that I'd ever seen one that close before, and it was very much smaller and neater but very much more business-like than I'd imagined.

The launcher was a ten-wheeled trailer, hauled by a Kenworth Transorient truck. It's firing-ramp was already raised on two shining hydraulic pistons, so that the nose of the missile was pointing up over the trees that surrounded the Jessop estate. The missile itself was painted white, with two stubby wings and a tailfin. It wasn't much longer than a family car. On one side, it bore the letters USAF, *Jessop Aerospace Industries*. Three engineers in blue overalls were crouched on the launcher beside it, making last-minute checks.

'There it is,' said Martin Jessop, unnecessarily. 'The instrument of our salvation.'

'It's so small,' said Sara.

'Oh yes, ma'am, it's small,' said Martin Jessop. 'But that's micro-engineering for you. In fact, it's forty-five inches longer than the Boeing cruise missile, but it has to carry extra payload, seeing as how it has to lift off the ground by itself.'

'How long will it take to get to Los Angeles?' I asked.

'Only a few minutes,' Martin Jessop assured me. 'It cruises at Mach 0.72 which is nearly three-quarters the speed of sound. This is the tactical version, which we guide into the air from our IBM computer right here. In mid-course, it flies by a

Lear Siegler strapdown platform and a TI active radar seeker.'

'I'm afraid that's all Greek to me,' said Sara.

'I'm sorry,' said Martin Jessop. 'I guess I spend too many hours of my life talking to aero-engineers. But you can take it that this missile is extremely accurate. In its strategic version, which has a range of fifteen hundred miles, we can guarantee to hit a target no more than one hundred and twenty feet in diameter. We call that CEP – circular error probability. That's with Tercom guidance, of course.'

'Oh, of course,' I nodded.

'I think we ought to get on,' said David, loudly. 'The convention opened at nine-thirty. The centre should be pretty crowded by now.'

I glanced back at the house. 'Does your father know what's going on here?' I asked Martin Jessop.

Martin Jessop stared at me for a moment. He had a slight nervous tic over his right eye. 'My father knows we're carrying out a test fire, of course. I expect he's watching from his study window.'

'But he doesn't know where the missile's programmed to strike?'

'That would spoil everything, wouldn't it?' Martin Jessop said, in a voice that was light and tense and almost threatening.

One of the engineers down at the launcher raised his hand and shouted, 'All okay with the launch system, Mr Jessop!'

Martin Jessop checked his stainless-steel Rolex watch. 'Right then, Mr Delatolla. I think we're all ready to fire. Don't you think we'd better sort out these contract problems first?'

'There *are* no contract problems,' I told him.

He stared at me. 'Now, just you hold on a minute. What do you mean, there are no contract problems?'

'Precisely what I said. The contract is fine. In fact, it's so fine that I didn't even bother to bring it with me.' I opened my coat and showed him that my pockets were empty.

'Then what did you come here for?' he wanted to know. 'Didn't you work everything out between you and Mr Sears here? Or is there something that doesn't satisfy you?'

'I'm satisfied.'

'Well, in that case, I'm going to have to ask you to leave. You've got to understand that this is all high-security stuff we've got here. And it's dangerous, too, for women and children. All deference to the ERA, ma'am,' he added, with a gratuitous smile at Sara.

'I think we'd prefer to stay,' I said, firmly.

'Now, I'm sorry, Mr Delatolla – I appreciate everything you've done to bring this occasion about – but I'd prefer it if you and your family would leave without any protests. This just isn't a suitable place for you right now.'

'Mr Jessop,' I said. 'If you oblige me to leave, I shall immediately call the police, the FBI, and the Pentagon.'

'And say what? This firing is authorised by the Pentagon, it is covered by all the necessary permits and insurances, and it happens to come under the heading of Urban Defence. Permission has been granted for a fire out towards the Pacific Ocean, overflying unpopulated areas, and you can call all the police you like but you'll never prove anything.'

'Mr Jessop,' I said, 'if I call the police right now and tell them where your missile is accidentally going to fall, ten minutes before it falls there, then you won't stand a chance.'

'I thought you had this guy tied up!' Martin Jessop shouted roughly at David. 'I thought you had him implicated in the death of that priest!'

'I do,' said David, rather weakly.

'He does,' I nodded to Martin Jessop. 'But if you don't let us stay, I'll still go to the police and that's all there is to it.'

'What makes you so damned anxious?' demanded Martin Jessop.

'I'm anxious because I don't believe you're actually going to do it,' I retorted. 'You see that chair? I'd rather face ten of your missiles than face that chair again. You know what I'm talking about. You've lived with the damned thing ever since you were a spotty kid. Well, I want to make sure that you get it out of my life for ever. I want to see you do it and hear you do it, first-hand.'

'Do you believe him?' Martin Jessop asked David, over his shoulder.

David looked away, as if he had suddenly seen something on the distant horizon that had interested him, like a purple-throated humming-bird.

'Can we trust him?' demanded Martin Jessop, more loudly.

David turned around and peered at me myopically. Despite my feelings, I managed to give him a quick, chummy grin, and one of those shrugs that means, come on, you know me, I'm not that much of a bastard really.

'All right,' said David, at last. 'He's bound by the contract. And he knows what's going to happen if the firing doesn't go off according to plan.'

'Sit down over there,' Martin Jessop told us, pointing to a carved marble bench at the side of the patio. 'Sit down over there and don't make a move until we're all finished here. You got me?'

'We got you,' I nodded, and I ushered Sara and Jonathan across the patio towards the bench. We sat down, and it was as cold as sitting on someone's overturned headstone. The sun was still struggling to shine through the grey morning fog. It would probably be a roasting-hot day later.

'I have to warn you that this launch is going to be real noisy,' called out Martin Jessop. 'So make sure you stick your fingers in your ears when we reach the count of launch minus three.'

'We'll stick our fingers in our ears,' I promised him.

'Okay, we're on launch minus sixty and counting,' said Martin Jessop, checking his watch again.

I took my eyes off the cruise missile and looked towards the Devil's chair. There was no doubt now that it was humming like a generator, and that the ground was trembling so much that it felt as if we were in for an earthquake. Sara held her hand out and I squeezed it as comfortingly as I could. We both knew the risks we were running, bluffing our way into the Jessop place. Anybody who could calmly arrange for the 'accidental' deaths of a hundred people or more, just for the sake of his own survival – well, they didn't bear thinking about. I knew exactly how much they didn't bear thinking about, because I was one of them. If anything went wrong with my plan this morning, then I would be just as responsible for all of those deaths as Martin Jessop and David Sears.

'We're on launch minus fifty-five and counting,' said Martin Jessop. Down at the bottom of the slope, where the missile-launcher was parked, the three engineers hurried away and hid themselves behind a temporary barricade of sandbags.

'You're sure we're going to be safe up here on the patio?' I asked, in the kind of naîve tone that a tourist from Idaho might use on his first trip into the spray of Niagara Falls.

Martin Jessop glanced at me in irritation. 'We'll be safe, don't you worry, Mr Delatolla. These missiles don't go off with much of a blast. Noise – but not much of a blast.'

David was staying close to the chair, and pacing about impatiently. He could feel the hum of malevolent power as well as I could, but to him it meant only one thing – his Jennifer was soon going to be restored to him the way she was before her accident. His long-dead wife was going to share his life again. The very idea of it made the hairs on the back of my neck tingle.

'Fifty and counting,' said Martin Jessop. Behind him, the sun was beginning to break through the clouds, and the first gilded light touched the dragon-scale tiles on the rooftops of the Jessop house, and sparkled on its windows.

'Forty-five and still counting.'

Sara said, 'Ricky – what are we going to do?'

'Watch,' I whispered. '*Watch!*'

The deep hum of the Devil's chair had become overwhelming, and sitting on the black leather seat there appeared to be a half-invisible presence, a transparent ripple of disturbed air. At first, it was impossible to tell what it was, but then immediately beneath the grimacing face of the man-serpent an outline began to gather itself.

It was the shape of the minotaur, the bull-creature. The Devil Himself. After almost two thousand years of banishment, He was so impatient to return that He was already beginning to take shape in the grotesque form in which He had terrorised Earth for centuries before the birth of the first of the innocents – the infant Jesus Christ.

David, mesmerised by the slowly-curdling currents of air that were now filling up the seat of the chair, gradually sank to his knees.

'Master,' he said. 'Master of everything.'

Sara pressed her hand to her mouth. 'My God,' she said. 'My God, it's the Devil. The actual *Devil*.'

Martin Jessop was staring, too, but in his efficient, mechanical way, he still managed to say, 'Forty and counting.'

'It has to be now,' I said to Sara. 'We've only got forty seconds left.'

'Ricky, you're not going to – '

'Sara, I have to! Look at that thing! The minute those people are blown up at that convention centre, it's going to take on real flesh and real life, and then this world's going to be cursed, I promise you.'

Sara didn't say anything. So I took Jonathan's hand, and helped him to hop off the marble bench, and then I led him across the flagstones towards the Devil's chair.

It was cold, close to the chair. It felt as if someone had left the door of a meat-freezer wide open. And there was a penetrating smell, too, like the smell of decomposing corpses, and unpleasant acids, and musty fungus. Jonathan glanced up at me, and swallowed hard to show me that he felt sick, but I simply smiled at him, and led him forward. At least, I tried to smile.

There was no question that the beast was taking shape now. I could see the wavering transparent curve of its horns, and the two dark smudges of its eyes, swimming in the air like the unformed eyes of an embryo chicken swim in their liquid albumen. And there was a *sound*, an echoing sound, as if someone were breathing down a long echoing metal pipe.

Above the crest of the chair, purple-throated humming-birds began to hover – only two or three of them at first – but then twenty or thirty, and more. They made a noise like swarming blowflies.

'Twenty-five, and counting,' said Martin Jessop flatly.

David, on his knees in front of the chair, turned around to stare at Jonathan and me as we approached. His face was already pinched with cold, and his eyes were as wide as a lunatic's.

'Get away,' he told us, and then he shouted, *'get away!'* because he must have sensed the purpose of what we were doing. But together, my six-year-old son and I kept walking closer and closer to the Devil's chair, until we were standing right in front of it.

The Devil, already half-formed out of the promises that David and Martin Jessop had made Him, stared at us out of the slanted darkness of His eyes.

'Why have you come?' He whispered, in my mind.

'You know why,' I replied.

'Your efforts are futile,' He said. *'It is already too late. My Kingdom is about to come.'*

'Your Kingdom will never come as long as there are innocents. And it will never come as long as there are people who believe in God, and do whatever they can to emulate Him.'

The cold, congealed air that was sitting in the Devil's chair began to ripple and shift, and I thought that I could see the shadowy outline of bones.

'You can never defeat me,' whispered the voice. *'You have no strength and no determination, and you have already contracted with Me to sell your so-called Christian morality. To every one of those pilgrims at the convention centre, my friend, you will be Judas.'*

'Not yet,' I said. 'Jonathan – I want you to sit on the chair.'

Martin Jessop said, 'Fifteen, and counting. What's going on there, David? Get Mr Delatolla away from there.'

I grasped Jonathan's hand, and led him to the chair. Jonathan's teeth were chattering, and he stared up at me in terror.

'Daddy, I don't want to. Daddy, there's something there. I'm frightened.'

I hunkered down. The cold was so intense that my hands were white. 'Jonathan,' I said, 'you remember when you were asleep? What it was like there? Well, the people who looked after you then will protect you now. I promise you. But it's very important for you to sit in that chair. It's the most important thing in the whole world. And if you're brave enough to do it, you're going to be a great big hero, bigger than Superman, bigger than anybody. Now, will you do it for me?'

Jonathan, trembling, nodded. And it was then that David grabbed hold of my coat and jostled me sideways, so that I lost my balance. *'Get away!'* he screamed. *'You're going to spoil everything! Get away!'*

I heard Martin Jessop say, 'Ten seconds, and counting.'

I rolled over in what seemed like slow-motion. For a split-second, as I fell, I could see two of Martin Jessop's blue-uniformed engineers running up the slope of the garden towards us – presumably to come and sort me out. Then I collided with the chair, and reached out a hand to stop myself. My fingers gripped the black leather seat.

I felt – I experienced – *Hell.*

No matter how many medieval paintings and writings talk about eternal fire and burning, Hell is cold. Colder and more painful than anything you can imagine. Think of pressing your head up against a block of ice until your actual brain begins to suffer frostbite. Think of every thing inside you shrinking and tightening up and prickling with agony.

I don't know whether I screamed or not. I heard someone screaming, far away, as if they were screaming in another city, on another world. And then I felt myself irresistibly drawn towards the back of the chair, towards that dark endless crevice into which every damned soul is tumbled. It was Jonathan's dream coming true – the dream he had told me about the first day the chair had arrived. The dream of his father disappearing down the back of the chair, lost and shrieking and gone forever.

I heard a deep blurry voice mouth the words, 'Eight . . . seven . . . six . . .' And as if I were able to be everywhere and anywhere at once, I saw people all around me, felt them jostling against me. I saw them crowding into a large hall, and taking their seats. I felt the warmth of their bodies, the palpitation of their hearts, their fears and their loves and their friendliness. I was cold, frozen, and suspended in darkness, yet I was amongst them. I could almost reach out for them.

I was actually *inside of the Devil's consciousness*, sensing the souls that He was about to take for Himself, relishing their vulnerable humanity like a fierce beast outside of a cabin door, relishing the flesh of the people he can scent inside.

Someone said, 'Mel . . . there's a seat here, Mel . . .' and someone else said, 'Isn't that beautiful . . . that cross all made out of flowers . . .' and I tried to reach out of my coldness and touch them but they were miles away in Los Angeles, and when the deeper voice said, '. . . four . . . three . . . two . . .' I knew that they only had minutes left to live before the roof came in and they would all be blasted into bloody pieces.

Then a brassy blaring voice commanded, *'Come back!'*

There was a moment when I felt as if my whole mind was being wrenched inside-out. Every memory of every day that I had ever lived, every word that I had ever spoken, every sunrise and every sunset, ripped out of my head like the multi-coloured wires out of the back of a television set. Then I was hurtling in slow-motion away from the chair, out of the darkness, and into the glare of the morning sunlight – falling across the stones of the patio with the awkward grace of an action replay.

Martin Jessop, in a voice so slurred that I could hardly understand what he was saying, said, '. . . one . . .'

I sat up with dream-like slowness. I saw David lunging towards the chair, his face contorted with fear. I saw the hideous outline of the Devil. And I saw my son, Jonathan, climbing on to the black leather seat with all the confidence of an angel.

Everything snapped back. David screeched, 'Jennifer! You promised me Jennifer!'

Martin Jessop said sternly, 'Ignition! Fire!'

And Sara was screaming, 'Ricky! Ricky! The chair!'

'No!' I yelled at Martin Jessop, but he had dropped his arm as a signal, and I heard the first ignition of the missile's engines, a popping, crackling bellow that frightened the birds out of the surrounding trees. It was too late. It was all too late. There was nothing I could do. The pilgrims at the Los Angeles convention would all die, and if Martin Jessop had anything to do with it, so would Sara and Jonathan and I.

Half-deafened by the mounting thunder of the missile, I turned towards the chair again. Jonathan was now taking his place on the seat as if he owned it – as if it were his own personal throne. He was actually sitting within the wavering shape of the Devil Himself, smiling, calm, and self-confident, and there was a radiance about him which reminded me of the brightness that had shone from his eyes last night.

David went down on his knees in front of the chair, scuffing and tearing his immaculate trousers. His face was extra-ordinary – crimson with anger, and knotted up with fear. He reached towards Jonathan as if he wanted to take hold of him and strangle him, but Jonathan simply smiled in his direction with all the composure of a Christ-child, and David seemed powerless to move any further.

'*Jennifer!*' raged David. '*Jennifer!*' And at that moment, the cruise missile roared away from its launcher on a stiff lance of blue-and-white flame, and disappeared over the treetops with more noise than I can ever remember hearing in my whole life. It sounded as if the whole world had been swallowed up by fire.

Jonathan stood up on the seat of the Devil's chair. Without a word, his eyes radiant with light, he pointed to an upstairs window of the huge Gothic building behind him. David, shaking like an epileptic, staggered to his feet and stared.

'Jennifer,' he whispered, 'Jennifer. My God. Jennifer. She's there. Martin! Jennifer's there! Martin!'

Shuddering with fear and disbelief, I looked up at the house. In the leaded window to which Jonathan's finger was so steadfastly pointing, I could see a woman, pale-faced and still. Sara came towards me, reaching for my hand as if she were blind. 'Is that really her?' she asked me. 'Do you really think that's her?'

'Martin, it's her!' shouted David, and began to run towards the house. Martin Jessop, confused, did nothing more than stare at me fixedly and then stalk as quickly as he could in pursuit. The two blue-uniformed engineers came puffing up to the patio, but when they realised that Sara and I were no longer of any apparent interest to anyone, they stopped, and looked at us with obvious uncertainty, and then gradually retreated back down the sloping garden towards the missile-launcher.

But Jonathan stayed where he was.

He stood on the seat of the chair, his face transfigured, his arms crossed on his chest, and he was smiling the most electrifying smile.

'Ricky . . .' said Sara. 'He looks like . . . I don't know . . . he looks like *God*.'

I could still vaguely make out the shape of the minotaur-beast. But then Jonathan raised his hands, and lifted them to the sky, and the shape began to twist and writhe all around him like a whirlpool. There was a grating, groaning noise, and gradually the shape began to lose its definition.

'*You will regret this*,' said the voice inside of my head.

I didn't answer.

'*You will regret this day until the end of eternity.*'

I heard a skin-crawling sound like living flesh being torn away from living bones, and then the Devil disappeared. Jonathan, his face triumphant, looked down at me from the Devil's chair, and he wasn't Jonathan at all.

'*Does it not say in the sacred book, "Who ever perished, being innocent?"*' he said, in a voice as clear as a trumpet. '*And does it not also say, in the same chapter of the sacred book, "They that plough iniquity, and sow wickedness, shall reap the same"?*'

He pointed towards the horizon, over the treetops north of Escondido. For a moment, there was silence, but then I heard a rumble, and the rumble grew louder until it sounded like approaching thunder. And Jonathan lifted up both of his arms, and out of the distance came the cruise missile, gleaming white, as fast as a bird, faster, with translucent fire burning from its tail.

My son, my six-year-old son, pointed towards the missile and the missile was totally in his control. The two engineers were staring up at it, their hands shielding their eyes, and one of them was speaking frantically on his radio transmitter. But there was nothing they could do. Jonathan kept pointing at the missile, and sweeping his little arm in a circle, and the missile thundered around the grounds of the Jessop house as if it were a toy kite on the end of a string.

Jonathan smiled. Then he laughed. And he made that missile circle and circle and circle again, his finger directing every move it made, every deflection, every twist and turn through the trees.

'*Jonathan!*' I shouted, but he didn't hear me, or wouldn't hear me, and I didn't dare to take him down from the chair in case he lost control of the missile and sent it plummeting down into the road, or into somebody's homestead.

An incredible voice in my mind said, '"*Whatsoever things are true, whatsoever things are just, whatsoever things are honest, whatsoever things are pure; think on these things, and the God of peace shall be with you.*"'

And then Jonathan raised his arm upwards, and the cruise missile began to climb. It climbed and climbed and climbed on its tail of fire, and the morning sky was so bright that I could hardly see it. More than anything else, I was conscious of the noise. It blotted out all thought, all sensibility, everything except the overwhelming idea that this, at last, was the moment of judgement.

Jonathan stood for one endless second on the Devil's chair, his finger directed at the sky right above him. Then he turned and pointed at the Jessops' Gothic mansion, and up above us the cruise missile tumbled and turned, and dropped earthwards.

As the missile fell, it momentarily broke the sound barrier. There was a weird echoing report, and I felt an expanding pressure on my ears. But that was nothing compared to the explosion that followed. A huge charge of devastatingly high explosive burst the Jessops' house apart, sending the cliff-like walls thundering into the garden, and whole towers and balconies collapsing into the main hall. Broken chimneys hurtled into the air, hundreds of feet up, and a blizzard of broken glass showered the lawns until they were sparkling and white.

For a few seconds, the framework of the house held together. But then there was another tearing crash, as joist after joist ripped away from its supports, like the ribs of a dying dinosaur, and brought the main roof sliding into the wreckage. The echoes of the explosion came back from the surrounding hills, and then came back again, until they finally died.

A huge pall of grey dust hung over the house, and then slowly began to stir in the mid-morning breeze. I heard a crackling noise as wood and furniture began to burn.

I walked over to the chair and lifted Jonathan down. He looked like my son again. He *was* my son.

'It's finished,' I said. 'It's all over.'

He looked at me for a moment and then he went over to Sara, and hugged her tight. There are times when a boy needs his mommy, and this was one of them. Down at the end of the garden, I heard the cough of the Kenworth Transorient truck. It sounded as if the engineers had decided they were better off someplace else. I didn't know whether they were planning on telling anybody what they'd seen today, but I didn't much care.

I took hold of the Devil's chair, tilted it on to its side, and dragged it over to the ruins of the house. There was a fire blazing quite close to me, part of a collapsed staircase, and I picked up the chair and threw it on.

It burned slowly, the chair, because it was solid mahogany. But it burned. I stood watching the flames lick up at the face of the man-serpent, and I thought to myself, *there you go, he who burns first burns hottest*. The face was expressionless, and the disappointing part about it was that I knew that it was nothing but wood.

I waited for nearly ten minutes, until the chair was reduced to a blackened frame of charred timber. I kicked it, and it fell to pieces.

Sara and Jonathan stood watching me. In the distance, we could hear the sound of fire-trucks, their sirens whooping as they sped along the road towards us from Escondido.

I put my arm around Sara's shoulders, and said, 'Come on. I think it's time we went home.'

*

It took six weeks for a special USAF Tactical Air Command enquiry to decide that the Jessop cruise missile had suffered 'a guidance complication' and that its devastating attack on the Jessop mansion had been an ironic but entirely accidental tragedy.

Escondido paramedics discovered in the wreckage of the Jessop mansion the bodies of Mr Sam Jessop, his wife, and his son Mr Martin Jessop. Their Mexican manservant had gone down to the basement at the moment of impact to look for a bottle of Châteauneuf-du-Pape, and had miraculously been spared. Also discovered in the ruins, with their arms around each other, were Mr David Sears, a British antique dealer, and an unidentified woman. The coroner noted with surprise that the woman's body was badly burned, while Mr Sears's body was completely untouched by fire, or even by direct blast.

Three Jessop flight engineers were questioned about their part in the disaster, but apart from voicing suspicions that the ground-to-sea test wasn't being carried out 'for any discernible aeronautical purpose', they all testified that they had noticed 'nothing unusual' during the launch.

Sara and Jonathan and I returned to our quiet and occasionally dozy life in Rancho Santa Fe, among the lemon groves. The leaves began to bud on our eucalyptus trees again, and our bushes began to flower, and the paintings in our living-room were as normal and as pleasant as Copley and Stuart could ever be. Only the charcoal outline on the Moreau painting refused to disappear, so I took it down from the bedroom wall and stored it in the attic. I didn't need any reminders of that week we'd spent in the company of the Devil's chair.

And one thing more – the grass never grew on the patch where I'd buried the Devil's trilobite, no matter how much seed and fertiliser I tried.

All this happened more than a year ago now, and most people around Rancho Santa Fe and Escondido have forgotten about the spectacular missile accident that destroyed the biggest and wealthiest house in the county. But, until last month, one tiny unanswered question always used to irritate me, and I would often sit for an hour or more by the side of the pool wondering what the hell the answer was, and why it had happened that way.

Then, when I picked up a copy of the *Los Angeles Sunday Times,* I was given half of a clue. On an inside page, buried in the Travel section, there was a photograph of a curiosity store in Bali, or someplace like that. And there, smiling at me from behind the counter of this junk-filled emporium, was the face of Henry Grant. Either him, or his identical twin brother.

I've never discussed it with Sara, but I've formed a kind of a theory that Henry Grant was somebody very special, somebody who brought us the Devil's chair because he knew it was part of our destiny to fight it and destroy it. That's why he left his office with strict instructions that we weren't to give it back.

And maybe some day, in some antique market somewhere, you too will come across a dealer like Henry Grant – a dealer who will offer you a bargain price on a chair or a table or a corner-cupboard. All I can advise you to do is to touch it, feel it, and maybe sniff it, too. Because, from my experience, some of these old pieces of furniture can give you a Devil of a lot of trouble.

GRAHAM MASTERTON

THE MASTER OF HORROR

It's late at night . . . the wind is howling around the door . . . the fire flickers eerily in the grate . . . and you're alone . . .

Now's the time to pick up one of Graham Masterton's spine-tingling horror novels, novels like CHARNEL HOUSE, the scarifying story of a house that's anything but normal, or REVENGE OF THE MANITOU, a tale of revenge more horrifying than you could ever imagine.

Read a Graham Masterton horror story tonight, but beware . . .

Enter the world of Graham Masterton at your own risk – you may never want to be alone again!

By Graham Masterton in Sphere Books:

REVENGE OF THE MANITOU	£1.25
THE WELLS OF HELL	£1.25
THE DEVILS OF D DAY	£1.25
CHARNEL HOUSE	£1.25